Throw Away Girls

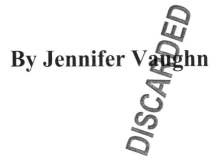

By Jennifer Vaughn

Published by Waldorf Publishing

2140 Hall Johnson Road

#102-345

Grapevine, Texas 76051

www.WaldorfPublishing.com

Throw Away Girls

The Jaycee Wilder Series, Book 1

ISBN: 978-1-944245-62-7

Library of Congress Control Number: 2015958503

Copyright © 2016

Printed in Canada

Dedication

This book is dedicated to my family. To my mom and dad, you remain my biggest cheerleaders, and I am beyond blessed for the life you created for us. I hope I have made you proud in return. To Brad, Brody, and Darby. Because of you, my heart is full. To the men and women who serve and protect, I also dedicate this to you. My stories are pure fantasy, while yours are real. Your courage humbles and inspires me to be better.

Chapter One

"You are heavier than you look, sweet thing," the man grunted as he hoisted the woman by the waist. Her knee caught a metal hook near the wall that held cat o'nine tails and ripped open. She groaned. Blocking out the stab of pain and the stark shock of having this enjoyable encounter rapidly degrade into a nightmare, Zoe Statler switched to survival mode.

"Don't worry, love, some poor slob will clean that up later." He swung his head around to motion to the trickle of red plopping onto the cement floor.

"One step ahead. You always gotta be one step ahead. Even if you bleed out here, there's so much DNA sticking to this floor it's contaminated before it even falls out of you." His hands squeezed her tender windpipe, choked off her air, and then released it. "The only thing splats of your blood will do is confirm you are one sick bitch to wind up at a place like this."

Zoe Statler squeezed her eyes shut. He was right. She wasn't merely a seventh-grade science teacher; she had a ravenous appetite for what was satisfied in places like these. She had encountered rough, rather enjoyed it that way, but she had never known sadistic or murderous. She had to get out of the room. She had to get away. She channeled her Zen yoga instructor, Marla, who taught her how to quiet her busy brain and focus on the richness of the oxygen that gave her life. Pull in through the nostrils, hold, and release. If she were to panic, her air would dry up; her nose had to control it.

1

Come on, she told herself silently. *Think!* Zoe refused to go down like this. Her eyes flew back open, searching up, down, and to each side, scanning for a weapon, a sharp object, something she could slam into this asshole's esophagus. The man's bony shoulder stole her breath as it slammed into her ribcage. He was manhandling her, hurting every inch of her, just because he could. Her clothes were off, and she was vulnerable, all parts of herself exposed to his cruel hands. His fingers dug into the soft flesh of her lower back as he threw her like a jackknife over his left side. Zoe winced. Her face bumped against the seat of his jeans before he heaved her spine first against the wall. Her bones rattled. Her teeth began to chatter, and she couldn't feel her legs. Using her fingers like claws, she crawled toward the door. The shadowy room kicked off gruesome, overblown images along the wall of her collapsed body hunched and lurching forward. She twisted back and started to yell. Surely, someone—even if he were caught in the throes of depraved passion—would hear her? She gurgled and sputtered, screeched and begged. Her raw warbles only echoed around grimy walls.

"Help me! Help…He—" Unbridled agony grabbed the air Marla had helped her find with such ferocity Zoe's eyes went wide with shock. A sliver of awareness opened like a picture book. Inside were the faces of her parents, her little sister, boyfriend and her best friend. Her people. Not only would they have to deal with her death, now they'd know her secrets, too. She thought of the parents of her students.

They'd be horrified that someone like her had access to their precious offspring. She wouldn't be remembered for the time and care she took with their kids. No, they'd only gasp when they found out where she spent her nights off. Her life reduced to a teaching moment of what *not* to do to get your rocks off.

Goddamn it! Fire erupted in her heart. *This will not happen to me, not if I can help it. Fight, Zoe, fight!* Her nails skittered along the slippery floor as she kicked backwards with every ounce of her soul, feeling giddy when she slammed into the man's thigh with her heel. She could see the door handle.

Just feet away.

"Bitch!" he growled, trying to tackle her down while he bent low in pain. She sensed an opening. He was wounded. She had to act fast to inflict more damage. Zoe engaged her core muscles, twisting like a caterpillar in a cocoon to slam her knee into his damaged leg. She hurled her full weight against him; her torso slid on a sheet of blood. She tried to rise and felt one foot connect with the floor. It was so weak it buckled. No! Forcing herself to find balance, she hopped backwards, away from the now doubled over man. She turned. The space between her and the door got smaller. She could do this. If she could just hobble away, someone would come. Someone would have to see her!

The ankle tried like hell. It twisted on needling discomfort and went down sideways. Zoe's hands couldn't catch her fall. She struck the cold cement hard, forehead first. Noise rushed through her ears, like running water, as white haze descended behind her eyelids. A swipe of her thick tongue revealed a jagged edge of the front tooth her dentist just bonded two weeks ago. The tooth was now almost entirely gone.

Using her chin to push upward, Zoe hauled herself back onto her chest and ignored paralyzing pain. Moving military crawl style until her nose scraped the wretched mixture of dust and grime on the floor, she forced her torso upright, and risked a backward glance to gauge the distance she'd achieved. It was minimal in the small room. Goddamn it! With a grunt of extreme effort, Zoe lead with her stronger ankle, jumped out a full stride and forced her damaged foot to take some of her weight. It held, but even better, the door was closer. She frantically slid one leg after another as fast as she could, hunched over and rickety like a wounded pony attempting a weak cantor; her fractured gait found a sort of broken rhythm she turned into a mantra.

Get-a-way. Get-a-way. *Get-* the strong foot smacked heavily. *A-* her weight shifted to protect the other ankle from a clumsy landing. *Way-* the jagged tooth sunk into her lower lip to swallow the ripple of full body torment. Even her tri-weekly TRX classes paled in comparison to this kind of physical depletion. She was exhausted. Only the power of her mantra pushed her on, lumbered step by lumbered step, toward the elusive slip of light in the dank hallway. If she could just round the corner and escape this hell chamber, there was hope the freak wouldn't pursue her in open space. If she could just…

Zoe heard a sound so piercing she didn't realize it was coming from her. Animalistic survival skills had her instinctively throwing her arms up around her head as she was roughly thrown onto her back. She felt warm liquid pumping from the base of her skull, like the spray of the shower when she rinsed the conditioner from her hair.

"Could've spared yourself all this pain," he snapped into her face, eyeballs blazing white between blood-streaked cheeks. "Your choice."

Zoe stared into his eyes. He had seemed so exquisite to her in the hazy lighting of the meeting room, a perfect creature for an impersonal yet mutually satisfying meeting. She chose him because he looked normal. Like her. Just with a sharp edge when it came to fetishes and desires. How wrong she'd been. Deadly wrong.

Trying to stop the heaving in her chest she attempted to speak, careful to look him in the eye to further create a connection. She wanted to make herself real to him. "Why are you doing this?" she barely recognized her own voice, distorted by the new space between her front teeth. "Please…you don't have to…my name is Zoe. I have a name, a family…."

"Shhh," he interrupted softly. "I admire your strength. You're feisty. You fight back. You're special, Zoe. Nice name, by the way."

The man straddled Zoe's waist. He plopped his rear onto her abdomen, forcing her to draw in a quick breath before another wave of pain tore through her. "Sorry," he said casually, "that probably hurts your ribs. You may have broken a couple when you fell. Makes it hard to breathe."

Fog pushed into Zoe's periphery. She couldn't bring in any air. Sensing her growing desperation, the man shifted himself slightly over Zoe's right hip and freed up enough room in her solar plexus to feed oxygen to her burning lungs. She grabbed for it in open-mouthed clips. "Please…" she sputtered.

"No can do, Zoe. It's just the way it has to be. Girls like you don't matter. You're dirty. This is your own fault, sweetheart. What do you expect in a place like this? See, with me, it's not just about the sex, although that was good, too. This is a place for all kinds of fantasies." He slid a finger down Zoe's bare thigh, collecting a thin rivet of blood. With her arms held in place by his body, he placed his finger inside her mouth and rolled her blood over her broken teeth. She gagged and pushed back, but he was stronger; she could feel her stomach heave and buck. He grabbed her battered head by loose strands of hair and forced her face close to his.

"I take a little from all my girls," he told her, as a sinister glint lit his half-lidded stare. He sucked on the finger coated with her blood. "You taste so good, Zoe, inside and out."

The bare light bulb on the ceiling flickered like Zoe's spotty coherence. She let go and allowed her brain to take her where it needed to in these final moments. She saw her mom, who baked the best tea cookies at Christmas, and her dad when he taught her how to drive a stick shift when she was fifteen. She saw her boyfriend, Sam, who loved her but just couldn't understand her attraction to exploitative sex with random strangers. He had wanted to be everything to her. She had wanted more. And now she was about to pay for that.

"You were right, Sam," she said, although she wasn't sure her mouth was moving. "I wasn't good enough for you."

Sam shook her shoulders. He was angry with her. But he needed to get away from here. Zoe couldn't help him. No, Sam, go away! It wasn't safe for him here. She tried to throw her hands out to stop Sam from coming back to her.

"Don't!"

Zoe's lips turned in; this was wrong. Very wrong.

She rolled her head from ear to ear. The hard floor was cold and hard like an arctic glacier. She turned sideways but met only resistance.

"Wake up, darlin'." A forceful smack to the cheek snapped Zoe's eyes back open. Instant recall. She wasn't baking cookies, driving, or kissing Sam's scruffy cheek; she was dying at the hands of some madman.

"Stop…" she whispered. "Please…just make it stop." The pain was relentless, a torment that began in her bones

7

and spread through every cell of her body. Zoe was broken, her spirit ready to disconnect. She muttered The Lord's Prayer, feeling more anger than comfort that she would be called home under such hideous circumstances. Her life was a good one. This sucks!

Summoning a final defiant burst of strength, Zoe jerked her right arm free and let it fly, her fingers hooked into a claw that connected with the man's flesh and sliced it open near his chin.

He muffled a roar, using one arm to pin her back down. With the other he wiped furiously at the bloody wound. She expected his wrath, found peace in her soul, and braced for the end.

He laughed.

"Good for you, Zoe. You're a warrior, and I salute your brave heart."

White teeth flashed in a wide smile. His face was too young to be so evil. Zoe tasted metal and swallowed the blood that pooled near her tonsils. Did he want a response? Validation for his sick compliment? Zoe said the only thing she wanted him to hear.

"Fuck you."

His grin lengthened into a line. A subtle twitch rippled the taut skin around his mouth. That brought Zoe deep satisfaction. She may not be long for this world, but she got to him first. She pissed him off, and that felt like vengeful divine intervention.

Moving with purpose, the man's arm went up. Zoe saw the steel blade. Even though she always watched the nurse plunge the needle into her arm when she had blood drawn at the doctor's, this time she looked away. As the knife slashed through her abdomen, splicing organs and bouncing off bone, Zoe found them again. Off in the distance, she saw her people: Her beloved family, her cherished co-workers, and those special kids she had the joy to instruct. The tallest figure filled the middle; the others let him lead. *Daddy*. Suddenly she became a little girl again and her father was hurling her into the air, his arms wide and ready to catch her before she fell. She placed trembling fingers to her bloody lips, softly kissed them and reached to take her father's outstretched hand.

"I'm ready, Daddy," she whispered, eyes locked on the first man in her life she loved. With a final gasp, her wounds drained her body of the precious blood it would need to survive. Zoe began to let go. She ignored her killer and the loping letters he formed on the wall with her expelled blood.

Throw-Away Girl.

In the time it took to die, Zoe Statler was surrounded by love.

Chapter Two

At some point overnight, the A/C unit in Jaycee Wilder's condo complex must have stopped working. She woke up covered in sweat.

"Ugh," she groaned, and then tapped her boyfriend, Van, on the chest. "Get up, the A/C is broken."

Van rolled over, ignoring her. She squinted at the digital numbers on the nightstand. 6:04. Van wouldn't be up for at least another five hours. When he had to close the bar after last call, Van didn't get home until after three a.m. In the few months they'd been shacking up together she'd learned this much: He was as communicative as a boulder until almost noon unless he had an audition to get to. Van was slinging drinks at a West Hollywood nightclub several nights a week but only until he became the next Bradley Cooper. As Jaycee saw it, that would happen anytime between tomorrow and never.

"Ugh," Jaycee moaned again. Tossing the sheet aside, she tumbled out of bed and headed toward the kitchen and her trusty Cuisinart coffee maker. Twisting her shoulder-length blonde hair into a messy, low ponytail, she completed the pre-brew ritual and flipped the machine to "on." It gurgled to life. Jaycee yawned, wiped her sweat-slicked brow, and thought ahead to another crazy busy day. She threw in a good stretch of her long arms and back to wake her shoulders and neck. High energy and good calf muscles were prerequisites for a job in the Los Angeles TV market that demanded fashionable heels, yet the willingness to destroy them—and your feet—while out in the field. Her special report on credit card identity theft needed one last sound bite, she had calls out on three new stories, and was scheduled to shoot a promo for the station's investigative unit. Her news director, Clare, was pushing the I-Team hard.

Hunting for fresh, cool air, she detoured to the front living room windows and threw them open. Her normally quiet condo buzzed to life—a frenetic, urgent soundtrack of car horns and the dull din of tires on pavement—the melody of human movement typically blocked out by the low hum of her air conditioner. The city was a notoriously early riser.

Three loud pings from the kitchen told her the dark roast was ready. The remote control sat next to the glass pot, forever on standby. Not a moment went by that Jaycee didn't need to know everything that was going on. As she turned on the TV and threw some wheat bread into her stainless steel toaster, she prepared for shootings, robberies, perhaps even a Hepatitis C outbreak at some medical center, the usual stuff that greeted greater Los Angeles viewers every day. Moving a layer of thick peanut butter lazily around the browned edges of her bread, she was about four bites in when the anchors came back around to recap the top stories of the day. They began with a domestic shooting in a nearby town. She listened for the details. Husband allegedly shot wife after a spat over the escalating cost of renovating their home. Husband arrested

11

after he held police at bay for five hours while his wife choked and sputtered on their newly redone hardwood floors.

"Gross," she muttered. The reporter finished the live hit from the street in front of the now cordoned-off house, and tossed back to Jill and Dan, her station's morning anchor team. They transitioned into a short weather report, which was the same as it was the entire month of July— sunny and hot—and teased a developing story: A horrific attack at another underground nightclub just off Hollywood Boulevard.

Jaycee leaned forward. This would make the third in six months. Three women butchered inside these no-holds-barred, stranger-on-stranger sex shops.

"The latest from the scene just ahead," they said, as a series of peppy commercials rolled across the screen. Jaycee sipped some coffee as anxious ripples erupted across her gut. Another girl lost.

She sat impatiently on the chair as inane grocery store and car dealership ads reminded viewers of hot summer sales and clearance prices. Finally, the glitzy open returned to alert the viewers they were watching The Eye-Opener on ABC 12, with Jill Jones and Dan Renner. The stuffy condo air was thick and bristly, hard to fit through her nose.

"Come on, come on!" she urged. An eerie foreboding shut out sounds, smells, and sense of time. Her foot bounced. Some family out there had just suffered an unimaginable tragedy.

"A story developing this morning. L.A. police are investigating a homicide. A young woman was found dead at a nightclub near the Alley Cat Pizza Shop off Hollywood Boulevard. Police say the woman was badly beaten..."

"Babe, what's this?" Van looked down at her, bare-chested and Adonis-like in form-fitted boxers. She gazed at the length of him.

"Shh," she said dismissively. "Another girl, sexed up and then sliced up. I'm trying to listen here."

"Sorry," he muttered. She felt bad she snapped at him. She reached her arms around his ripped abdomen. "Just listen, okay?"

"Police have not yet identified the young woman, but do say she appears to be in her early to mid-twenties. At this point, there are no suspects. This is the third woman to turn up dead at these so-called fantasy adult nightclubs in Los Angeles. Two other women, Sarah Walsh and Mackenzie Drew, were also murdered in locations near or along Hollywood Boulevard."

Jaycee shook her head. "I know it sounds dramatic, but I'm starting to think there's a serial killer out there, Van," she said, as she moved away from the TV to refill her coffee mug. "Some sick asshole targeting girls at clubs. These are not cases of rough sex going too far. He's making them bleed." Jaycee had begun watching it closely. After the first girl turned up, a gory slaughter that implied murder over mishap, she was intrigued.

13

"I'll bet she fought for her life, maybe they'll have fingernail scrapings to work with," Jaycee whispered to herself, surprised to hear Van agree with her. Returning with her iPhone, he placed it on the kitchen table and pulled up a chair. "Here, just in case you want to check your Twit," he said.

"It's *Twitter* and thanks."

"Whatevs. You know I only do Instagram. Keeps my face out there. So, at what point do you think this girl realized she was fucked. And not in a good way?" Van's eyes skated left and right. Even though he was a bartender-slash-actor, emphasis on the former, he did occasionally get bit parts on TV shows. Ever since a stint on Criminal Minds last year, Van had fancied himself a hard-edged crime sleuth. Mostly, it was something Jaycee teased him about though he did track down some dude who drank and dashed from the bar using nothing but witness interviews and gut instinct. Jaycee shifted into ignore mode as Van started pacing the tile-floored kitchen. His arms waved while his jaw flapped about forensic evidence and DNA testing. Van was working to insert new buzz words into his somewhat limited conversation style.

"Could be just a thrill kill," he continued, "obviously given where it happened. But what if she was being watched by someone like in that episode of *Law & Order* I read for, remember? Killer wanted to bone some lawyer chick, so he followed her until he knew her routine and...*wham*...one day just whacked her, right there on the steps of the courthouse."

She waved Van off. "This is real life, Van, three girls are dead. This isn't a script. It's totally happening." At times, Jaycee really didn't have the patience to debate someone who had the brainpower of a ferret.

Sufficiently smacked down, Van mumbled another apology and walked back into the bedroom.

She reminded herself to deal with him later with an apology of his choice. There was no need to be so bitchy, but distress blanketed her heart like a smoldering fire. Something about these murders deeply bothered her. The victims would be written off as sloppy sex seekers who got what they deserved. If the public barely valued them, the killer gained power to carry on. Why stop with three?

Jaycee had the awful feeling this was just the beginning. She looked at the clock, 6:20 a.m.

And another girl was dead.

Chapter Three

The soaring ceiling of the church made Jaycee dizzy.
Sound reverberated through the old cedar wood, and the
summer air was uncomfortably dewy. Her kneecaps pulled
tightly together, she sat way in the back, the pews packed
so deep her elbows and thighs were sticking to someone
else's. It wasn't the first time she had attended the funeral
of a murder victim she grew to know through her job, a sort
of crude fascination that helped her tell their stories. Jaycee
covered all her bases, even the unseemly ones.

She heard immature voices asking nervous questions.
Zoe Statler's students. She fought an urge to ask the
families for an interview because the setting was
inappropriate. Her news director, Clare, warned her to be
inconspicuous and would have her head if she made herself
an issue for the grieving family. "You keep your lips
sealed, Jaycee," she told her. "You think you need to be
there, fine, but don't agitate anyone, and for shit's sake,
don't be pushy! Respect your surroundings. You may be on
your own time, but you still represent this station.
Remember that."

Jaycee believed that in order to give proper coverage
to a murder victim, she needed to get to know her. It wasn't
something every reporter liked to do on the weekends; in
fact, Jaycee was the only reporter here as far as she could
tell, even though it had been several days since Zoe's
identity was confirmed by police. She had called the church

and asked permission. The family hadn't objected, as long as there were no cameras inside.

Much like the other two sex club victims, Sarah and Mackenzie, Zoe Statler wasn't just some slutty skank. She had been a well-liked educator, and a beloved daughter. Sarah was a waitress in Sherman Oaks, and Mackenzie had been a single mom from Burbank raising four-year-old twins. Each young woman had a loving, supportive family that had professed shock upon hearing the details of their deaths. It must be dreadful to learn your precious little girl ventured into dark caverns where pleasure and pain intertwined with one's own exploitation. What a shitty way to go. In a cold place that invited the darkest parts of a person's soul out to play.

In the front row, Zoe's mom shook on a fresh round of silent, racking sobs. Jaycee had learned she was a bank teller, her father a regional sales manager, and her little sister a senior at Cal-Tech. Ultimately, Jaycee wanted an interview with them, a chance to sit down under carefully shaded lighting, and let them open up on camera about the girl who had lived a double life. Pictures of Zoe were scattered through the funeral program. She had been a beautiful young woman, with the same exotic looks of her dark-haired mom. Her sister, Anna, clad in a black pencil skirt and yellow eyelet sweater was entirely her dad. With sweeping blonde hair and sharp cheekbones, she was gorgeous in an all-American kind of way. If Zoe was the orchid, Anna was the sunflower. Two lovely young women from an upstanding family marred forever by the shame of Zoe's death. It was just so tragic.

Closing her eyes, Jaycee shut out the holy words intended to bring comfort. Heat burned through her body, spreading moisture like shower beads beneath her bra and across her shoulders. Even her ankles, crossed beneath the pew, felt slippery.

She returned her gaze toward the front, noting how two long-haired heads leaned toward the other, the outline of a broken heart. Zoe's mom and sister took comfort in touch. Jaycee's eyes traveled the length of their hunched backs, remembering a super-smart psychologist she'd interviewed a while back when an entire family was wiped out by one diseased relative and a butcher knife. Ceaseless sadness. That's what she had called it. A level of human suffering so intense it was emotional quicksand. So entirely consuming, its victims flailed and fought, but eventually tired and faded to black. The story had haunted Jaycee for weeks. When the investigation revealed a deep and long-standing history of mental illness in the family, the media set out like a pack of dogs. Jaycee's task was to uncover the killer's inner torment. The story had earned her an Emmy, but it had taken a toll, smashing her reporter's impartiality toward the victims and reducing her to tears in her shower. A professional line dangerously close to being crossed, she had strayed beyond learning about the people she covered. She had become attached to them even in death.

The good doctor was right. Ceaseless sadness can be as deadly as an AK-47.

* * * *

"I've just started going through Zoe's apartment," Mrs. Statler whispered, *choked*, to mourners as they passed through the family receiving line. With the service over, Jaycee hung back at a respectable distance. She scanned for stragglers, anyone who appeared alone or especially focused on the family's grief. Truly perverted killers often attend the funerals of their victims. She'd covered a story like that years ago in Maine. A tow-truck driver would listen for distress calls and then get there first. He'd left four people to bleed out and die in their trunks and then brought flowers to their caskets. It was a sick world.

"I know there are things she would want you to have," she overheard Mrs. Statler tell a lovely young woman with reddish hair. "And I have to figure out what to do with Tanner." A sad grin distorted her face as she went on to explain Zoe's baby was a rescue dog, a zippy pit bull mix banned in many tony suburbs after too many kid-faces were ripped off by their powerful jaws. She heard her dad tell someone that Tanner would need an owner who had a lot of energy. Jaycee looked away, feeling like a nosy interloper. She walked back into the belly of the church. She approached the casket with soft steps.

Yellow roses sprayed out across the oak casket, Zoe's favorite flowers. The lid was closed. Zoe's wounds were too grave for the traditionally open casket of a Catholic service. Jaycee moved slowly, carefully on her thin metal heels, heat rose up her neck like spindly fingers. With a shaky hand, she touched the cold, polished wood, trying to connect with the young woman tucked away inside.

"Help me," she said inside her head. "Help me find the man who did this to you. Help me find your clues. Let me tell your story. I know you were more than just a victim."

"Jaycee Wilder?"

She jumped back, eyes snapped open in surprise as her hand reached for the fold of her gray shirt near her startled heart. "Excuse me?" she murmured to the man in a dark suit about two sizes too small. She'd noticed him a while back. He had been alone, just like her. "You startled me. Yes, I'm Jaycee. Have we met?" Her eyebrows knitted together. She was used to getting recognized and didn't like the idea of being a distraction.

"Detective James Barton. L.A.P.D. Homicide."

"Ah, yes, I see you had the same idea I did." She didn't recognize this guy, certainly no one she'd interviewed before. Jaycee had a good memory for faces. This one was paunchy, with gauzy hazel eyes rimmed by thin lashes and a sloped forehead. He looked like he spent more time in bars with rusted beer taps than combing the streets for criminals.

"I'll likely be covering Zoe's murder for ABC 12," she told him.

He opened his eyes wider, revealing yellow, jaundiced eyeballs, a telltale sign of a man who battled the demon at the bottom of a bottle. "Then I guess you'll be talking to me. I'm heading up the investigation on Zoe."

Jaycee moved her lips sideways, not particularly thrilled that a boozy, fat-ass slouch was leading the charge to find Zoe's killer. She reminded herself not to assume the worst.

"I didn't see anything weird going on here, did you?"

"In terms of suspects?" he narrowed his eyes at her and figured it was okay to continue. "No. I don't see anything of interest."

"Obviously, Zoe is the third victim killed in a sex club setting. I think you have a serial killer," she quipped, all done with pleasantries. "What do you have on that?"

Barton shot her a curious expression but followed it quickly with his typical cop dismissive. "Once you start thinking a certain way about your evidence," he chastised her, "you risk bending the entire case around to support it."

Jaycee sighed. She would not be put off.

"Three dead girls along Hollywood Boulevard. Six months. You have a serial killer, and you know it." She was willing to risk being more right than wrong.

He analyzed her with narrowed eyes and a sudden spark of respect. Maybe this news babe had more than just a nice rack. It wouldn't hurt to hear her out.

"Off the record?" he started, because he would say no more if she couldn't guarantee him a clean conversation. "You reporter types have burned me before."

"I don't work like that. Ask anyone. I value my sources, and I'm not just a reporter type. Until you instruct me otherwise, I will consider this and any fact-sharing discussions we have entirely off the record. Tell me this freak left something behind. Something you can work with?"

Barton nodded, impressed with her assessment. He looked left and then right to ensure no ears were open and ready to receive. "You keep this quiet now, right? I don't need this shit hitting the screen or the paper. Not yet."

"Yes."

"Killer left behind a mess of Zoe, but the human forensics in that place is off the charts. Same with the other two. Sure, we probably have his DNA, but it's all scattered in there along with four dozen other dudes. And Zoe hadn't been with just one guy that night. That gives us a conflict in body fluids if you know what I mean. It will be awhile to catalog all that…stuff," he coughed on the word.

"So, you couldn't press charges," she offered, nodding along with his point. "One would cancel out the other."

"Potentially. I would want more than that anyway. Again, all that is out at the lab but forensics backlogs being what they are, you can expect that to take some time."

That pissed Jaycee off. These girls deserved better.

"Even though there was enough blood to power a dialysis machine, and partial prints up the wazoo," Barton moved his hand across his wide abdomen in a sweeping motion. It forced Jaycee to notice a missing button on his shirt. Sloppy. "It's all irrelevant unless we can find one that matches all three fucking scenes. I'm just not there yet. 'Scuse my mouth." Barton had a habit of blurting out offensive words no matter the company he was keeping. At least he remembered to apologize for it.

"Are you pulling fibers, fingernail scrapings, or talking to witnesses?" Even as she said it, she realized that the people who entered these places were ghosts.

A blank expression under droopy bottom eyelids confirmed exactly that. "Yeah, we're trying. I got a guy whose name is on the lease, but far as I can tell, he doesn't exist. The clientele isn't required to leave their names and addresses behind. Everyone pays in cash, no receipts to follow, and no one checks in or out. By the time we got a call from a pay phone to report Zoe's death, the sun was rising, and whoever had been there was long gone. They're like vampires, these people. The light of day burns their skin off. It's a subculture. Things like this happen all the time when you subscribe to a certain type of lifestyle. People die, or end up missing, and too often we can't figure it out."

Zoe's murder was getting old. It didn't take a tired cop in the back of a church to convey to Jaycee that precious time was passing too rapidly.

"So, that's it?" she asked him pointedly. "That's all you got?"

Barton stared hard at Jaycee, a silent reminder to tuck this away from public consumption.

23

"Not exactly," he said.

"It stays between us," she confirmed, "you have my word. But from this point on, I want yours. I get your exclusives on this. Something breaks and you call me first. Okay?"

He shuffled fat feet jammed into worn loafers. "What's in it for me?"

Jaycee was far past flinching. She barely registered a blink. She sometimes made her sources look good on television. It was no big deal, a win-win without compromising her own integrity or theirs.

"Professional exposure," she began, "and guaranteed coverage when you break this case one clue at a time. I'll be there telling everyone how awesome you are. And I'll keep you honest." Jaycee couldn't resist a flirty wink. That always helped seal the deal when she needed a coveted male source on her side.

Barton considered her offer. It would be nice to make a name for himself in the department. Lord knew he had some making up to do.

"Deal," he said, thinking that up close this young woman looked like she could be David Beckham and Christie Brinkley's love child.

Jaycee reached for his hand to shake on it. Barton met her outstretched right hand with his left. An odd choice, she thought.

"Back to a serial killer," he began. "Why would you go there?" Jaycee sensed he was feeling her out more than considering this an original idea.

"Simple logic, really. I cover murders almost weekly. Gunshots, stabbings, what-have-you, but these are three dead girls, in a short time span in similar locations. No suspect, yet hideously violent deaths, and that's just what we know from the press releases. I'm sure it's much worse. How could you *not* start thinking about the possibility?"

"I'd say it's more than a possibility. I'd call it a probability. But we're not going there. Not yet. Once you pull that alarm, every sick motherfucker out there tries to clog up the system with bogus tips and it slows us way down. 'Scuse my mouth." Barton again looked around to ensure privacy. This was a bombshell they were keeping quiet for now.

"Strictly off the record for now?"

Jaycee nodded. "Of course," she told him.

"Our killer uses his victims' blood to leave a message."

Jaycee's mouth pinched around her teeth. Her juices flowed; fingers tingled in anticipation. "A message in blood?" she asked, but more just to repeat it to herself. "What does it say?"

"Throw Away Girl."

Jaycee's neck snapped back.

Throw Away Girl.

25

"What the fuck does that mean," Jaycee asked him. "'Scuse my mouth."

Barton shook his head. A few stray dark hairs he'd tried to strap down across the shiny globe of a head caught the sunlight through the stained-glass windows of the church and gleamed pure white.

"As of right now? We have no idea. But when we find our serial killer, we'll be sure to ask him."

Chapter Four

Metallica's "Fade to Black" boomed from cheap speakers on a dingy bureau. The man sat in front of a long mirror, lining his eyes with black kohl, and adjusted the sideburns along the edges of his ink-colored wig. His knees bobbed inside of tight pants, nervous excitement circling around the dark desire that had been doing a slow burn inside of him for days. He desperately needed another release. The sensation was becoming more difficult to deny, and Los Angeles was like a ripe cherry: sweet and delicious.

The basement-level, one-room apartment was gloomy and loaded with cobwebs that climbed from the baseboards to the edges of the drop ceiling. An overhead bulb seeped out yellowish light in a blinking tempo, its wires weak and barely connected. The bed against the wall was stained and bare. He only slept there occasionally, when his appetite grew and he required a feeding, a temporary detour from his life as a fine upstanding taxpayer and all-around Good Samaritan. No one knew about this place. He rented it under a fake name and paid in cash. Just as he'd done elsewhere, in other cities, at other times.

Untraceable.

For quite some time, his sporadic visits to this cave had been enough. That had allowed him enough time to become acclimated to the scene. He'd allowed salacious but otherwise tame releases of the sexual tension inside him to push back the urges he tried to suppress. Then, suddenly, inexplicably, a switch flipped up and the longing grew more demanding. It gnawed him raw. Why deny it? When he was a child, he quenched the thirst with animals. A stray cat, a slow squirrel, a chubby puppy, whatever he could inconspicuously get his hands on would suffice. He'd start with a paw, transferring his own pain to the creature. He'd remove its tail, or a tooth, only feeling better about himself once the animal felt its own agony. When the shock wore off and the pain became blinding for the creatures, the man would end it. He was in control, a god in his own right.

Pictures of a blonde-haired woman poked out from the wooden frame of the mirror. In some, she was smiling wide, happy, and lively while she chatted into her cell phone. He liked those; they made her look innocent and fresh. The other pictures were artsy and distorted. Taken from a distance, they revealed lines on her forehead as she sat in thought, muscles flexed in her forearms as she wrote something in a notebook. Those made his lips quiver. His camera magically caught an overwhelmingly sensual glimpse at the intensity of this stranger's personality. He had noticed her outside a coffee shop recently. This was L.A., so when he'd snapped off a few clicks with his superzoom camera, no one took notice. Hell, he looked like all the other paparazzi staked out in West Hollywood. She photographed beautifully, just as he knew she would. The light softened her sharp features and shadowed a full mouth and long, graceful neck. Her body was slim and tight, indicative of five–mornings-a-week spin class. Her eyes were green, her nose straight and strong. He had thought endlessly of every part of her since. How he wanted to touch her perfection, appreciate it, and then hold her down while he tore, dented, and destroyed it. The blonde woman's pictures were similar to others hanging in bunches around the room. He spent many hours behind his camera. He found images of his future victims everywhere: in the grocery store, in line at Starbucks, at the animal shelter he volunteered at, even at work. He took their pictures without their knowledge. Some were brunettes, while others were auburn-haired lovelies. The man was discerning in his types, but he appreciated the full-color spectrum of a woman's beauty. He loved women. But sometimes he had to kill them. Only some of them. The bad ones.

The Throw Away Girls.

Throwing a worn leather jacket over a black t-shirt, the man locked the door of the cramped apartment and walked up one floor to ground level. Making his way down streets filled with Los Angeles' unique creatures that only came out at night, he counted out one, two, three blocks and took a sharp left down an alley that looked identical to the ones before and after. Two skinny girls leaned against the stucco wall, smoking cigarettes held by long fingers with chipped nail polish. "Hey," they said in slurred unison.

"Hey," he tossed back, barely acknowledging them. Not his type. He pulled on a metal handle and slid through the bulky door. Sparkly light oscillated from a disco ball, tossing orbs of color through the large main room. Guitar-fueled rock music thumped through him like a pulse. He walked across stained industrial grade carpet, breathing in the smell of seduction and sweat. Rolling his knuckles, he plodded ahead past bodies intertwined and bent over sideways and then stepped over discarded undergarments thrown around in random haste. He kept his eyes straight ahead, preferring not to watch. He had mild disdain for those who engaged in public stimulation.

A bar set up around a half-wall hid a tender tucked behind the wooden counter wearing a muscle shirt that showed off intricate ink on both arms. His earlobes gauged and filled with black, circular disks. Small metal hoops lined his eyebrows, nostrils, and lower lip. The man could only speculate what else he had going on with the body parts he couldn't see.

"Lookin' for Olive," he yelled over the driving beat of the music.

"Who the fuck are you?" the bartender challenged. He was protective of Olive, that was okay.

"Tell her Slade is here. She'll know who I am."

He slumped onto a sticky barstool, not giving much thought to the bodily fluids his pants were absorbing, and reached for a small plastic straw. He tucked it between two back molars, chewing mildly to absorb some of the electricity flowing through his body. Fuck, he needed this bad! It had been growing like a blister, a monstrous urge to release, conquer, and savage the worthless. Tonight was about the danger, but he would not risk it with Olive. Although he yearned for something blonde and lean, like the girl at the coffee shop, that release could wait.

Olive was not a Throw Away Girl. She was strong and powerful; she would live. He deemed it so.

Two naked men sauntered by the bar, stopping for refills of some honey-colored liquid poured into red Solo cups. The bartender returned from a back room where Olive shuttered herself away between clients, holding up one finger to communicate a short wait time before she appeared. He topped off the two men and then returned to his perch in the back of the bar where he perversely watched all the action with the built-in excuse that it was his job. Sick bastard. The man gazed away from the bartender, squinting in the foggy air that grew more humid and acrid with the addition of several more barely dressed bodies. L.A.'s underground sex playgrounds were thriving, some of the best he'd ever seen. Strangers lived out fantasies with nameless partners who didn't give a shit about overdue mortgage payments, or fucked up childhoods that carried dysfunction into adulthood. Real life stuff never mattered here. It was all about the anonymity, the pleasure, and yes, the pain.

The man watched a young woman circle another, gliding a spiky fingernail down her arm and hooking it around her wrist. They moved together to the driving timbre of the heavy metal song, untying flimsy knots behind their backs that hold their shirts in place. As they

31

stepped out of jean shorts and low-waisted thongs, he turned away. Only Olive could give him what he needed right now. He would save the rest for some blonde girl on another night. One who resembled the flashy fashionista he'd been savoring recently.

He smelled her before he saw her, a sultry blend of sweet mint and sandalwood that made his mouth water. Clad in a flowing black robe open at the neck, Olive was a vision of extremes. A complete opposite of the blonde beauty he had been obsessing over, Olive's jet black hair sat upon ivory white skin clear of tattoos or piercings. Olive would never defile her temple. Her long nails and round lips were blood red. A small raised line near her full lower lip caught his attention. Someone must have gotten a bit rough.

"Come," she hissed like a snake into his ear. She walked in front of him, a slow, slinky gait accentuated by five-inch heels. Her hips coasted along with each step, wispy fabric swayed over lacy lingerie. The moans and high-pitched squeals from the main room faded the deeper they ventured into the cavernous tunnel of small, square rooms reserved for special clients with specific needs. Anything went here, as long as cash exchanged hands and no one wound up dead or permanently maimed. You were, however, allowed to come close. With Olive, he often did.

She led him into a smoky room. Before she closed the door behind them, he saw two women in corsets and fishnet stockings lead a man attached to a chain, blindfolded, and naked from the waist down. The man had shriveled skin and knobby knees. No wonder he had to pay for it. With a heavy thud, the door closed behind them and Olive sashayed over to one wall, where a bondage apparatus swung slowly, waiting for some action.

"Come here," she ordered, reaching for a thick rope. The man shook his head.

"Not tonight, my princess."

"What do you want, Slade?"

"Pain."

"That can be achieved," she drawled, turning from the rope to a braided leather whip. "Take your clothes off."

The man walked toward Olive, violating the rules of bondage by approaching his dominatrix without permission. Olive flinched at his advance. "Back, savage!" she exclaimed in a husky, trained voice. He respected Olive. She managed this place, was smart enough to use it rather than allow it to use her. He would never consider her a Throw Away Girl. Therefore, Olive would live, but she was about to learn how close she could come to the edge.

The man grabbed her elbow and spun her around until her spine was against his chest. "Shut up, slut!" he jeered. "The pain is all yours."

Olive didn't panic yet. She was familiar enough with his erotic fantasies that sometimes bordered on the delivery of discomfort. Some nights, she quite enjoyed that. She relaxed her backside against the man's wiry hips, undulating slowly back and forth. This was a bit disrespectful to her role, her back to him, but this client had demonstrated a range of desires in the past that teased her limits. What the hell, she thought, he was attractive in a high fashion sort of way and always left her a huge tip. She would zip her mouth and endure his Type-A control freak indulgences because they always paid off.

He laced his fingers through her hair. She moaned as if on cue. He told her to shut up. "Do not instruct me," she argued seductively, as if reprimanding her petulant student. "It is I who dictates your pleas—"

Olive's air suddenly dried up. She couldn't speak. Her eyes began to swim. "Sorry, Queen Bee, I don't think you're in any position to tell me what to do, yes? Do you like that I can control whether you live or die? Am I scaring you?" His voice sing-songed, taunting her with its glibness.

Her hands scrambled to loosen the chokehold on her windpipe. Her legs searched for balance, those stupid metal heels slid on the cement floor, unable to grab any traction. She attempted an elbow to his gut, but there was no force behind the strike. He merely stepped backward and introduced more space between their bodies. The fingers tightened, squeezing the life right out of her.

Until, inexplicably, they let go. Olive slumped to the floor, her lungs heaving while her eyeballs bulged from their sockets. She tested her voice and heard only croaks. Sweat pooled along her brow and rolled in rivers down her back.

Club music blared outside the room. No one would hear her if she screamed. For the first time since she was old enough to defy her strict Catholic upbringing, Olive prayed. Her mother was right. She should have become a lawyer.

She clutched her knees to her chest, inhaling her own scent that suddenly reeked like a whore's calling card, her left cheek flush with the cold floor. Several hundred dollar bills fluttered down onto her head. The man walked calmly to the door and stepped into the hallway without looking back. Only when she was sure he wasn't coming back did she let herself fall apart.

About five minutes later, she stood up, brushed herself off, and got back to work. The night was too young, and there was still money to be made.

Chapter Five

"Jaycee, you're late!"

She wasn't, really. But in Clare Chatworth's world of deadlines and live shots timed to the second, on time was showing up two hours in advance.

"Nice to see you, too, Clare," Jaycee huffed, dropping her overstuffed Hermes bag onto her desk. The plush, red leather beauty had been a gift to herself when she landed the job in Los Angeles a few years back.

Clare slid the expensive bag two feet to the right, making room to thrust her burly forearms onto Jaycee's desk. She wiggled her wide rear into the chair opposite Jaycee, as its wheels squeaked in protest.

"Anything of interest at the funeral?" she asked.

"Not really reportable, no. But I'm working a new source."

"My office. Now." She lumbered out of the chair and hobbled on two thick ankles toward the glass doors of her office, or The Fishbowl, as it was more commonly known among the unfortunate reporters hauled in for a tongue lashing while the entire newsroom pretended not to watch.

Jaycee chuckled. She liked Clare. The older woman had been like a mentor to Jaycee, she may have a salty mouth and a crusty disdain for incompetence, but her heart was as deep as her ass was wide. Most of all, she was always fair. If she called you out on something, she always listened to your side. That's why Jaycee was certain Clare would understand her need to pursue her hunches.

"Sit," she commanded, once they were inside her office and the door had sealed shut.

Jaycee sat. "Clare, I want this story."

"Derek covered the other two girls," she reminded Jaycee. "And you're on that identity theft special—don't roll your eyes at me—it may not be sexy but the old timers will love it." Derek was her lead investigative reporter and head of the station's I-Team. Jaycee was just the latest addition to it. If Clare played the seniority card, Jaycee's hand was a dud.

"I get that. But Clare, there's more to this than Derek will point out. You know he's…" she looked down at her lap. It was disrespectful to trash a colleague to their boss, but this was too important. Derek was lazy, and too wrapped up in his new twenty-four-year-old play thing to do the extra legwork involved in a heavy story like this one.

"…Well, let's just say he's not as motivated as I am. Plus, think of this as good exposure for the I-Team. I need to earn my keep, right?" She held a firm stare into her news director's deep brown eyes. A gazing contest ensued until Clare cocked her head and brushed firmly at her short bangs.

"Fine. But not today, I need you elsewhere. You're on a tough one. Stray bullet. Shitty area near Watts. Little kid goes down last night, shot up right through his bedroom wall. The dead sluts can wait. You okay with that?"

"Of course. Live for both the 5&6?" Jaycee felt almost giddy. The story was hers to pursue!

"Ronaldo will talk to you about the rundowns, but you'll be A block in both shows. The truck will meet you later this afternoon. Don't plan on coming back here and for Christ sake, don't bring that million-dollar, bright red bag that screams *"Go ahead, mother fucker, take it."*

Jaycee laughed and stood up. She needed to check in with the assistant news director, Ronaldo, to discuss her live shot location and then make some calls. "Okay, I won't. I have a Nike bag in the car. Please tell me B-Rod is here? He didn't return my text last night."

Ben Roderick, whom she had affectionately nicknamed B-Rod after his baseball crush, Alex Rodriguez, whom he lusted after with all the power of a hundred-mile-an-hour fastball, was Jaycee's favorite photographer and good friend. They'd been together for about two years now. Ben was what they called a "market-hopper." He jumped around from one city to the next, banking experience and skill at different stations, and never sticking around too long. Ben told her he wanted the big time, network television, or perhaps something life-affirming like a National Geographic project. Jaycee had no doubt he was good enough to get there. Together, they had found a mutual respect for the other's work ethic. Ben was a genius with his camera, finding unique angles and beautiful touches that brought a story to life. He had become like the goofy cousin you sat next to for Thanksgiving dinner and pretended to drop boogers into each other's mashed potatoes. She could be real with Ben. He'd spent a few days off in Mexico with a new guy he'd described as a knock-off version of the real Yankee.

"He's like one of those Louis Vuittons you buy out of some Mexican dude's trunk," he'd joked to her. "Still fits on your shoulder but the zipper sticks."

"Yeah, he's back all right." Clare did a series of three quick snaps in front of her bouncing boob shelf. Ben was a diva, but he was fantastic at his job. Whenever she could, Clare paired Jaycee with Ben and together they brought beautiful images and thoughtful storytelling to her award-winning news team.

"Great, a little bit of Ben is just what I need today. I'm off," she gave a little salute and hustled toward the glass door.

"Jay-Jay," Clare called after her. "Be careful out there, girl. Smart…"

"…and safe," Jaycee finished the station motto they all muttered before heading into possible peril. "See you on the TV."

"Uh-huh." Clare watched her rising star reporter take brisk steps toward Ronaldo's office, feeling a sense of unease she couldn't explain. Kid was hungry; that was a given. She just hoped Jaycee had the good sense to temper that with caution.

Clare could only worry for so long. Her office phone was jingling like a wind chime and her cell was vibrating its way right off her desk.

"Jesus fucking Christ!" she spat. Picking up the black plastic handle next to her flat screen computer, she plopped into her chair and kicked off her day with a fiery, "This better be good."

There just wasn't enough time in her world to worry about Jaycee Wilder.

Chapter Six

"Los Angeles Police Department," the female voice stated. "Officer Tollson speaking, how can I direct your call?"

"Detective Woodson, please," Jaycee told her. "It's Jaycee Wilder, ABC 12 News."

"Hold," she said, unimpressed, clicking over to a pleasant male voice that rattled off a canned message. "The Los Angeles Police Department depends on you. Help us make our communities a strong and safe place to live, for you and your fam…"

"Woodson," the detective's growl cut off the automated monotone. He may sound menacing, but the fifty-something, gray-haired cop was one of Jaycee's favorites. He covered the southeast community police station, difficult spots like Parkside Manor, Hacienda Village, and Watts. Detective Woodson maintained an upbeat, friendly nature in spite of the vile human behavior he was exposed to daily.

"Mornin' Detective, it's Jaycee."

"Hey, kiddo, let me guess, you're on the Watts shooting today?"

"Yup. Got time to give me some quick sound?"

"For you? Of course. I'm heading over to the scene in about a half-hour. Meet you over there?"

"Sounds good. Thank you." Jaycee hung up and quickly ran to her car to exchange bags. She signaled to

Ronaldo that she was leaving and told the assignment editor she was taking Ben.

"No shit, Jay Jay," he shot back, crooked glasses blinking back sallow newsroom light. "Thanks, I wouldn't have known that."

Jaycee and Ben, the A-Team, Always Together Through All Kinds of Weather. The silly slogan stuck after a series of dangerous late winter storms that pummeled the Southland last year. They hunkered down together in L.L. Bean anoraks and rubber boots, going live for wall-to-wall coverage of flash flooding, mudslides, and pounding hail that tormented residents for days, both of them refusing to clear the scene or clock out until the worst had passed.

She heard him before she saw him. That detached lilt in his voice, an uppity east coast drawl that had her half-smiling with its familiarity.

Jaycee made her way through the photographers' garage, where the news SUVs were parked and the cameras, batteries, and lights were stored. The cement walls kicked back a stench of stale cigarette smoke, exhaust, and greasy fast food bags. Photographer's rigs were infamously unkempt. Sandy floor mats collected muck from crime scenes, every nook and cranny stuffed with stained napkins or crumpled notepaper, and potent odors poked through even the most powerful Christmas tree-shaped air fresheners. All rigs, except for the navy blue Ford Explorer Ben drove every day. It was meticulous. Jaycee longed to slide onto the soft cloth seat Ben washed

42

down every night after work and bask in the warm shine of the dashboard that smelled of an all-natural almond cleanser. Ben's rig, her second home, was her safe place when the world outside was so ugly and twisted.

The big engine was already rumbling as Jaycee swung the door open and climbed in. Her blue eyes found his. "Get in, you hag," he started. "Didn't you eat since I last saw you? You are like, heroin chic skinny right now; it's El Pollo Loco for lunch today, my treat. Gotta plump up that skinny ass."

"Don't worry, asshole, the camera does that nicely on its own."

He ruffled her elbow, handing over the oval Ray Ban metal-rimmed glasses she kept in his SUV. "Hater blockers on…" he stated dryly.

"…World out," she completed their daily mantra. Pulling out of the garage bay, Ben tossed his own Oakleys over the chestnut brown hair strewn across his forehead and asked where to.

"Watts shooting. Defiance Ave. Kid takes a bullet through the wall."

"Bummer."

"Woodson is meeting us at the scene. We'll get him on camera and then I'll try the mother. And a baby daddy if one happens to show up. You never know, we could get lucky."

"Or not."

"Yeah, or not. So how was vaca? You and Blake have fun in Me-hee-ko?" she asked cheerfully. Ben glanced over at her, a salty expression darkened his angular face. His strong chin sported a thicket of new whiskers over pink skin.

"Oh, ouch. Jeesh, do I have to call this guy and tell him to tone down the rough sex?" she grimaced at the fading scab.

"Yeah, not exactly," Ben pointed out several spots of raw skin on his face and neck. "It's the other way around, trust me." Ben's right wrist tilted down only slightly. He didn't give off many clues about his sexual orientation, but Jaycee had always had a keen eye. She picked up on his vibe immediately and couldn't care less. In fact, Ben being gay almost made her love him more. There was no creepy tension between them, no ogling her when she got caught in a rainstorm in a tight sweater, or weird zooms on her boobs when he was shooting her live shots.

"This is from the spa bee-atch in Cabo who gave me a glycolic peel. She took half my face off. Cost me a hundred and fifty bucks, too."

"Oh, my poor Benny-Boo. I'm thinking that I'd like to meet him," Jaycee stated. "If he's important to you, I want to know him. It's time."

"Yes, mom. Hey, it's not like I'm hiding him. He's in software sales. Dude's busy; he's always in a plane. Mexico was just a layover for him. He's in Japan right now, probably getting one of those fish pedicures."

"Eww, remember we did that story last year? At that nasty spa in Paramount? It shut down after that."

They moved on to the weather, *flawless*, Jaycee's shoes, *way too fabulous to feel good*, and Ben's new agave lip moisturizer, *a total splurge*. Eventually, during the drive over to Watts, she brought up the death of Zoe Statler.

"No way?" he asked sharply. "For real, another one? Didn't Derek do a story about some other hooker in a fleabag club recently?"

Sarah Walsh. It had been a mostly vague report, uninspired and half-assed, and strictly off the press release with zilch extra effort. Derek had yet to even bother with a follow-up. Jaycee wanted to change that.

"Yes, he did. Sarah Walsh was the first. Not a prostitute, though, just a waitress who liked to go to those weird fetish clubs on Hollywood Boulevard. Another girl, Mackenzie Drew was next, same kind of place. Now, this one. Her name was Zoe Statler. She was a seventh-grade science teacher in Long Beach."

"And apparently liked to run her own experiments at night?" he joked.

"Apparently," Jaycee confirmed but didn't laugh along. "I think there's more to it."

"More to what? Three dead girls found in bad places?"

"Yeah, here's the thing. This isn't kinky sex takes a deadly turn, Ben. I think there's one killer out there targeting these girls."

His eyes registered shock. "What? Jay Jay, seriously, turn your suspicious reporter radar down a notch. How do you *think* you know that?"

"Don't you ever watch TV? Listen to our newscasts?" she huffed. "Read a newspaper?"

"Does the Stars Without Makeup edition of the Enquirer count? If so, then, yes, I do read newspapers."

Jaycee looked at her friend with a half-smirk. "Good thing you were born beautiful and talented, my friend. 'Cause your brain isn't gonna pay the bills."

"True dat, sista," he drawled. "So anyway, getting back to your theory. Tell me more."

Jaycee played with her phone. It wasn't easy to put theory into convincing fact. She remembered Barton's remark that if you force it hard enough, evidence can take any shape you want it to. "I don't really have more. Again, just my suspicious reporter's hunch."

"Why aren't we covering this today, then? Didn't you push Clare to let you into the story?"

"I did. She promised I could have the follow-up. Starting tomorrow, I'm making calls and knocking on doors. Today, we're stuck with a little kid and a stray bullet."

Chapter Seven

"Ben and Jaycee, stand by."

Jaycee was still, listening through her tiny plastic earpiece to the anchors setting up her story back in the studio. Ben's eye socket pressed into the rubber around the viewfinder; his tripod aimed high to elongate Jaycee's frame. A little trade secret in the field—always aim down, never up—the talent preferred it that way. They began with a short intro about the shooting and then tossed out to her.

"…Our Jaycee Wilder is live tonight in Watts. Just tragic, Jaycee, where does this investigation stand?" Jorge Pelloni used his concerned voice. Jaycee envisioned him in his thousand-dollar dove gray Armani suit, sitting on the set shaking his head at the injustice of it all, his mouth turned down in sadness and despair. Such a buffoon.

"Jorge, it is tragic. A young mother put her little boy to bed last night, never imagining it would be the last time she saw him alive. Now, police here in Watts are scouring the neighborhood for clues, determined to track down the person who shot him."

Roll package. Package was up.

The producer's voice in her ear told Jaycee her story was rolling. She heard her own voice tell the woeful tale of a nineteen-year-old girl living in a shithole, trying to raise three kids with three different fathers. But now there were only two. Because some punk pissed off at some other faceless twit just because he called himself a Blood and the other stooge called himself a Crip decided last night was a

good night for him to die. One, two, three shots fired, two
miraculously missed the moron on the sidewalk, while one
wormed its way through the flimsy particleboard wall of
the apartment's front bedroom housing a hand-me-down
crib with a sleeping child tucked into threadbare blankets.
A direct hit through his tiny forehead. An expert marksman
couldn't land this shot, yet some bonehead with a juvenile
brain mash of pride and brotherhood lands it just right with
a stolen Glock.

Disgusting. Unfair. Just fucking wrong.

Jaycee hated herself when she thrust her microphone
into the mother's tear-stained face in the doorway of her
Section Eight house, asking awful questions she knew she
had to. "Tell me about your little boy. Is there anything
you'd like us to know about your son?"

In her ear, Jaycee heard Detective Woodson, in
practiced cop-speak, declare this a terrible night for this
family, and for Los Angeles. He made the vow that they
would find whoever did this to bring closure for this
mother. His voice, then followed by a sound bite from the
tormented mother who was more of a child herself. How
she tucked in Shayjawn, kissed him goodnight, placed his
stuffed elephant by his side—he just wouldn't go to sleep
without it—and moments later heard that sound, that awful
sound mothers around here grow painfully used to. A gun
firing. When she rushed back in, Shayjawn was still. His
sheets were bright red when they should have been polka
dot blue.

48

Jaycee stopped listening, tuning out everything except the out-cue that would alert her when her story ended, and she was up live again. Ben put one hand up to the right of the camera while he refocused his shot, his fist clenched as a sign for her to standby. When his fingers made a circle in the air, she began to tag her story.

"Police tell me they are pursuing a few leads. A neighbor gave them a description of a car speeding from the scene and the gang unit has been called in. Little Shayjawn will be laid to rest this weekend. Reporting live in Watts, Jaycee Wilder, ABC 12 News."

She held her gaze into the lens for a count of four and waited for the producer to set her free. "You're clear, Jaycee, thank you. See you at six," the producer signed off from the booth back at the station, reminding Jaycee of her next live shot for the six o'clock newscast. She had about forty-five minutes to finish her package. She took her seat next to Ben in the live truck, while the engineers checked cables and tightened wires, stopping for regular smoke breaks near the hood of the live truck to make sure the rabid bystanders didn't get too close to Jaycee. In this part of town, her crew was her only protection.

"Hey, pretty lady!"

"Sweet tits!"

"Come on, mama, I'll show you my cock, oops, I mean my Glock!"

Hisses, sputters, obscene remarks and gestures were nothing new. Jaycee got it all the time. She never acknowledged the rants, but Ben couldn't resist.

"Hey, I'm rolling here, losers," he shouted out the door. "I'm sure most of you are out on parole, so fuck off before I turn the video over to the cops and they throw your asses back in the pen."

"Fuck you, man, you lame fuck." Middle fingers thrust into the warm air, high-top sneakers kicked up dirt, and cigarette butts jumped like firecrackers set loose on the ground. Most of the gangbangers were barely of driving age yet already boasted a criminal record that would make John Gotti look like a pussycat.

They walked on, tossing more f-bombs back over their skinny shoulders hanging out of tank top basketball jerseys.

"Jesus Christ," Ben sputtered, plopping into the seat next to Jaycee. "You really gotta do something about your hotness, dah-ling, or I'm gonna start demanding hazardous duty pay. Fucking baby bang'ers can be more savage than the adult version. All right, let's slam it together." Ben pulled the editing keyboard toward him on a small, flat surface with two miniature TV monitors mounted above.

Jaycee was scrolling through the messages on her phone. Her mother sent a text with the usual request for money. She sighed.

"What's up? You okay?" Ben asked, so tuned in to Jaycee that he sensed her mood shift.

"Mom," she held her phone out on top of her palm. Ben nodded.

"Your own fault for giving her your digits. Haven't we already discussed the peril of the needy mamas?"

"Many times," Jaycee relented. Hours together in the news van had revealed cracks in their badass news personas. Ben had shared that his family was uninterested and uninvolved. Jaycee admitted that she only pretended it didn't bother her that her family hailed from a nest of duds. Her mom, somewhere in Vegas, trolling casino floors for rich, old men with high cholesterol and fat bellies, would only call Jaycee when funds ran low. Her dad was too busy raising his new family in some crunchy Utah enclave to worry about his old one. Jaycee was damaged but way too strong to admit it.

She wrapped her hair into a ponytail and rolled it through two fingers on her right hand, an absent habit when she was putting a story together in her head. "Sorry," she said quietly.

"Don't worry, you know that I am perfectly balanced despite being raised by a pack of wolves in the woods," he joked. "Wanna talk money? I got you beat. My next of kin are blowing through my inheritance at some over-fifty-five community in Florida. It's like a little tribe of old people. They putter around in their golf carts, bitch about their hip replacements, and live on the edge by having sex after a heart attack."

"Hmm," she giggled, "nice visual." Getting back to work, she suggested a few changes for their six o'clock story. "I'm thinking we just switch out the Woodson sound bite and one from the mom. I'll pitch it more from the investigation perspective, less emotion. Although when your kid is shot up in his own bed that is a bit like burying the lead. Work for you?"

"Absolutely," Ben agreed. She watched his fingers twirl masterfully around the buttons on the edit board, cutting video over the audio bed. Usually, Jaycee was all over this part, suggesting different shots, or asking for a specific cut-away in her story. Not now. She was sitting awkwardly with one long, slim leg tucked beneath her rear end; sweater pulled tight like a vice around her torso. She was still.

They talked without looking at each other. Ben fast-forwarded and then rewound the images on his computer to fit Jaycee's script. She pointed to time codes on a sheet of paper between them, directing Ben to where the video would be.

"Here, grab it from…'we showed up on scene…' I'll tell you when to cut sound."

"Got it. You're thinking about those dead hookers, aren't you?"

He knew her so well. "Kinda. And they're not hookers, Ben."

Ben mumbled something without any vowels. It was how he communicated when he was distracted with work.

"Are you good with the changes I want for six?" she asked.

"Yup," he said.

"I'll be right back."

Ben's fingers stopped spinning across the control panel. His eyebrows drew together. "Where you goin'?" he demanded to know. He didn't like it when Jaycee wandered around a dangerous scene without him.

"Just to find Woodson. I'll be right back, I promise."

She winked back at her friend, appreciating his concern for her safety. She gritted her teeth after stepping off the last metal stair of the live truck in her heels. There would be blisters tonight for sure. Unwrapping the loose ponytail, she fluffed out her hair and tucked in her shirt. Jaycee took great care in her appearance. She considered it an act of respect for the station she represented, and the people she interviewed. Detective Woodson deserved better than messy hair.

She spotted him near the Crown Vic that had been on scene all day. He was writing something down on a pad of paper while resting one hip on the side of the hood. She knew this bothered him deeply. He would make the most of his police resources and his own stamina to search out the little fucker who had taken down a baby.

"Detective?" she said quietly, not wanting to spook a man with a gun.

He looked up from his notes and smiled at Jaycee. When he did that, deep creases squeezed his lower eyelashes into oblivion. "Hey, kiddo, what's up?" He had already given Jaycee all the sound bites she needed for her story.

"Can I ask you something? Totally off the record?" she always kept her word, Woodson could be certain of that.

"Well, sure, but you know everything I know here…"

"No, not about this," she put her palm up to stop him. "It's something different, another story I'm working on."

"Oh, okay. Not sure if I can help you, but fire away." Again, his eyes were warm and squinty. He liked Jaycee. She was one of those reporters who pushed, but she did it with a smile on her face to take away the sting. It worked for her. Others in her line of work, not so much.

"Between you and me," she began. "Do you know a James Barton, L.A.P.D. Homicide? I think he's new." Jaycee began her probe already expecting a blank expression and a dead end. Woodson's face revealed the exact opposite. In fact, he did a rapid shuffle off the hood to stand sturdy on two legs.

"Are you doing a story on Barton?" he surprised her with the question.

"*On* him? No, no, not at all. I'm looking into the murders of three girls. I think they're connected by one killer."

"What three girls?" he asked.

"Sex club killings," she told him.

"Ah, yes," Woodson nodded. "Barton on this?" he seemed surprised.

Jaycee nodded in the affirmative. She narrowed her eyes, watching his unease grow. What the hell had she just stumbled into?

"If I'm making you uncomfortable, Detective, I apologize. I'm only asking because I met Barton and found a few things about him sort of odd. That's all."

"Odd? Like what?" he pressed. Obviously, if Jaycee were to get anything out of Woodson, he'd prefer if she lead him.

"Well, for one, how he shook my hand was weird. And I didn't like that he came off as sort of jaded."

Detective Woodson typically tolerated reporters. This one, though, he rather enjoyed. Jaycee Wilder always got the story but didn't burn the bridges that helped her tell it. Although he firmly believed in having a brother's back, he trusted her not to exploit the family. Settling backward against the bumper, Woodson gave Jaycee some information. But only the kind that would lead her to her own answers.

"Google him," he started. "Throw in the words Cambridge and Vietnamese and you'll find it all. Suffice it to say Barton is getting his second chance out here. A friend of a friend and all that. He's connected to someone high up in the department, but that man has been through hell."

Jaycee had her instructions. She could barely get through her six o'clock live shot, the anticipation of what she'd find nipping at her until her skin felt like it was on fire.

Chapter Eight

The TV blared some stupid late night talk show with lounging celebrities so tightened and stitched they appeared almost translucent, much like everything else out here. James Barton was not a West Coast kind of guy. He was a doughnut-eating, Irish barstool-sitting dude who swallowed his "r's" and belched out Boston pride. He was drowning in this land of bottled water, pet massages, and skinny jeans no real man should be found dead in. This place had no soul.

Barton took the tip of his pen and made three sharp lines forming the letter Z. He stared at his notes until the words blurred. If he got lucky, forensics could separate the consensual bodily fluids from the criminal ones, but it was a long shot up a high pole. Nothing about the murder of Zoe Statler and the other two girls would give him a tidy case to solve. Tough shit. He was lucky to have a case at all. One misstep and the short chain they kept him on would snap his neck. He could not fuck this up. He'd already been warned that a ticket back to Boston awaited him after his first strike. He no longer deserved a full count. In fact, maybe they had given him this case simply to concrete his short-timer status.

He leaned his bulk back in the chair and then winced at the whine of the bolts trying to keep the thing together. It was late, and he felt like shit. His head was exploding and his blood burned like an army of angry ants was on the move. A solid month without the juice was like a million years of hell. He had no choice. This cold turkey bullshit was his punishment, and like the peasant he'd become, he would take it up the ass just to make sure he still got to see his kid every other Saturday and every third Wednesday night. He'd followed his ex-wife to the West Coast when she'd landed a job at a posh plastic surgery recovery center. Her college roommate happened to have a grandfather who was once an important fat cat in the L.A. police world. He promised to stay clear-headed and professional and begged for the strings to get pulled. He bit back the hate because the payout was enormous. If he wanted to see Mason more than twice a year, he'd have to do it in California. And, he'd have to be sober.

His small apartment back home on Mt. Auburn Street in Watertown, Massachusetts, had few hiding places. Just before Debra confirmed the decision to pack up and head out, their five-year-old reached for a towel in the hallway linen closet and disrupted the resting spot of a half-empty bottle of Glenlivet. Down it came, clipping little Mason's left eyebrow along the way. Three stitches later, she was threatening lawyers, restraining orders, and rehab. It was an accident, of course, but Barton barely had enough shaky ground beneath him already to withstand another earthquake of the magnitude she was threatening. With her angry brother watching, his burly arms crossed, ready to report back to his sister, Barton dumped all his goods down the stained drain in his kitchen, suddenly noticing how slow the pipes were and wondering what the fuck had happened to his life.

As he stared out at a concrete and palm tree landscape that was decidedly different from the heavy tree limbs and historic brick facades he was used to, Barton stopped fooling himself. He knew exactly what had happened. His rapid dismantling had begun on that brittle November day a few years back. Mason was just a little guy then, still sucking away on his bottle, struggling to hold his legs steady on the edges of their wooden coffee table. Debra worked per diem at Brigham and Women's in the cardiac care unit, a nurse who spent most days measuring the red-tinged fluid that flowed through tubes attached to lifeless heart patients. She made a good living and never complained about her work, but being home with Mason made her most happy. They laughed together often in those days, cooked chicken Marsala on the weekends, and took in the occasional Red Sox or Bruins game. He maintained the ability to detach from the horror of his job, to separate the world into two spheres: one that held his family and heart, the other that stored the danger and devastation of his police work. That November night, the fragile barrier between his two worlds shattered like a bullet through bone.

The call came in around dinnertime. All units were told to respond to a high rise in Cambridge, a few blocks from the Charles River. It was in a decent area, lots of young professionals and families who were still working their way out to the burbs. The voice calling into dispatch spoke rapid Vietnamese making it nearly impossible to get a read on what was happening. Then a few tinny *pop-pops* and the line went dead.

Ninth floor, gunshots fired, proceed with caution!

Barton and his partner happened to be nearby on Soldiers Field Road doing some busy work on a separate case when they heard the call. They didn't care about dividing lines among precincts or which city's emblem was on the cruiser door, a cop was a cop and jumped in wherever he was needed. They were the second patrol car to pull into the roundabout drop-off area near the front entrance. Dusk was falling fast. Sirens wailed in the distance; others were on their way. Barton set his scene and marked his location, staying in constant communication with the others but unwilling to wait for them. Just not his style. He admitted to being a bit rogue at times but only when time-sensitive situations demanded immediate action. He entered the building and found the stairwell, taking the steps two at a time. In those days, he didn't drink more than a Sam Adams or two at a backyard barbecue; his body was fit, lean, and hard-driving. If he had to haul himself up nine flights of stairs today, he'd drown in a pool of his own puke.

His partner was on his right hip, another officer with gun drawn just behind him. They stopped outside apartment 904. Pressing an ear to the door, Barton heard the muffled whimper of a small child. With a powerful front kick, he tore through the entrance without a single clue of what he'd find on the other side. He announced his presence in clear terms…*Boston Police, drop your weapons!*

The young cop behind him immediately turned tail and gagged up his lunch. The stench was inhuman. Windows sealed shut, the galley kitchen littered with what looked like hunks of sidewalk meat decaying on the linoleum. The living room was dark. Long panels of cheap curtains were squeezed together to block out light and air. It was sweltering inside. Instantly, Barton's skin was shiny and slick, lines of salty water poured in fast rivers down his face, stinging his eyes. Taking quick swipes to clear them, he first noticed something stacked up in one corner. He moved closer, squinting in disbelief. No, can't be. Can it? Two arms, a foot, and several long thin fingers scattered between them. All bloody stumps that appeared freshly dismembered. Heaps of gray near the kitchen caught his eye. Barton walked closer, bending down while breathing through his mouth. Skin. Slivers of ashen flesh pulled back from muscle and tissue that had hardened and shriveled. Stainless steel pots and pans were nearby. He peeked inside, dreading what he would see. Puckered and opaque, multiple eyeballs bobbed in some murky liquid that resembled toxic gel, the life they once held long lost.

"Jesus Christ," Barton muttered as his partner called for his quick attention.

"Barton, here!" came the order from the left side of the shadowy square room, near the windows, pushed up against the wall. The source of the anguished juvenile voice was discovered.

A small Asian man was sitting calmly in the center of a paisley-print couch. In his right hand was a small black revolver that had obviously done significant damage to the face of the woman slumped next to him. Barton's gaze zipped to the left side of the man. His bony shoulder was slung around a tiny form under a Tinkerbell blanket, the shiny glint of a military style knife extended from his left hand, just above the torso of the small body laid out on his chest. *Fabulous,* Barton thought, *a dual threat*. Gunshot or knife slash. Both equally deadly.

The rusty blade followed a slow, slicing pattern, a clear warning from this deranged maniac that he was prepared to cut more. Barton saw it was already sticky with drying blood of which God only knew the source.

"Put your weapons down," Barton moved slowly toward the man, expressionless under dead eyes. "Just let us take the child. We won't hurt you. We just want the child."

Protocol would demand he stall. Talk to the suspect, defuse, force a retreat, or wait for SWAT and hostage negotiators to wrap things up. Only as an absolute last resort would Barton fire. His finger gripped the trigger. Protocol could fuck itself.

A beastly grin revealed black spaces where teeth used to be. Barton made a pushing motion to the officer behind him, an indication to keep arriving forces back. This man was too volatile for any quick movements. That goddamn knife could maim the kid with just a flick of his wrist. The officer slowly made his way back toward the front door. Two others, including Barton, left in the living room.

"They move, too!" barked the man in a heavy accent, motioning with his head to the officers behind Barton.

"No way," Barton clipped.

The man pulled the knife back slightly, a cocky tilt to his eyebrows that told Barton he was in control as long as this child was within striking distance.

"All right, all right. Do not hurt that kid!"

Radio transmissions buzzed. Barton held his stance, his gun out straight, aimed at the man's head. Could he take the shot? The kid's skull was only inches away. Shit! It was still too risky. He told the younger officer to move back, ignoring his attempt to protest. "Do it," he said calmly. "Give me the kid," he made a come-here motion with three fingers on his left hand. The man watched his hand; an evil idea took shape.

The rot inside his mouth appeared again, along with a baleful giggle. "You want girl. You give me finger."

"What!?" Barton snapped in disbelief. He took a quick look behind him to see if anyone was still there. This might be more than he could take on. They needed a sniper to put a fucking bullet in this guy's brain, stat!

"Finger," he confirmed loudly, but his eyes were already rounding in sick anticipation of what Barton might be willing to do. He licked his cracked lips with a thin tongue, obviously hyped up. "Or I kill." He shrugged, like it was no big deal. The blanket covering the form next to him on the couch slipped down, revealing two spiky ponytails held together by pink ribbon. The tip of the knife perched about an inch from the tiny bulb of her nose and wickedly close to her carotid.

"You sick fuck!" Barton spat. "You give me that kid, or I will take you down with one shot."

"Finger," he whispered, stretching out his elbow to force the blade across the girl's neck in one rapid motion. She gasped as it split her tender skin. A torrent of red opened, but the wound wasn't deep enough to cut her air.

"No, no, stop!" Barton screamed, instinctively approaching the couch and reaching for the bleeding child. The door burst back open, the hallway teeming with a sea of blue, weapons locked and loaded. Barton threw his arm at them. "No!" he yelled out in a gravelly voice, fearful the distraction would snap this asshole's focus.

"Back, back!" the man screeched, his voice rising, whiny and needling. "Finger, now!"

The knife again made contact with the girl's open wound. Barton narrowed one eye, aiming above the lank bangs fanning the man's forehead. His hands were unstable. Fuck! He might miss.

"Screw you," Barton whispered, aware of fat splats of sweat falling off his cheeks. His mouth tasted like old cheese and flat Coke. He locked eyes with the little girl. Her tiny hand pressed to her chest, blood spouted vertically through two fingers, her chin quivered in fear and pain. Not much older than Mason. He couldn't let her die.

"Motherfucker! Fine, give me a fucking knife. Do not cut her again!"

The reptilian smile returned. The man motioned to a Swiss army knife folded into itself on the table. Barton knew instinctively it held a mighty blade inside. His hand shook, fingers were slick with sweat, as he kept his right arm level and squatted with his back straight to grab the knife. Flicking it open with his pinkie nail, he noticed the blade was brownish with what must be old blood. The glassy eyes followed his every movement. The only sounds Barton heard were the panicked gasps of the girl and his own heartbeat booming in his ears. He barely registered the scuffing boots near the doorway or the frantic exchanges on their transmitters. He heard them ask again for SWAT and a negotiation team but Barton knew this wouldn't last long enough for them to get there. They had no clean shot. Nor did he. He had to make this work.

He glared at the small-framed man in his white button down shirt streaked with other people's blood, and he wondered what special kind of crazy made a person inflict such devastation.

"Do it," he squeaked again, his voice pitched with giddy anticipation.

"Loosen up your hold on her," Barton instructed, trying to resume control. "I want her on the edge of the couch."

The man swung the child over one knee, placing her bottom on the ragged edge of the cushion. She was too afraid to look at either of them. Barton saw a pink Hello Kitty t-shirt. A rhinestone bracelet. Two sparkly earrings. Someone loved this little girl. Was the dead woman on the couch her mother? This crazy fuck her father?

Barton held the knife in his left hand, his gun in his right.

"No, no, other. Other!" the greasy killer commanded. Barton's mouth gaped as he realized he wanted him to cut his gun hand. Bastard! The man's twitchy body suddenly bounced, he impatiently shook the child until she howled. Barton was rattled. He watched the man raise his knife again and tug the child's chin upward, triggering a fast rush of clumpy blood from the slit on her neck.

"Stop," he screamed. "Stop, no more! Do not hurt her or I will fucking fire!"

"Finger!" he yelled again but refused to release the child. The girl's eyes rolled back as her mouth fell open. Barton knew he was losing her to shock or her little kid brain was simply shutting down. Who knows what else this poor child had seen. He had to act.

Then the man screeched like a Japanese ninja, his eyes wild, blazing with a renewed thirst for more blood. The knife changed trajectory. It moved back toward the girl's ear to widen the cut. Barton was dizzy, the next slice would slit her windpipe. Hello Kitty was now drenched in red, the ponytails drooped, their ribbons loose and hanging free. He jumped onto his toes, the tension in his calves shot up his spine. He forced the man to look at him, to stop the carnage. His voice quaked.

"She's just a kid. Stop! It's all right. Here, see?" He took the Swiss army knife and held it between his thumb and forefinger. The savage was mesmerized, temporarily distracted from the bloody child, his mouth frothy with a mixture of sweat and saliva.

"Do it. Other one," his voice was a mere whisper, the devil inside him fully aroused.

Barton's eyes locked on the kid. One deep breath. Two. It must be quick. He might pass out if he got stuck on the bone. Tucking his weapon into his waist, he trusted that once he could open some space the guys behind him would take the shot. He had to move her just one foot. Two if he could. They needed a clean target. He could do this.

His eyes glazed, he passed the blade under his chin, toward his right hand. The silver metal stopped below the knuckle. The man was still, mesmerized, his breath reduced to sharp bursts. Thankfully, the child was not watching.

Barton dug in, puncturing his own flesh, felt the bone halt the motion, and then exerted more force until it gave.

There was no pain. Not yet. The tiny man's mouth hung open in fascination; his muscles slacked just enough for Barton to act. In a flash, he moved. Flying over the coffee table, he grabbed the girl's arm and pulled her down onto the shaggy rug beneath the couch. He threw both arms around her, trying to wrap her in a human shield. She weighed nothing, so small and fragile. He exhaled. She was safe.

Instantaneously, the man was jerked to his feet; his body heaved left and right under the force of the bullets striking his head and torso. Unfortunately, he was also at the perfect angle to deliver one final blow. His body quickly lost blood and strength, though it had enough of both in reserve to stab straight through the back of the Hello Kitty shirt. The blade reached all the way to Barton's shirt but didn't draw blood. Not from him anyway.

The little girl's downy eyelashes flew open and then slowly lowered as a final breath passed out of her like a gentle breeze.

Until you've had a child die in your arms, Barton thought as he made lazy loops around Zoe's initials again, *don't you dare fucking judge.*

* * * *

At about the same time in her own concrete building with darkened views of palm trees swaying in the balmy Santa Anna breeze, Jaycee Wilder shut down her laptop and stared out at the black sky.

Detective James Barton. One time hero cop. Now, a survivor in his own right.

She had judged him too early. And she had been wrong.

Chapter Nine

Karena Statler sat stone-faced, her unpolished fingertips gently kneading the edge of her skirt until it resembled a narrow tunnel atop her thigh. Her husband, Tom, seemed to be studying the tops of his loafers. Both husband and wife waited patiently for Jaycee and Ben to set up, but Jaycee knew that if either had a choice to be there with her or stranded on an iceberg drifting through the Arctic, the Arctic would have two new residents.

"I apologize for this," she began quietly. "Ben is fast but meticulous. He just wants to make sure the lighting is perfect for our interview."

Karena didn't respond. Tom merely nodded. Between them on the worn coffee table stood a heavy glass frame with their dead daughter's college graduation pose. A wide grin pulled back to reveal even white teeth. Her cheekbones were fragile, like her mother's, but her chin was strong and prominent. Jaycee had to pull her own eyes from the frozen gaze, as sadness threatened to disrupt her focus. She hadn't had to beg for this interview; it was granted upon her first request to the family. Clare was already alerting the promo department to start blasting it out as an "exclusive." No other station had been granted access.

Tom had answered their home phone, recognized Jaycee's name after she identified herself and reminded him she was the reporter who had attended Zoe's funeral. In a sad voice, he agreed to an interview only to tell the world that Zoe was much more than just a sexual deviant and didn't deserve to die.

Jaycee promised to be fair. "This is your chance to set the record straight, Mr. Statler," she had told him. Although, the record was pretty straight already. You can't argue with the fact that young Zoe was killed because of the desires she was obviously embarrassed to tell her family of. Jaycee had also reached out to the families of Sarah and Mackenzie. She had yet to receive a return call and doubted very much she ever would. Her experience as a reporter yielded a fifty-fifty split on getting a loved one on camera. Either a grieving family shared memories because it was cathartic for them, or they completely shut themselves off, refusing to ever speak publicly about their loss, and ignoring media requests entirely. It was one or the other; Jaycee had yet to see a middle ground on this most difficult of topics. In fact, if a family member objected, Jaycee never pushed. She backed off and did so with grace, apologizing and disappearing forever. She loathed the door knock after a family had suffered a tragedy. It made her feel like an insensitive bitch.

If, however, someone granted her the opportunity, she told their story honestly and with passion. Car accidents, murders, fires, whatever the calamity and no matter the deceased, she and Ben took a series of their photographs and transformed them into a visual eulogy. Her words and his technique were used in careful combination to give back to the families more than they had taken from them.

She would do no less for the Statlers, her parting gift to them in exchange for trusting her with the story of Zoe's life.

Ben tapped her right shoulder, a quiet signal that he was set up and ready to roll. She took a deep, cleansing breath, and began.

"Zoe was your oldest. What about her made her so special?"

Jaycee chose to begin with a softball, the kind of question that would allow for an emotional release from Zoe's parents; a mother and father reflecting on a child they will never see again. Their firstborn. Their little girl.

She propped them up when they faltered, and fed them prompt words when weeping blurred their own out. When they caught their breath again, Jaycee carefully redirected the interview back around to the tough stuff, their daughter's darker side.

"Mr. and Mrs. Statler, I know talking to me like this is unimaginably difficult. I also appreciate that you both wanted the public to know that Zoe's lifestyle choices were unknown to you, before now."

Mr. Statler reached for a tissue and handed one to his wife. They both took a moment to wipe noses and eyes. "Yes, it was," he started. "And despite the fact Zoe was an adult, we were shocked." He reached for his wife's left hand and pulled it into his right. Jaycee knew instinctively that Ben was tightening the shot, slowly zooming in to close around Tom Statler's red, tear-streaked, grief-ravaged face. On television, the visual would be both empathetic and impactful, a powerful moment for viewers.

"Her mom and I want everyone to know that despite where Zoe was found, and—and—and…"

He lost himself for a moment. "Can I do that part again?" he choked. "I'm sorry."

Jaycee felt hot tears sting her own eyes and before she could stop herself, dabbed a finger to the outside of her eyelid to pull the drop of moisture away from her waterproof mascara.

"Of course, Mr. Statler, we edit all of this. You begin again when you're ready."

Wanting to be strong for his wife, Tom Statler dug deep to find strength and resolve. He kissed the back of her hand, still entwined with his, and winked. "For Zo, right?"

Mrs. Statler could only nod in sad confirmation. This poor woman was on empty, her tank entirely drained. Jaycee wished she could deliver to them the man who had taken away their baby girl and replaced her with scorched dreams and undying agony. "Here," she'd say. "Have at him."

If only.

"Of course, Zoe's mom and I know where she was found. We know what happens in places like that. And even though the police are doing their jobs and trying to find out who did this, we just don't want to see this…" he looked down and swallowed hard. Jaycee watched his Adam's Apple bob and then settle. "…Ever happen again.

Please, if you're a parent, talk to your kids, ask them questions even if they're uncomfortable. If our Zoe was involved in this sort of lifestyle, then anyone can be. Even if your little girls are grown up, talk to them and warn them. Don't let this happen to you, to your little girl, like it did to ours."

God bless this man, Jaycee thought, as her chin quivered. He held it together until the very end, unflinching and unabashed, determined to use his daughter's death as a warning for other parents. He was smart, brave, and yet completely and irreparably broken.

Jaycee's calf muscles groaned when she attempted to rise from the wooden backed dining room chair they had set up for her across from the couch. She had been so tense and disturbed, her limbs felt shaky. Reaching for Mr. Statler's hand, she shook it lightly but didn't pull back when he awkwardly wrapped her into an embrace. Mrs. Statler touched her hair and whispered her thanks. Zoe had been just a few years younger than Jaycee. Perhaps they saw bits of their own child in her.

Delicately, she commented on how beautiful Zoe was, that she wished she'd had the chance to know her. At times, when the camera stopped rolling, some of the most pertinent and critical information was revealed. The reporter in her listened for cues, but Jaycee's heart ached for the Statlers.

"She had a boyfriend recently," Mrs. Statler began, speaking in such a low volume Jaycee leaned into her personal space to hear her. "A very nice boy. He used to play basketball in the driveway with Zoe."

"Yes, Sam," Jaycee nodded. "I remember him from Zoe's services."

"He's not doing very well," Mr. Statler interjected. "He truly loved Zoe. And she didn't love him back. Such a shame, all these other boys she was talking to…"

Jaycee's expression tightened, her ears pinged on a potential clue.

"Other boys, Mr. Statler?"

"Well, I think so anyway. Her phone was always bleeping with names of different boys at the top of her screen. I may be getting older but my eyes are still sharp."

Jaycee could imagine Mr. Statler peeking over his daughter's shoulder pretending not to read her texts. It was what any good father would do, no matter how old his daughter was.

"So the police have that phone now, correct?" she asked. Standard procedure.

"Actually, no. It's still right over there on the kitchen counter, right where she left it."

"Zoe didn't have her cell phone with her the night…" Jaycee hitched on the rest of the sentence. *The night she died.* Thankfully, Mr. Statler rescued her.

"She left it here. It was an absent-minded habit of hers. I was always running things over to her school. Stuff like class charts, papers she'd been grading here at home, project printouts she'd prepared for her students. Her phone usually went everywhere with her, but not that night."

Jaycee considered this. A cell phone could be an important piece of evidence. Why had the police not asked for it to be turned over yet?

"Mr. Statler. I know this sounds odd, but is your name on Zoe's cell phone account? Do you pay the bill?"

The older man grinned, as though he had just been caught doing something silly. "Yes," he confirmed. "I still have both girls on my car insurance, on my health plan, and I pay their phone bills. It was just my way of trying to take some financial pressure off them. They're still kids, really. Well, Zoe was a kid…to me anyway."

Jaycee heard Ben's bag zip, along with the ruffle of lens films being tucked back into his gear bag. She had a few more minutes until he'd be ready to go. It disturbed her that Zoe's phone had yet to be analyzed, but given it was in her father's name, it was obvious the police simply hadn't yet gotten around to filing a search warrant to seize it. This was her shot.

"Would you allow me to see Zoe's phone?"

Mr. Statler's chin dropped. He wasn't following her and didn't seem poised to hand it over.

"Let me explain. It's nothing I would use on television. Are you aware that two other women have been killed in the same type of nightclubs Zoe was at?"

Mrs. Statler inched closer to their conversation. "Tom, that's what I was telling you last night. Two other girls, right around Zoe's age."

"I assume the police haven't yet discussed that with you?"

Both Statlers shook their heads. "Why would they?" Mr. Statler asked. "And we don't watch the news—no offense—because it's just too painful."

Jaycee struggled with what to tell them. And then Ben was by her side with his gear packed, bags hanging off his shoulders and elbows. He would hear everything she was about to say, too. And then he would sharply reprimand her in the car for inciting a conspiracy theory.

Oh hell, she had to risk it.

"This is not official. It's merely my own suspicion…" She paused. Ben loudly cleared his throat, his way of warning Jaycee that she was stepping out onto a pond covered with thin ice. Wouldn't be the first time Ben had tried to keep Jaycee safely onshore.

"But, I'm looking into a possibility…a disturbing one…that someone may be targeting girls like Zoe at these places. And if I'm right, I'm worried there could be more to come."

She did not say the words *serial killer*. She didn't have to. Her point was made.

After pondering this for a few seconds, Mrs. Statler turned and walked over to their tidy kitchen with red and gray patchwork curtains over a white farmers sink. Near the toaster oven, atop a bright blue cookie jar with an animal print and the warning "Paw's Off" was Zoe's white iPhone 5. Mrs. Statler reached for it. She walked back to Jaycee and handed it over.

"Take it. Please. I don't know my way around all of this technology. We wouldn't know if there was anything important on there. Do what you have to do to get answers, Jaycee. Don't let this happen again."

She clutched the phone, wrapping her own fingers around Mrs. Statler's. The two women let their fingers touch in solidarity until Jaycee pulled away with Zoe's phone tucked into her palm.

"Five minutes," she told the Statlers. "That's all I need. Keep this handy. The police will want to see it."

They nodded at Jaycee and allowed her some privacy to work her way around the apps. No lock screen, that was fortunate. The very first thing she checked was Zoe's call history. She scrolled through a mixture of nicknames and regular names, sadly noting multiple calls to Mom & Dad, and her sister. Several calls made to Sam. Nothing looked weird or out of place, but given Zoe was a stranger to her, Jaycee wasn't entirely sure what she was looking for.

She clicked on the "messages" icon. A flurry of emoji's and hastily tapped out text abbreviations filled the screen. Most referenced work, restaurants, or held innocuous conversations about being tired or hung over. Jaycee scrolled further down, squinting at the phone, waiting for something to jump out at her.

And then, something did.

Jaycee's stomach lurched. On the screen was a simple command. *Take a right after Alley Cat Pizza.* Wasn't that the area of the club where Zoe was killed? She was almost sure of it!

She held the phone closer. The sender was identified as "Zander," and the message had been sent to Zoe two days before she was murdered. Another message followed.

Good place -try it out -highly recommend.

Holy shit! Could it be?

Zoe's cell phone was a lucky hit, and Jaycee was the only person who knew about it. For now. She handed it back to Zoe's parents, telling them to keep it safe until police asked for it. "Trust me," she told them. "They'll want to look into this."

Chapter Ten

"Girl, you straight up cray cray!" Ben fired at Jaycee as he threw the seatbelt over his shoulder and pulled out of the Statler driveway. "What the hell are you thinking? If Clare finds out you did that, she'll rip your eyes out. Not to mention, the police. Isn't that like screwing around with an investigation?"

"Don't start, Ben. Just haul ass to City Hall."

"City fucking Hall? What the hell for?"

"There's someone there I want to talk to."

"About this stuff?"

"I'm not sure yet."

Ben sighed in exasperation as they pulled out of the neat and tidy middle-class neighborhood with painted mailboxes and manicured front lawns. Clare was giving them a wide berth to gather interviews and video for Jaycee's upcoming story on the Statlers. She'd have the remainder of the day to write it and then hand it off for Ben to edit. With their deadline extended, they had the freedom to spend some time doing reconnaissance. Ben was used to Jaycee's enterprising ways out on a story, but her digging around like this bothered him. This wasn't some zoning board controversy they were covering, this was serious shit, and he was her last line of defense.

"You are like a Chihuahua with a diamond collar trying to sneak into a pit bull fight club," he admonished. "Tell the story, Jay Bird, don't *be* the story."

"Duh," she grunted back. "I get that. It's called investigative reporting, my friend. That means actually investigating."

Ben sucked in a retort. He knew it would fall flat. "All right, fine, but you know I don't like showing myself near city officials. I'll be lucky if this car doesn't end up with a big metal boot on it for unpaid parking tickets. This job, killin' my rep."

"Oh stop, they're all work tickets. Your rep is fine." Driving around in a news vehicle all day chasing stories resulted in a flurry of parking violations. The photogs would hand them over to their managers each week and who knows where they went from there. The operating costs of a television station probably had a column on the spreadsheet dedicated solely to employee violations and fines accrued in the field.

Jaycee placed a call to Detective Barton. Voicemail. She hung up. This was not the kind of information imparted in a message. Jaycee would attack this herself, and then fill him in after. Asking for forgiveness was always easier than asking for permission.

"Do I even want to know what spooked you on her phone?"

"No," Jaycee replied, staring out the window as they passed one neat ranch after another leaving Long Beach. Zoe Statler came from classic Middle America, with two loving parents, and a job teaching children in her hometown how to read cells in a Petri dish.

How the hell did someone like her end up hooking up with strangers in some freak show palace and then left slaughtered on the floor?

"I'm going to tell you anyway. Do you remember last year when that city councilor was rung up on charges that he smacked his wife around?" she asked. She wanted Ben to be somewhat aware of what they were about to do.

"Of course not. Just another scumbag to me. I just shoot 'em, honey, I don't have to remember their life stories."

Jaycee shot him a look. "Again, Ben, you really need to take an interest in what's going on around you. Like, beyond your *eye* hole." She couldn't help but smirk.

"I'll take that under advisement, my queen. Now, what about the wife beater?"

"It's not him. It's his staffer. Some dude who was sending out press releases and giving interviews on his behalf."

"Lowly city councilors have 'people'?" Ben joked, hooking his fingers into air quotes. "I swear, only in Los Angeles."

"I know, right? Sometimes young wannabe politicos attach themselves early to a potential hot ticket candidate and wait for the meteoric rise to begin. Boy, did he hitch his wagon to the wrong horse. Jesus Christ, how do you *not* remember this, Ben? We even tried to interview the councilor's wife. Come on! Remember that short little Puerto Rican spitfire who threw her water bottle at us?"

"I got nothin'," Ben answered, nonplussed. "Ain't the first time I've stirred up a hot-blooded Puerto Rican, doll. Sorry. And really, Jay Bird, how am I supposed to remember everyone who's thrown shit at us in this friggin' job? Too many to count."

Jaycee sighed. "Anyway, the staffer's name was Zander Butant. About six weeks after the councilor scandal broke, Zander switched his allegiance to the City Council President. He signs all the communication sent out to the media. It's such a stupid name. How can there possibly be more than one Zander out there."

"Seriously? Again, this is L.A." Ben's jaw moved sideways, an indication that he was in thought. "And this has to do with Zoe's cell phone *how*…"

Jaycee began speaking faster, her words jumbled and excited with the possibility of a link.

"I looked at Zoe's text messages. There's one from someone named Zander and it includes an address. Well, a vague mention of an address, but it's the same general area as the club where Zoe was killed."

Ben turned onto the freeway and shifted into a middle lane. He was quiet for a few minutes. Jaycee could tell he was disturbed.

"I'm trying to get a head start here, Ben. That's all, I promise." Jaycee could read him too well.

"You're not a cop, Jay Bird. You carry a cell phone and a tube of lipstick, not a revolver or a badge. You could end up pissing off a very dangerous bad guy."

"What's he going to do, Ben? Kill me in City Hall?"

* * * *

Skirted women and suited men dotted the steps leading into the Los Angeles City Hall. No matter the time of day, it was a bustling building and Jaycee's direct path was interrupted twice as people recognized her.

"Oh my, you're Jaycee Wild!" one woman exclaimed, reaching out to touch Jaycee's elbow.

"*Wilder*, and yes I am. Hello, there, nice to meet you." Jaycee gently pulled away from the woman's grasp but wasn't rude about it. She just didn't like to be groped.

The woman stared, looking Jaycee up and down. "You're so skinny in person! Sorry, but all you people look fat and old on TV. You're so much prettier in real life."

Ugh, here we go, Jaycee thought. The typical *sorry, not sorry* she always got from strangers.

"Thanks, glad you're watching. Bye now."

Jaycee took two more steps before a young man carrying a stack of papers tried stuffing one into her hand.

"Jaycee Wilder! Are you here to cover our efforts to stop Los Angeles police brutality? Can I talk to you for a minute? Are you aware that every thirty seconds in L.A. an innocent person is harassed by pol—"

"Another time," Jaycee let the paper slide from her hand and moved past him curtly. She even pretended she didn't hear him mutter, "bitch." She'd been called worse. Part of the job.

Once inside the building, Jaycee and Ben climbed to the fourth floor, where the offices were located. She knew where the council president's chambers were, and was going on hope that Zander Butant was in the vicinity.

The door to the office was open, featuring a coat rack to the left and a Poland Springs water cooler on the right. In the middle was a squat, square-shaped woman typing away on her computer.

"Help you?" she asked without looking up.

"I'm looking for Zander. Is he in?"

"Who's asking?"

"Jaycee Wilder."

Still supremely focused on her computer, the woman removed one hand from the keyboard and pressed a button that allowed them through a low gate and into the space beyond her desk. So much for security concerns. Jaycee made a mental note to pitch that as a special report for November sweeps.

"Go ahead, second office on your right," she instructed. If something happened back there, this woman would be an empty witness with zero worth. Frightening.

About four strides down a narrow hall, a booming voice echoed from a half-open wooden door with worn stain chipping off near the brass handle. Ben stepped around Jaycee just as she had started to push herself through the doorway.

"We can still leave," he said firmly. "That fat-ass out there has already forgotten we were ever here. This could get weird."

She appreciated Ben. Like always, he had her back. This certainly wasn't the first time he'd put her well-being ahead of a TV product. "Thank you, Ben. But this is important to me."

He never expected a different answer, so Ben was already moving out of the way for Jaycee to enter Zander's room.

"Knock, knock?" she announced, opening the door wide and greeting the man seated behind a sleek Ikea desk. "Anyone home?"

Zander Butant worked in Los Angeles city politics; he was hardly one to get caught off guard. Instantly, the thousand-watt smile was on display and the palm outstretched in warm welcome. He hung up his phone with a curt, "Gotta go," and turned on the charm that was usually a showstopper with the ladies.

"Hi there," he began, recognizing Jaycee, but looking beyond her at Ben. "I know Jaycee already, but I'm not sure we've met. You do look familiar, though." He narrowed his eyes, trying to recall how and where. "I'm Zander."

"Ben. I'm usually carrying a camera. So, this is out of context." Ben had both hands pushed into the pockets of his Lucky jeans. His camera was like an appendage; he felt awkward and uncomfortable without it. "You've probably seen me trailing this one around." He nodded toward Jaycee.

"Ah, yes, of course." Zander bounced back quickly. He stood up, stretching out his six-foot-two frame on purpose. Zander liked being imposing to people. His stylish haircut allowed for some movement around the forehead. Jaycee noticed gelled pieces of dark blonde hair sticking to one eyebrow. "What brings you by, Jaycee? Is this about the parking lot ordinance near the convention center site? You guys doing a follow-up?"

Not so much. Jaycee didn't want to play for very long. She needed this to be quick and direct.

"No, Zander, this is personal. And consider this a warning that right now, I am the least of your problems."

The cuff on Zander's slacks quivered slightly around his ankles, the only subtle sign that his ramrod straight posture had just slipped. Otherwise, he came off as entirely unnerved and impatient, the consummate politician's mouthpiece. He did, however, shut the door between his small space and the larger office of the council president behind them.

"Clearly, Ms. Wilder, I don't appreciate being put on the spot—"

"Can it, Zander," she interjected, noting how quickly she had gone from Jaycee, to Ms. Wilder. She didn't fall for the uppity bullshit and was hardly put off by it. "You need to shut up and listen to what I'm telling you." She felt a small trickle of sweat tickle her neck. Ben's warning rang through her head but so did Zoe's face. She gritted her teeth and stepped into his space. "If you don't answer some questions for me I will fast-track this at work to make sure your pretty face is leading the newscast tonight at six." She ignored Ben clearing his throat in warning. This was risky, but Jaycee was not leaving this office without answers.

"What do you want?" he asked, his dark blue eyes gleaming with disgust.

"Information," she replied.

"On what?"

"Zoe Statler." Jaycee watched his reaction carefully. Zander was a tough nut. His public image required strict emotional control. If she could rattle him, he may crack.

Zander Butant pushed back. He kept his composure and played the party line, slipping back into spokesman mode. "Oh, yes, of course," he tried to sound sympathetic and concerned. "It is horrific for this city to be marred by such violence…"

"Shut up."

"Excuse me?"

"I know, Zander. Before I take it straight to the viewers, I want more information."

She watched him. He did not move, cower, or apologize; he simply transitioned into the new phase of their conversation.

"I don't know a goddamn thing!" he growled.

"Not true." Jaycee pushed. "I'm not saying you killed her, Zander. But you sent her there. Why?"

Zander's face broke out in a sheen of nervous perspiration. He leveled a frigid glare at Jaycee before eventually, the facade crumbled and Zander Butant became what he was all along: a poser. Once he knew he was over a barrel and about to pull a hammy, he broke wide open. He pressed his hands over his chiseled cheeks, rubbing furiously to encourage this bad dream to end.

"Jesus Christ, Jaycee!" he cried, throwing his weight back and allowing the rounded edge of his low desk to catch him. He seemed to shrink before their eyes. She could hear Ben's breathing escalate. Her own, too. In truth, she had no idea what role he played in Zoe's death, but watching him squirm and skit around like a baby deer on new legs proved something. He didn't have the stomach for murder.

"Might as well spill, Zander. The police will be seizing Zoe's phone and your weird-ass name is front and center in her text messages. How did you know Zoe? Why did you send her there?"

Zander stared beyond Jaycee and Ben. He was formulating his plan, searching for an escape hatch. If he gave her anything, he would ask for something in return.

"I want my side out there. And I want your word that you'll be fair."

Jaycee scoffed. "Being fair to you is hardly more important to me than being fair to Zoe. She's the victim here. You're just...well...I don't know what you are yet."

"I'm no killer, Jaycee! You have to believe me. I would never hurt Zoe, or any woman. That's bullshit!"

His lips were loosening. Jaycee worked his emotion, waiting for something to slip out, an often-used reporter trick during intense interviews. Only this time, Ben's camera wasn't rolling, and this was about bloodshed. "Why did you send her there? How do you even know about a place like that?"

He squirmed around, clearly hating the admission he was about to belch out.

"I want your word, Jaycee. I will deny everything I just said here unless you promise me an interview and a fair shot at getting my side out if my name is released. I have a future to think about, you know!"

That pissed her off. Even though her professional integrity meant she would give Zander what he requested, she couldn't resist reminding this self-serving puke that Zoe no longer had a future.

Zoe was dead. And he was the one who sent her straight to her killer.

"And Zoe doesn't." She gave him a fiery look, what Ben called her RBF, Resting Bitch Face, a stony don't-fuck-with-me laser beam into a person's soul that usually forced her interviewees to cough up a few more details.

He did a slow nod. "I know that." He collected himself. "She was a sweet girl. Really smart and funny. I met her at a club in Anaheim last year."

"A sex club." Jaycee skewered him again with her tone, hoping to make Zander sweat some more. She had been scouring the internet to learn more about these types of places. Her home laptop revealed the more lurid results because her company computer had blocks in place to keep such smut out of its network. It didn't take Jaycee long to realize that if someone were seeking guys, girls, dogs, donkeys, or parakeets, Los Angeles had a club for that.

"Yes, Jaycee, a sex club. Zoe and I became friends and *no* not like that. You don't go to these places to find a BFF, but we had a definite connection. Whenever I found a hot new club, I'd tell her about it. She did the same for me. That's all. I swear to God."

"Were you there? The night Zoe was murdered?"

"Of course not! I found out about this when everyone else did. How do you think I feel? Do you think I don't know that if I hadn't sent her there, Zoe would still be alive today?"

"What constitutes a 'hot' club? Can you tell me more about why you liked it there, and why you thought Zoe would, too?"

He uncomfortably scratched his head, a clear sign that the batteries in his moral compass weren't completely dead. At least Zander had the grace to be embarrassed.

"You wanted to talk, remember? Your side?"

Zander cleared his throat. "Just like bars, there are some clubs that bring in a higher level of clientele. You get me?"

"Yes," Jaycee nodded. Zander liked his nameless sex partners to have a certain look.

"The club I told Zoe about was nice. High-end. Good options."

Jaycee inadvertently flinched at the meat market reference. "You mean, highly attractive people."

"Exactly."

"So Zoe preferred that as well."

"She did. She was a beautiful woman. Just makes sense."

"So this place, the one Zoe was found in, only lets in the sexy people."

"Pretty much," he confirmed.

"How many times have you been there?" she asked.

"Just once," he replied.

"Zoe had never been there before, as far as you know? What about the other dead girls? Do you know anything about them, or the clubs they were at?"

"As far as I know, I'm the one who told Zoe about that club. I don't know the other two at all, and I've never been to the clubs they were found in."

"Okay," Jaycee digested that. She believed him. "Back to Zoe, since you knew her. Was there a certain type of guy she went for? Did she like dark-haired guys, skinny guys, tall or short?"

"Good lord, Jaycee, I don't know. I never asked her that. She just liked, uh, guys in general, I think."

"So, there are private rooms inside this club? Have you ever seen anyone get violent? Any guy ever strike you as odd? Well, more odd than the rest of you freaks?"

Zander sighed. "You'd be surprised by the 'freaks' as you call them. There are all types of people enjoying the freedom of these clubs—"

"Spare me," Jaycee interrupted coldly. "I'm not your mother or your priest. I just want to know if you've ever seen anyone acting particularly weird."

Zander nodded slightly. "Yes, there are odd things that happen, and yes, at times, it can get physical…but usually that's what they went there for. As far as private rooms, yes, there are some totally private, semi-private, or even group rooms. Whatever you're into, there's space for that. The rule of thumb is to leave a closed-door closed. You can be sure that Zoe knew her way around these places quite well."

"Charming," Jaycee said with disdain. "So, basically you're telling me that given Zoe was found in a private room that she presumably entered willingly with this psycho, because she was expecting that night to be like all the rest, we'll never know how long she laid there, bleeding out, crying for help before someone finally found her."

Zander seemed to study Jaycee's face, his eyes traveling from her eyes to her downturned mouth. Eventually, once the full weight of her statement had sunk in, he nodded in confirmation.

And then Zander did something that blew Jaycee away.

He sat back down, lowered his head toward the giant calendar that detailed a very busy life, and sobbed his heart out.

Jaycee extracted her business card from her purse and placed it next to a framed picture of Zander with his arm around a set of aging parents, two brothers, and a posse of tiny nieces and nephews.

"Call me when you're ready," she told him. "I'll give you a fair shot, you have my word."

Chapter Eleven

"Don't get pissed at me, okay? I may have overstepped." Jaycee's voice was weary. She'd stayed late at work to finish writing her story on the Statlers. Emotionally, she was flat-lining, but she remained alert to pass along the developments of the day.

Detective Barton had to admit this was a first, a reporter providing a key point of a murder investigation to him. Jaycee Wilder was proving herself to be far more than just a pretty girl with a microphone. She was tenacious like a wild boar hunting for truffles, calling him seven times in three hours.

"Jaycee, I'm not pissed," he told her into the phone. "But I am concerned. This Xanadu guy could've been dangerous."

Jaycee coughed out a brittle laugh. "His name is Zander, not Olivia Newton John."

"Whatever," Barton replied. He wasn't in a jovial mood. Jaycee had learned he could get quite snippy at times. Even with her, and they barely knew one another. She wondered if that was the result of his failures and frustrations, or just the kind of cop he had always been.

"And you know," he continued sternly. "You can't fuck up a police investigation by messing with evidence. 'Scuse my mouth. That's not part of our deal. We're going to call your access to Zoe's cell phone 'semi-inadvertent.' Given you didn't purposely tamper with it and we hadn't

95

yet seized it. That made things slightly complicated because Zoe's phone was not in her name."

"I know. It was in her dad's."

"Don't tell anyone you know that," he instructed.

"The Statlers know that I know that."

"They're grief-stricken, they'll probably forget. I won't pursue it with them."

"So you're not pissed?"

"No, I'm not pissed."

Jaycee was standing above a boiling pot of water, about to dump in some whole grain pasta for dinner. It was pushing ten o'clock and this was the first time she'd been able to make contact with Barton since her run-in with Zander.

"When is your Statler interview going to air?" he asked her.

"Monday." It was Friday and the wait time wasn't ideal. "We don't air big stuff on the weekends, and they are teasing the hell out of it. The story is good, but I want more. I haven't been to the scene yet with my photographer. We have video from the day after the murder—when it was cordoned off—but I'm hoping to get inside. And you're up next. I want you on camera with a juicy clue released only to me."

"If you think you're going to find something at the crime scene, think again. There's nothing left. The scene is clear and the club is back open. I firmly doubt you'll be able to get inside. They have a strict no-camera policy."

Jaycee knew it was a long shot. It didn't mean she couldn't try even though she probably sounded naïve to an investigator.

"I'm surprised it's back in business, lickety-split, after a girl is murdered," she said. "You guys can't shut that place down?"

"How could we? Crimes happen everywhere. We can't close a convenience store just because it's been robbed, can we? Same principle here. We checked it out. Liquor license is up to date, rent paid, and we can't prove anything illegal was happening there. Far as we know, it's a nightclub, same as any other. Once the scene was processed, they're free to resume activity."

"I assume your witness list is still short?" she asked.

"Try non-existent. I've been going building by building looking for security cameras that could have caught people coming and going from the club. So far, nothing. Jeesh, back in Boston every goddamn building had a camera attached to it. 'Scuse my mouth. I'm also trying to get a read on the person who called it in from the pay phone."

"I know the autopsy report is coming out," Jaycee said, stirring the pasta in the rolling water and letting the Boston reference slide. "Will that matter?" They always updated murder cases on television with the official cause of death.

"To the public, no, not really. What we'll do next is search for a wound pattern among the victims. We won't be telling your people that, of course."

"Of course. You mean, like, slash wounds versus blunt trauma injuries. That kind of stuff?"

"Yes, and more. If we can match blow sites on the victims' bodies or identify a death blow as being identical on each girl, that helps build our case that one killer is responsible for all three. It may even reveal if he's right- or left-handed. I will tell you, between us, in Zoe's case the wound patterns are all over the map. She has hacking cuts, slices, and welts indicative of hard blows with either a fist or object. The other girls weren't quite as mutilated."

Jaycee grimaced, thinking of the sweet face in the picture frame. The beloved daughter wrapped in love and wholesomeness. She shut the stovetop off and wandered away from the pasta. Her appetite was gone.

"Jaycee, you there?"

"Yes. You need to know I'm not the only reporter making a connection between the girls. It's being suggested in the papers and even the tabloids. You need to address that. When will you be speaking to Zander?" Jaycee figured Zander was expecting them. Barton, too.

"We will assume he has a newly retained lawyer and that he'll be marching in bright and early tomorrow morning. We'll dig around a little but you know we can't charge a guy with liking kinky sex and telling a friend where to go to get it."

"He wants to do an interview, to get his side out."

"Why?" Barton asked.

"I think he's worried about this leaking. Even a benign association with Zoe would reveal his wild side. Dude wants to be Mayor someday; this could handicap him pretty good. No one would vote for a dirty boy who likes to be whipped around and called Big Daddy."

Barton couldn't suppress a mild laugh. "Are you going to do it? An interview?"

"I promised I would, in the event his name gets out, in exchange for the info about Zoe and the address on her cell phone."

"The fact that he gave it up so easily implies something…you get that, right?" Barton was testing her. Seeing how perceptive she was in thinking like an investigator.

"That he's a pile of mush under pressure and certainly not our killer."

Barton smiled into his phone. He knew she was a keeper. "So he knows this particular club, huh?"

"I guess so," Jaycee confirmed. "He told me he's only been there once but thought Zoe would like it. I never knew this, but apparently there's a class system for sex clubs. Zander is a good-looking guy; Zoe was pretty, too. Seems the beautiful people stick together, even in places like that. From that, we can assume the killer isn't butt ugly."

"Neither was Ted Bundy, Robert Chambers, or OJ Simpson. Being good-looking doesn't preclude a person from being pure evil on the inside. It helps a little, but doesn't really reduce our suspect pool." Barton said.

"I get that, I just thought it was interesting. You're not looking for the Elephant Man."

"No," Barton agreed. "He uses his looks to lure his prey. He likes that. It gives him power."

"Sounds like three-quarters of the guys in L.A.," Jaycee scoffed.

"Jaycee, there's something I want you to do."

She didn't hesitate. "What?"

"I don't regret our agreement but to go deep in something like this you need to wear your protective gear. Kinda like a scuba diver thinking his oxygen tank is just an accessory."

Jaycee had also learned that at times, Barton used clever analogies to make his point. His mind may be sharper than she first realized. "I get it. You want me to be safe."

"When these stories hit, ninety-nine-point-nine percent of the time, our killer is watching. He's flipping around the channels, reading the papers, and pretty much relishing the fear and anxiety he's creating. Notoriety gets him off. The fact this guy left a message in the victims' blood is indicative enough that he likes attention, maybe even wants to mock authority or society in general. Perhaps it's his way of explaining why he does what he does. But for some creeps, the allure of sin is as intoxicating as the sin itself."

Jaycee could grasp that. "Are you trying to scare me off?"

"Not at all. I just want you to understand that as you dig around and become your station's face of the investigation—which sounds like that's exactly what you want to be—he may not like that, or he may love it. He may become interested in you. Either way, when we start putting out information that other reporters may not have yet, I'd bet your big salary that'll pique his interest."

In other words, Jaycee, watch your back!

"I'll be careful. I promise."

"I'm not sure how much you know about police work. I assume you've gotten to know a few of the patrolmen here, they speak highly of your work." Barton skipped the other things they said about her. That was just guy talk. "But you need more."

"Okay," Jaycee was fine with that.

"Get yourself some mace and make sure it's with you when you're out in the field."

"No problem, I already have some." Check one.

"May not be a bad idea to consider buying a gun."

Jaycee swallowed hard. Check two sounded ominous. "I'll consider that."

"This is legit, Jaycee, you need to be aware of the intangibles, the risks you invite when you become attached—by design or accident—to a case. You can't expect to defend yourself against a homicidal maniac with nothing but your wits. Let someone know where you are at all times. Serial killers are cruelly fickle. They may love the public's obsession with their work one minute and then seek retribution the next. This guy feels showy and big to me, like he fancies himself a grand power. He's sticking to the script on location…seeking out women at these clubs he perceives to be worthless, but that doesn't mean he won't become irritated by your coverage. Look up psychological analysis of something called *mission-oriented* murder. It'll help you understand his possible motivation. If it's up to him to enact justice on these girls, anything keeping him from his task is an obstruction. Here's the thing: his justice is motivated by sex which makes him even more dangerous for someone like you."

"You mean, because I'm a woman?"

"Well, an especially lovely woman, I'd say. But listen, if I were an investigative reporter, I'd be wondering if the cops were looking beyond L.A. Are they starting to poke around other cities for unsolved murders of prostitutes or runaways, or even sexual mutilations in the same geographical area? There's too much skill and knowledge here. Big group settings make evidence a tossed salad. He knows that. Look around. Are there stories that surfaced for a while and then disappeared? Notes left behind? How close did reporters and police get? And this one is big: Did he escalate in either manner or shortened time span just before the murders stopped?"

Jaycee's head spun. What a brain dump! He wanted her schooled, and damn fast. She'd be lying if she said she didn't feel her heart jump with nerves. He was almost fearsome with an authority she had yet to experience first-hand, gone were the sarcastic remarks or wise cracks. This must have been how Barton performed, pre-Cambridge drunken meltdown, ruthless in pursuit of his target.

"Sure, I can do that."

"About the messages left in blood," Barton said.

"Let's go with it?" Jaycee half-asked, half-stated.

"Yes. Tell your viewers that a source within the investigation is confirming that a message has been left at the scene of Zoe's murder. Don't mention the other two girls yet. We're about to announce a task force assembling to investigate all three; we'd like to withhold that for a while longer. Then I'll go on camera for you."

She was right! Finally, the forces were gathering to treat these deaths as a serial crime.

They agreed to talk early next week. Jaycee hung up but was restless and agitated. She reviewed what she'd learned so far and where she needed to go.

Barton seemed to be sober and alert. A good start. Their victims, Sarah, Mackenzie, and Zoe, were among a thriving group of attractive, sexual thrill seekers taking advantage of Los Angeles' bustling nightclub scene. Hollywood Boulevard was a hotbed. That meant the suspect pool could be huge, but given what Zander had revealed about the club Zoe was at, chances were good the killer was at least decent-looking. The girls had liked him and trusted they were safe. They likely engaged with the killer in anticipation of a good time, it didn't appear any of them were forced into a private room. Among them, they left behind three sets of parents, two motherless children, scores of friends, and even dozens of traumatized seventh graders. She was about to put Zoe's story on TV, and announce a lurid clue: A message scrawled in blood. She had just heard an investigator tell her the cops had no idea who was doing this, but that he may have done it elsewhere, perhaps even in bulk, and that she should really learn how to watch her own ass.

Was Barton right? Would the killer be watching? She told the stories of murder all the time, and then went home and resumed her life, never giving a second thought to her own safety. But this felt different. For the first time in her entire career, Jaycee felt uncomfortably exposed.

Was she making herself a target? Was it worth it?

She closed her eyes and thought back to when Mrs. Statler had clutched her hand, a mother's desperate attempt to connect with a physical being not unlike the one she had lost. She recalled her dad's unwillingness to throw his daughters into the world without a safety net.

I still pay their bills. Zoe was still a kid...to me.

Was it worth it?

Abso-fucking-lutely! This was personal now. She had seen the pain up close.

Jaycee rolled a strand of hair through two fingers, keenly aware of knocks and pings in her quiet condo that normally wouldn't have bothered her one bit. She was alone here all the time. Now, she jumped and bucked as nervous tension had her hyper-aware of her surroundings.

She needed a human connection. A voice on the other end of the line.

Ben's phone rang once, twice, three times. Before it went to voicemail, Jaycee hung up. Ben was probably already zonked out for the night. He had told her he'd be hanging out with a bottle of Shiraz and the Property Brothers on HGTV.

"They can hammer my walls anytime," he'd joked, as they said good night to one another after a long, arduous day.

She dialed Van's cell. The bar was loud and busy; he wouldn't even hear his phone ring. She left a voice mail.

"It's me. I know you're at work, but if you get this, I'm planning a beach day tomorrow. You're not sleeping in, so come home as early as you can."

She hung up. Her girlfriends told her she ordered Van around like a servant. So what? She liked being the guy in the relationship as long as Van took over those duties when it mattered.

She had no complaints there.

Jaycee sighed, realizing the only company she had was a wretched sense that something else was about to happen.

* * * *

Detective Barton was having an equally difficult night. Once he hung up with Jaycee, he heaved the remnants of a sausage and pepper sub into the toilet. The monumental effort to represent himself as clear-headed had tapped him out. Hell, this entire case was tapping him out. He was sweating through his Red Sox t-shirt, his body angry and begging him to give it what it needed to make the pain stop. The pink skin stretched over the gnarly stub on his right hand barked in agony. Phantom pain, his shrink called it. How the body reacted when a piece of it suffered a trauma. If you're lucky, it'll go away, he'd been told. He sure as shit hadn't been born with a four-leaf clover up his ass, so why would this be any different?

He stumbled as if on a pre-determined trajectory into the kitchen and tried to rip open the cabinet beneath the sink, the fingers on his left hand fumbled with the child-lock holding the two wooden panels together by their bronze knobs.

He tugged furiously. He braced one foot against the cheap molding and pulled. His sweaty grasp let go, sending Barton's bulk hurling backwards into the wooden kitchen table his ex-wife had borrowed from a co-worker. '*No son of mine is going to eat his breakfast on a kitchen floor,*' she'd stated. '*Here, take this, on loan.*'

One of the four legs on the hand-me-down table buckled and snapped.

Barton sat there, his chest burning and his legs splayed toward the kitchen cabinet that had locked him out, afraid to remove the only thing holding up the heavy contents of the tabletop: his back.

Fuck my life, he thought to himself.

Angling his head to the right, he looked through the thin sliver of space he'd managed to open between the two cabinet doors. He saw the gleam of a glass bottle, his old friend, and most formidable nemesis.

His mouth watered in desire and defeat. He loved and loathed it in what had become an epic paradox that rocked his sensibility and destroyed his resolve. It had robbed him of everything, and yet he longed for its nectar like a liquid life force, the only thing powerful enough to keep him alive in a hopeless world where children died in your arms, and young women became bait for a diseased predator.

Chasing a serial killer, trying not to fuck up in front of his new boss, and now feeling obligated to protect the reporter helping him, James Barton dug deep. He came up with just enough strength to look away from what was secretly stashed in the kitchen cabinet and live to fight another day.

Chapter Twelve

The man was buoyant. The tomb-like darkness of his dingy room illuminated the beads of sweat on his forehead as he inspected his face in the mirror. His body was zinging with energy. He felt like a king, the ruler of his own universe.

This was the night. He was a god again.

Rolling the tip of his Kohl liner over his top eyelid, the man did himself up for a Friday night on the town. He would not return to Olive's; he wasn't naïve enough to think she would welcome him back. He was also wise enough to know she would never report their meeting to the police. Even though professional whores had their limits, they also had an allergy to authority. It worked well in instances when he simply needed to feel powerful and strong. The alpha male, omnipotent and untouchable.

The man pursed his lips into an 0, enjoying how a light touch of gloss set off his full lower lip. Tonight he would finally select a blonde. One who resembled the girl in his photos. He'd been craving a chance to taste her golden innocence. It was time; he'd waited long enough. The city was crawling with opportunity and police were chasing their tails. Amateurish, bumbling fools who thought he was simply an over-aggressive lover. They had no respect for his life's mission to seek out the trash mistakenly sprinkled into this human experience. It was his duty. He took it very seriously. He would pursue them forever.

He climbed into tight skinny jeans and replaced his golf shirt with a white t-shirt. Hiding the black wig under a backwards baseball hat the man made quick time to the club, his dick already pressing against the slim zipper of his pants. Holy shit, this was going to be good! Sixteen blocks down Hollywood Boulevard, he entered a bland-looking Chinese restaurant on the right. The place was foul, but the club below promised good vibes and a bounty of delights from which to choose. The man had done his research.

Sour smells leapt at him from the oily kitchen as fast-talking Asians stood behind a stainless steel table, smacking and rubbing spices onto muscle-toned flesh that could have come from a variety of hosts. He hustled through the kitchen, swung open a creaky, insect-ridden screen door, and stepped down six steps into a cement-floored basement. Reddish brown stains decorated the walls. He heard a hint of heavy guitar and base. Following the noise, he adjusted his crotch and fingered his balls. His junk was throbbing.

The air changed. The cool kiss of air-conditioning gave way to stinging humidity. He filled his nostrils with the pungent, sweet odor of sweat and sex, adopting a new swagger in his hips he never managed to display in real life. He was just a character here, free to be all the things he tucked away every day: a savage, a sexual deviant, a killer. It didn't matter here. People didn't come to judge, and every last one of them was as depraved as he. Especially the girls.

The Throw Away Girls.

Stepping into the belly of a large room with artificial light, the man stopped and seductively scanned the crowd. A woman approached from behind, cupped his ass and pressed her naked breasts into his back.

"Wanna fuck?" she whispered with breath tinged with cigarette residue and hard alcohol. Her fingers kneaded at him, but he stepped away without responding. Instinctively, he knew, she was not the one. The girl he met tonight must be willing to play.

He took a swig of flowery-smelling liquid from a cup passed to him. It was probably laced with some psychedelic shit so he swallowed only a small amount. He preferred to remember his encounters, to stay clear-headed enough to relish the exchange. When he spotted a blonde-haired, half-naked woman near a blinking exit sign, he knew immediately.

He had found her. His pulse quickened.

Wavy hair splayed over a dragon tattooed on her shoulder. When she laughed, she tossed her mane back, revealing a spray of ink resembling fire. Yes, he knew it. She was a fighter.

Words were not necessary in this land of fantasy, so the man simply caught her eye and beckoned for her to follow him. She scanned him up and down and then decided she liked it well enough. The man felt his heart skip, his stomach jumped. He watched the dragon dance as she began a languid trot a few paces ahead of him. The rule of thumb was to walk by doors that were closed, and feel free to join in when they were left open. Preferring privacy, the man took the lead and walked the woman to the last room on the left. The door was thrown wide open to advertise a shadowy, yet empty space. They were alone.

He lead her by him, seductively dipping his tongue into her ear as she passed. A low moan escaped her lips. He pulled back. No need to get her worked up so quickly.

"Take it easy, my pet, no need to rush."

He shut the door. The woman was ripped, her ab muscles clenched and released as her breathing sped up. She placed a hand atop a pile of plush blankets that sat next to an assortment of riding crops, handcuffs, gels, oils and condoms. He shook his head and reached first for a terry-cloth towel. Circling it around in the air a few times, he achieved a line of twists and snapped it against the woman's lower leg, inciting a swell of red on her pale skin. She flinched, but didn't rush for the door. A good sign. Her sinewy thighs carried her toward him. Maintaining silence, he handed it to her, signaling a challenge. Round one was underway.

* * * *

A half-hour later, the blonde-haired woman was blind and choking on her own blood. One eye socket had been broken apart so completely it could no longer contain the slippery round eyeball. She cradled it in her palm. Her right ear lobe was there, too, after being gnawed off and chewed into thin tatters. Her chest, kicked until she heard ribs crack. Air rattled and groaned on shallow tugs of breath.

"Hurts, huh, cookie? Hurts like a bitch, I'm sure. Sorry 'bout that, but what do you expect when you come to a place like this? It's a cruel world, so you should consider this a gift. A chance to end the cycle right here." He closed his eyes, pleased with himself and fully aroused. The air was sweet with the metallic aroma of blood and death. He breathed it in, allowed it to fill his lungs, and eventually exhaled with a flourish. He was back on the circle, always moving, forever transforming.

"You're welcome," he kissed her forehead.

The woman felt the soft kiss, but her spirit was sinking. She tightened her fingers into fists and pushed them against his flesh. "No," she growled through pain and anguish. "Don't touch me…" Her last conscious words were defiant, and she faded out to the beloved image of a blonde-haired little girl who deserved better than to wake up tomorrow morning without a mother.

The man grabbed the towel and stuck it beneath his shirt, feeling no need to leave anything extra behind.

Circling the crumpled body like a vulture, he bent low near her head, matted with blood and flesh, and swept a finger through the ragged circle of skin where the woman's eye used to fit. He poked inward, feeling the warmth of soft tissue, coating his finger with her blood. He then fit it between his lips, to take from her one final time. Such a waste of a woman.

Another Throw Away Girl.

He applied moderate pressure to the blocked concrete wall, crafting short letters in careful script with his pointer finger, the same one that had just been inside the woman's head. When he was done, he stepped back to survey his work.

It was perfect.

The man opened the door and stepped into the empty hallway. He could hear others in the throes of pleasure and pain, and moved swiftly back into the open cavern of the club where unions were just beginning to form among the guests. He kept his chin tucked low, his blood-stained hands stuffed into his pockets as he made his way back up and through the kitchen, riddled with new yet equally offensive scents.

He turned back onto the main street and disappeared into the night.

He hadn't left much behind, except for one thing.

A Throw Away Girl who wasn't quite ready to get thrown away.

Chapter Thirteen

"Autopsy results are pending."

"What about the tox report?"

"Another ten days, at least. The ME can confirm the knife blade was serrated and approximately six inches in length." Van cleared his throat when silence replaced the line he was supposed to hear next.

"…I said…approximately six inches in length. Jay Jay, you're up."

Jaycee tossed the script onto the striped beach towel. "Really, Van? Isn't there some other role I can help you read for? Puppy breeder? Football coach? My heart really isn't into all this murder and mayhem right now."

"Okay, let's take a break. Sorry. I'll work this script on my own."

Van laid his head on Jaycee's flat abdomen, lightly toying with the butterfly stud in her belly button. "Wanna swim?" he asked.

"Not yet."

"Wanna eat?"

"No. Maybe. I don't know."

Jaycee pushed up onto her elbows and gazed out at the endless stretch of the Pacific. The sand was crowded, but she purposely chose Venice Beach for that exact reason. She wanted noise, laughter, weird sites, and hard bodies to distract her from herself. Her week had been intense and overwhelming. She saw Zoe everywhere; her tender face was haunting her.

"When is your audition?" she asked Van, ready for a change of topic.

"Next Friday," he told her. "I've worked with the director before. I think I have a good shot."

"Oh, great. Do you want to run lines again? I can totally rally. Come on, Van, bring on the slash wounds."

"No, I want you to relax." Van placed his palm over her hip bone, preventing her from reaching for the folded pages of the script.

Jaycee murmured an agreeable response. She stroked Van's brown hair and gently kneaded his raised deltoids. His body stood out for its perfection, even on Venice, the premiere Southern California eye-candy playground. Hot summer air tickled her nostrils with beach scents like coconut oil and open Fritos bags. Van heard her stomach rumble and reached for the Igloo cooler he'd packed at home. Small steady steps that showed Jaycee a new side of her boyfriend. He'd even been learning to cook more than quinoa, mashed carrots, and plain chicken breast. Sustenance, he'd told her, for this stressful time at work.

Van plopped onto his rear and placed the cooler between his legs. He pulled out some of Jaycee's favorites—Doritos, Baby Goldfish, chocolate chip granola bars—all things he would never eat but she put down daily. "Did your fingers burn packing this?" Jaycee joked. Van refused to even touch her junk food in the kitchen pantry. His body was his temple, and in Hollywood, his best asset.

"No, but I felt my arteries closing. You need to fatten up a little. You think I don't know this brand new H&M bikini fit you fine last month? Lucky girl with the metabolism of a giraffe." He grinned, pulling on loose fabric around her ribs that used to be filled by her ample curves. His touch set off a little flutter in Jaycee's stomach. She sat up on the blanket, crossed her legs and threw both arms spontaneously around Van's muscle-bound upper body. "Thank you. You've been really good to me lately."

"Wow, a public display of affection," he said, sliding a hand up and down her naked back. "And I haven't even opened the Doritos yet."

"No one on Venice Beach watches the news," Jaycee joked. She kept a very low profile in public, shunned hand-holding and make-out sessions out of respect for her job and image. "It's safe, wanna get naked?"

"Don't I always?"

They laughed. Jaycee knew her guard was down with the amount of energy she was pouring into Zoe's murder. Logically, she was more likely to seek physical and mental comfort. Van was better with the physical, but could moderately cover both.

"I think Ben's irritated with me," she muttered, flitting around to another new topic. Her brain was jumpy. "I invited him along, but he was acting weird."

"Ah, news flash, Ben *is* weird."

"He's just artistic," Jaycee said, defending her friend. Van and Ben were both men. That was about all they had in common.

"If he's acting weird, then tell him to fuck off and get over it. You guys are attached at the hip five days a week. Why would you invite him to come with us on a day off?"

"I'm not complaining about Ben. I'm just…concerned…that's all. He has this long-distance boyfriend, no family to vent to, and I dragged him around a lot last week. You know, put him in some tough…spots." She reached for the right word, without revealing too much to Van about her undercover work. Ben had taken up his position by her side—both with Zander and the Statlers—but that didn't mean he appreciated being forced to do it. At times, it took her a while to realize that her aggressive traits could compromise another's.

"You know," Van started gently. "You're a lot to take on, Jay Jay. If you've been bossing Ben around this week trying to solve a murder, maybe the boy needs a break from you?"

Jaycee considered that. Van was right. "I'm a lot to take on, huh?"

"Yup, you are. But I like it."

Jaycee adjusted her sunglasses and tucked stray pieces of hair behind her ear before they stuck to her lips. Suddenly, the noisy atmosphere was overwhelming. Jaycee felt herself becoming smaller, turning inward as another rush of emotion billowed through her. A young woman jumped a short wave about six feet from Jaycee's towel, laughing with the man holding her around the waist. She had brown hair.

Like Zoe.

Laughing eyes.

Like Zoe.

Two little kids joined them. The man grabbed one and hoisted him high while the woman splashed the little girl wrapped in a ruffled, pink polka-dotted bikini. Jaycee felt rage bubble in her gut. Zoe would never know the joy of having a family. She'd never fall in love with a man who treasured her entirely, who could show her that she didn't need anonymous sex in a dark room to feel loved. Suddenly, the smell of Cool Ranch Doritos made her stomach roll. She looked away from the happy family, realizing the woman didn't resemble Zoe Statler one bit.

"…You okay?" Van asked, leaning in over Jaycee's folded elbows. He pulled them apart and forced her chin up. "Jay Jay? What's up?"

She shook her head. "Zoe," she whispered.

Van rubbed her arms. "That girl's gettin' to you."

Pushing him away, she flipped onto her stomach, and changed the subject yet again. Volatile thoughts shuffled through her head at a dizzying pace. Like an old-fashioned paper rolodex of names and contact information, she rifled through disjointed faces until she landed on the jaundiced image of Detective Barton. Van knew she was working with someone, but had yet to hear the disturbing details about his fast journey from decorated officer to nine-fingered town drunk. Oddly, she felt telling him would be cruel.

"Let's go over some info again," she said, inhaling the breezy Arm & Hammer detergent scent stuck to their beach towels. "About Zoe. I need to talk this out."

"Sure."

"Murder scene appears to provide few clues about the killer."

"DNA stuff is still pending, right?"

"I guess so, but Barton suggested the killer's DNA would be all mixed up with other dudes'. They have a ton of prints, but…they have a ton of prints. See what I mean? It's all right there, but may be useless. Tainted."

"That's just nasty," Van shrugged. "What about Zoe's fingernails? She must have skin scrapings."

"Nails were swabbed, of course, but again if there were other men…"

"Right." Van rubbed his eyes. "Club doesn't take names, like no one makes a reservation or uses a credit card. No paper trail. What about surveillance cameras?"

"Not that I know of inside the club itself. Although Barton is trying to dig up some that would reveal who called it in from a nearby pay phone. Nice work, Van." He surprised her sometimes with sparks of intelligence.

"Did Zoe's colleagues report anything new? How about her parents? What about a strange new boyfriend? Anyone showing up at her school, or her house?"

119

"Zilch."

"Okay, back to the scene. Anything else police can work with, a stray piece of clothing? Remember that movie I did last year? Yeah, yeah, I know it went straight to DVD, but the writing was solid. Such a travesty. Anyway, bad guy killing people. He left a piece of his shoelace behind once. That was all they needed to find his sick ass."

Jaycee kissed him lightly on the lips. "There may be something else," she admitted, "even better than a shoelace. I'm sorry. I promised not to say anything. This is top secret until next week."

Van rolled his eyes at her. "You and your trust issues, Jay Jay. Who do you think I'm going to tell? My bar flies have a combined IQ of about forty-five. They're into tequila and Botox, not exactly the sleuthing types. But, hey, if you don't want me to know…" He held up both hands in surrender. His sexy smirk tugged at Jaycee's chest.

"All right, all right. Barton, my cop friend, gave me the green light to go with this after the interview with Zoe's parents airs. It links Zoe's murder with the other two girls I told you about."

"That serial killer stuff?"

"Possibly. The killer leaves a message behind in the girls' blood."

Van shirked backwards. "For real?" he asked. "Jesus Christ! That's some creepy shit." He gave that some consideration. "Two thoughts…" he said eventually, holding up two fingers on his right hand. "First, he's trying to build a rapport with police, or he's totally fucking with them. NYPD Blue, season four, serial killer leaves notes at the scene for the sole purpose of intriguing the police. Turns out, he flunked out of the academy and that pissed him off. Killer's got some balls."

"Second?" Jaycee asked.

"He's sending a personal message," Van replied, his handsome face expressive and sincere. "CSI Miami. Four random women butchered and nearly decapitated. The killer left a note at each scene with bizarre statements and dates. Turns out he was taunting a former girlfriend. TV stations and newspapers went bat shit releasing all that, which was exactly what he wanted."

"That's why Barton's not putting the note out there to everyone just yet."

"Hmm, smart. What about the other two girls?" he asks. "Anything attaching them to a particular guy?"

"Not that I'm hearing. For now, my focus is on Zoe, and she never mentioned anything about a creeper on her ass. Her parents would've reported that. I can't get anywhere near the other two families. I've tried. They aren't playing."

Van drew lazy lines in the sand. Maroon 5's "Moves Like Jagger" blared out from a radio nearby. Kid giggles floated by on the moving wind. "Barton," Van began. "May not be a total fuckup?"

Loaded question. Jaycee wanted to be fair. "I think he's only halfway fucked up."

"I know you're working with him, but if he's not all there, why is he on a murder case? I thought L.A.P.D. homicide is, like, a supercharged, only-the-best-of-the-best pack of beasts."

"Long, sad story," Jaycee explained. "I did some research. He's the real deal, just sidetracked by an extraordinarily bad incident. He's from Boston, actually, not sure how he ended up here. When the call came in that night, Barton may have simply been the next guy in the rotation. So he shows up, but doesn't necessarily know it's a big case—or linked to the other girls—until after it's been assigned."

"But if he's even a partial fuckup, why is he still on the force?"

Again, Jaycee struggled with revealing the torment Barton endured to earn that battle scar. "Not sure. I do know he's not the only one working the case, and I'm not prepared to condemn him yet. Maybe Barton will surprise us. And don't forget, he's been good to me so far."

Empty the chamber. Load, reload, Jaycee's mind whirled and tumbled.

"Did I tell you Clare's going bat shit with the Statler interview? It's been promo'd about a hundred times."

"Are we done with the investigation?" Van asked, rolling slowly onto his back and slipping one finger under the elastic waistband of her bikini bottom.

"Don't rub my ass in public," she warned him.

"Can't resist such a sweet booty."

Jaycee wriggled over a few inches. "Stop!" she ordered, becoming testy. Poor Van, she knew she could be a twisted bitch sometimes. "Sorry, just stop for right now, okay?"

"Okay."

"Back to Zoe's parents. Clare is all hopped up about it. She gets giddy with exclusives, and I haven't even told her about the new information I'll be releasing in my tag."

"I don't know, Jay Jay. All this sleuthing around. Is anyone watching your back?" Van scoffed. "Remember that episode of *The Mentalist* I did last year. Pretty TV reporter ends up in the crosshairs of a police investigation. A skilled freak likes her look and makes her the next victim. Scary shit!"

"You're cray-cray," Jaycee smiled, placing a soft kiss on Van's cheek, and not revealing Barton's concern for exactly that. "Don't worry about me." She yawned.

Hot sunshine often worked better on her than an Ambien. Jaycee was exhausted. She'd gotten just two hours sleep the night before, searching around online for stories of murders and Throw Away Girls. In Detroit, someone killed sixteen prostitutes in 2007 and proceeded to tuck their limp bodies around tree trunks in some gory nature tribute. And then the killings simply stopped. Never solved and no new murders reported since. Over in Philly, a year later, seven young women with heavy crystal meth addictions met their demise inside an abandoned slaughterhouse. Also unsolved. Up in Norwich, Vermont, four college students went missing over three years. Never found and never solved. She read of gruesome savagery until her eyes glazed over, desperate to make a connection but spooked by Barton's warning the first time she met him.

Once you start thinking a certain way about your evidence, you risk bending the entire case around to support it.

But then, one case grabbed her by the hair and jerked her to attention. A frightening history of death tucked deep within the archived pages of The Miami Herald.

Spring 2009

A fourth young woman turned up dead last night, her body badly mutilated and almost unrecognizable.

And this:

Miami police suspect all four deaths are linked. The women were known heroin addicts with heavy criminal records. A note scrawled in what appears to be blood deemed them all: Unworthy.

Not the same, but undeniably close. The murders in Miami, also unsolved. Four women, all targeted and punished for their sins. Could it possibly be the same man? Was there a psychopath moving systematically from one place to the next, enacting his own justice on those who represented worthlessness and debauchery? It was almost unthinkable, and yet as Jaycee had sat there on her couch, listening to the noises of the night and nursing a glass of Pinot Grigio, she felt suddenly struck by the possibility.

Barton was right. The killer was like a traveling salesman: anonymous, and yet entirely driven by a purpose, a self-imposed God complex that granted him the right to act as both judge and jury. Finally, she dumped the wine in the sink and tucked her head under the covers of her bed. Her mind raced with gritty images of dirty alleys and bloody remnants of used-up girls. They tormented her dreams.

Jaycee reached for Van's fingers, giving in to her heavy eyelids and the warm breeze. Van stared at her tan back, stroking the skin just below where her bikini was tied. His girl was going through hell with this story. Van rolled sideways and before long his jaw went slack and he snored lightly.

Even if they were still awake, neither Jaycee nor Van would be able to hear the shutter clicking on the Panasonic superzoom camera perched on a nearby picnic table.

Click, click, click. The man adjusted his focus and zoom. He captured Jaycee at her most vulnerable: eyes squeezed shut, lips gently touching in the middle. She was a vision. He'd driven by her condo, waited for her to leave. These public personalities were so stupid. Protected and private? Yeah, not quite.

Once her car pulled out, he followed them, two lovers who wanted to lounge the day away on the beach. It was a pleasant enough detour, even though he wouldn't stay long.

He watched her chest rise and fall through his lens. His crotch tingled. She was smart, but maybe a tad too smart. Her desire to tell a story was treading too close. Of all the reporters covering the murders, Jaycee seemed the most invested. Her station had gone on a promo-palooza to tout her delicious interview with Zoe Statler's parents. A modern-day witch-hunt played out on the tube. Worse than a *Keeping Up with the Kardashians* marathon on E.

Reporters were typically a hyperactive bunch, always prowling around for an edge but too easily distracted by the next big thing. This one, however, could be trouble. She had an annoying yet undeniable staying power. Admirable, really, but only if she kept her distance.

Jaycee Wilder was not a Throw Away Girl.

He would prefer not having to make her one.

It was time to send her a warning.

Chapter Fourteen

"I like how you dissolved that," Jaycee told Ben as they sat in an edit bay watching her finished story with the Statlers. It was exquisite; the typical perfection Ben achieved when his creativity was unleashed. They watched Mr. Statler's face fade into his daughter's, a gentle technique useful for emotional moments. She wondered if the killer would appreciate how much Zoe had resembled her dad.

"See, there?" He paused the video to point out why he chose that effect. "I wanted her face to be the last thing you see." Again, the killer had already exploited that privilege.

"It's perfect. And sad. Thank you, nice work." Jaycee pushed out of her chair and left the stuffy small room. She needed air. They'd been working on the story for hours, each of them coming in early to carefully add or delete shots, throw in a new audio track, or revise how they used a cut-away of Jaycee.

The Statler interview felt like old news before it had even aired. The promo department had pulled various sound bites and added dramatic music to up the ante. The station had slapped a big fat embargo on the interview until after it aired, a legal hands-off to other stations and networks looking to grab it unscrupulously and claim it as their own. Jaycee knew the interview was a huge "get" for her, but it felt empty and shallow. The case was still open. Justice for Zoe and the others had yet to be delivered.

"I can't wait to see that!" the health reporter Maggie Severson gushed, walking by the glass door of the edit bay and glimpsing a preview shot of the Statlers sitting together on their couch. "I can't imagine what they're going through. Good job, Jay Jay."

"Thanks," she muttered. Her colleagues were a supportive bunch, mostly, and despite Derek getting his ego rocked by losing the story to her, they were complimentary of her hard work. Everyone was covering this now; the station was competing with other stations, print reporters, and even TMZ to be out there first with this ongoing story. Jaycee's exclusive with the Statlers had secured their spot, at least for a day, in the ratings war. She would follow that jab with a resounding right hook. It would be breaking news to tag the Statler interview, a highly enticing piece of investigative information released to only one reporter. A bloody message left at Zoe's murder scene. Clare wanted to source it out to the L.A. Police Department. Jaycee persuaded her to go with "law enforcement official close to the investigation."

"He's good to me," she explained earlier during a meeting in Clare's office.

"Fuck that. You know I like to source my shit." Clare was her usual bombastic self.

"I appreciate that. But if I reveal too much too soon, I'll screw him. He's on camera with me tomorrow. Not sure yet what the next peg of the story will be, but he'll do an interview."

"Do you trust him?" she asked, willing to give Jaycee some leeway.

"I do."

"What will you be able to get on the record?"

"As much as possible. Don't put me in the rotation tomorrow. I don't want to cover some fire or robbery; I'm on the murders. Plug the I-Team, you have a good audience now with our exclusives."

Clare relented but watched Jaycee closely. She also warned her to be careful and in no way was she to engage a killer. "If you have doubts about a location or an interview, send Ben in first," she'd told Jaycee.

Jaycee tapped some fake milk powder into a styrofoam cup and followed it with some hot, light brown coffee. It looked weak and tasted worse. She dumped it out and opted for a Diet Pepsi from the soda vending machine. Nervous energy consumed her. She returned to her desk and clicked around the rundown for the night's news shows. A smaller version of her story was written for the five o'clock hour, with the full report airing at six. She read through the anchor lead.

Tonight, an ABC 12 exclusive. The parents of a young woman found murdered in a nightclub are speaking out for the first time. While police scour the city for her killer, her mom and dad want other families to be on alert. The type of nightclub where Zoe Statler was killed is more common than most realize. ABC 12's Jaycee Wilder has the emotional interview.

Jaycee played with words and phrases. She added and then deleted, at least, a dozen times before calling it done. She moved onto the tag.

There are breaking developments in this investigation. A law enforcement source is now confirming to ABC 12 that the killer left behind a message at the scene of Zoe Statler's murder, though police will not yet release what it says.

Jaycee hunched over her computer. She read the lines aloud to gauge their flow. The tag worked. She added a breakout reader for the anchors about the cause of Zoe's death, loss of blood, but that did little to add to the overall product. Barton was correct on that, to the average viewer that didn't really register. Murder victims bleed. Los Angeles was used to that.

Her cell phone jingled.

Barton.

"Morning, Detective," Jaycee said. "We need to schedule our interv—"

"How fast can you get to Cedars-Sinai?" he interrupted. Something was happening.

"Uh," Jaycee stood up; her eyes scanned the newsroom for Clare. "I think I can finish up here soon and…"

"Jaycee, do whatever you have to and get your ass over here. Now. Do not, I repeat, do not tell anyone where you're going. Make something up. Get here, now, no camera, and make yourself…less…yourself."

Barton hung up on her.

130

What the hell?

Jaycee raced over to Clare and pulled her away from the rest of the team circled around the table discussing plans for the day. "Can I have a couple of hours to check something out?"

"Is this about Zoe?"

"I'm not sure yet. It may be."

"Where are you going?"

"Can I let you know that when I come back?"

Clare sighed; her rounded shoulders slumped into her chest. "I don't like this. Is your story done? Take Ben."

"No, I'm going by myself. Yes, everything's finished and in the rundown. There's nothing new to put on camera yet."

Clare nodded. "Take until two o'clock. You need to come back and order the graphics for your package tonight. There's some stuff made already, a background image with Zoe's face, but you need to add the text."

Jaycee noticed Clare's drawn face. She was balancing concern with intrigue. "Don't worry, I'll be fine. Be back in plenty of time to polish up the story. I promise."

Jaycee moved swiftly back to her desk to grab her purse, cell phone, and the Dodgers baseball hat she wore when she preferred not to be recognized. She assumed that's what Barton meant, her visit to the hospital was not to be an official work event.

Clare returned to the morning meeting but noticed the morning's mail pile. A few envelopes had *Jaycee Wilder-*

ABC 12 printed on labels attached to the front. She shuffled through the rest of the pile, found a few other mailers with Jaycee's name and brought the contents over to Jaycee before she left.

"Here," she said, handing over the envelopes. "If your mysterious journey takes you to the 405, you're going to sit for an eternity right now. At least, open your mail. You're not good at getting back to people. And I have to listen to their shit after you ignore them. Do not let one story monopolize your job."

Jaycee grabbed her mail and promised Clare she'd get back on track with return calls and messages. Clare was right; she had been preoccupied lately.

"Will do," Jaycee told her, and then rushed out the garage door where the photographers were packing up their rigs for the day. Ben was huddled over a mug of green tea in the room where all the camera batteries charged overnight. He caught a glimpse of gray pants, pink sweater, and flowing hair tucked beneath a ratty baseball hat swiftly moving out to the employee parking lot.

Jaycee?

Ben sighed. What now? He was growing more concerned that Jaycee's mounting obsession with the dead girls was about to put her in the direct line of fire.

Jaycee took long steps out to her car, juggling her keys, purse, and mail in an awkward grip. She threw the door open and tossed everything onto the passenger seat, and then huffed at a slip of brown tucked beneath one windshield wiper. "Really?" she blurted to no one. It annoyed her when fans attached letters or messages to her car. Too often, she worried that one day some sicko she exposed as a child predator or tax evader would attach a trip wire to her engine and blow her to smithereens.

Sighing loudly, she grabbed the square envelope addressed neatly to her and threw it atop all the other mail waiting to be opened. One more thing to talk to Clare about—workplace security. With killers running around this city, can't a girl get into her car without worrying about a parking lot ambush?

Chapter Fifteen

Tubes connected clear liquid to veins. There were too many IV lines to count. Compact, white machines on narrow metal posts beeped with timed alerts monitoring oxygen level, heart rate, and blood pressure. The girl's face was a swollen patchwork of stitches and gauze with tufts of matted blonde hair splayed out over a thin pillow. Puffed lips poked out like sausages from between bandages covering the length of her face. The torso was still, but both legs twitched and shook. The girl was obviously struggling against the medicated cocoon wrapping around her.

Jaycee had seen car accident victims dismembered and nearly decapitated. She'd been first on the scene of fires that had scorched human beings into ash. She'd sat on hard wooden benches in stuffy courtrooms, staring at overhead projector pictures of crime scene photos used as evidence in trials. She'd watched homicide victims get loaded into black shiny bags and then disappear forever.

This, however, was different.

The air in the ICU smelled antiseptic yet rotten. Noises, dings, and muffled sobs filled the floor that hooked like a U around a central nurses' station in the middle. Jaycee was in the doorway of room 601. Four other officers were on either side, with Barton directly behind her. She only knew how close he was after he braced her back as she swayed into him.

"Breathe," he told her. "Just breathe."

Jaycee took half a step toward the bed. The room was small and square, almost every inch of it filled with equipment working to save this girl from further agony. Bags of liquid pumped in drugs to quell the pain, more medicine to stabilize her heart rate, and droplets of blood were delivered one by one to make up for what she'd lost. The effort to save her was almost as grisly as the one to kill her. Critical care certainly wasn't a pretty business.

"He did this?" Jaycee whispered as tears threatened to leak out. "When?"

"Late Friday night," Barton told her. "Near 1873 or so Hollywood Boulevard. Cleaning crew called it in Saturday. It's a miracle she hung in there that long."

"Who is she?"

"Her name is Fiona Cooper. She's the office manager of a tattoo shop on Melrose. Has a kid and an ex-husband, both parents dead, no siblings. Closest next of kin—a second cousin—is flying in from Virginia as we speak. Including you, that's about ten people who know that she's here. If anyone asks, you're also a distant cousin."

"Will…she," Jaycee gasped on her horror, and then swallowed hard. "Survive?"

Barton nodded. "My gut tells me yes. The doctors say she's been fighting the drugs all weekend. She's made it through two surgeries already. Her face is really…not good."

Jaycee's head snapped. Barton was, at times, unnecessarily cryptic. "Beaten, you mean?" she asked.

"More than that, Jaycee. She lost an eye and an earlobe. Come out here, I want you to step away."

Jaycee stumbled behind Barton into the family waiting room area. She felt hot but her skin tingled with goosebumps. She wrapped her arms around herself, squeezing as if to connect to the moment. She really *was* standing in the ICU, feet away from the latest Throw Away Girl.

"I'm not reporting on this, am I?" she said, already knowing the answer.

"Not yet. Do you understand why I brought you here?" Barton was leaning against a pale pink wall near the elevators and a water bubbler. It struck Jaycee that even though she'd seen him not long ago, he looked suddenly lean. His skin had gone from the ashen gray she remembered at Zoe's funeral to a warm scarlet. He was becoming what he used to be, she thought, struck by the realization that a serial murderer was the catalyst to what could be his new and improved life.

Jaycee closed her eyes. "I'm going to tell her story. Eventually."

Just like she was telling Zoe's.

"Yes, when it's time. Right now, she's in protective custody. You need to sit on this. Nothing about another attack, and absolutely zero about a survivor." Barton's gaze into her eyes was the clearest she'd seen yet. He was definitely not juiced up on anything but adrenaline and anger. She smiled warily at him. Detective Barton, resurrected.

"It's good to see you like this," she said, before she realized it was wildly inappropriate. "Uh, what I mean…"

"I know what you mean," he interrupted. "Boston isn't too far from Los Angeles, if you're looking to find it."

Jaycee didn't take it as a slam, just recognition that Barton knew she'd read his story. She merely nodded. "Is there anything else I need to know?" she asked.

"You're still a go with the Statler interview tonight? And the release of the note?"

"Yes, both airing tonight. I will assume a note was left here, too?"

Barton nodded. "That, and there's something else we're following that you may be interested in pursuing yourself. Maybe get a head start. I'd say we'll be looking into a new lead sometime later today. A few hours from now, at least, I still have some paperwork on this to get in. Of course, I won't be available to go on camera until tomorrow, as you know, but if you really wanted to do some investigative reporting…"

Jaycee's stomach muscles clenched. She was about to get another exclusive detail.

"I'm ready," she confirmed.

"Olive," he told her softly. "Go find Olive. Tell her Fiona sent you, and for fuck's sake, don't go alone. 'Scuse my mouth."

Chapter Sixteen

The 405 was a monster and Van wasn't answering the phone at home. Shit! Jaycee was shaking behind the wheel. It was unsettling to know of another attack without being able to tell anyone. Ordinarily, once she uncovered a news tip, it hit Twitter, Facebook, and her station's website within seconds. It's how a reporter remained competitive and relevant. She lived each moment of her day working to expose things, and this was eating at her stomach like an acid-laced handful of Tums.

Her name is Fiona Cooper. She's the office manager at a tattoo shop.

Find Olive.

Ripples of sadness and frustration gripped her body as Jaycee stared—her hands wrapped around the steering wheel, despite sitting at a dead stop—out the front window of her car. The killer was emboldened. He was escalating. She remembered a National Geographic special she'd watched a few years back; a former colleague had earned an Emmy for it. It was a documentary on the psychological cycle of a serial killer. The piece dissected the traits of a man who'd been convicted of ten murders over a span of ten years. The last three, however, occurred within seven months of each other.

"Sometimes, a serial killer will suddenly and inexplicably escalate his attacks. We can't say why, only that many of them—under guidance from mental health experts or trained interrogators—will admit the final murders before they were caught were exceedingly brutal or rapidly executed, as though they felt a previously unknown urge they couldn't ignore."

Jaycee could hear the audio and see the video in her head: A short, balding man shown at trial, seated behind a wooden desk and watching witnesses testify against him with a vague, detached expression. He appeared not to toil in guilt as the details of his dirty acts were broadcast to a courtroom filled with reporters and devastated family members. No, he was merely disappointed there could be no more killings. The story cut to a videotaped interview the man had with a court-appointed psychiatrist, casually answering questions about torture and sex assault as if they were inquiries about whether he preferred watermelon or grapes.

"Why kill the last three women before you raped them?" the psychiatrist asked. "You preferred your earlier victims alive through that act."

The man had stirred slightly in his metal chair, the handcuffs that bound his wrists together jangled on the stainless steel table between them. You could hear jail guards shuffle in the background. Otherwise, Jaycee recounted, the video was thick with silent expectation and the shameless visage of a ruthless killer.

"I couldn't help it," he eventually told the woman with shiny gray hair wearing a no-nonsense navy blue suit. "I just had to kill. It felt like if I had only an hour left on Earth, I had to spend it killing someone."

139

The shot had tightened until the killer's unflinching and unapologetic face filled the entire screen. His eyes were brown, with tinges of green around each iris. He looked like a janitor, or a bus driver, maybe even a data entry desk nerd. The entire point was this: he didn't look like a man possessed by wicked intentions and hell bent on acting on them as quickly as possible.

And yet, that's exactly what he was.

The Throw Away Girls were piling up. The killer's hunger and savagery were intensifying. This had to stop!

She called Van again, impatiently waiting through four rings before he answered the phone with a groggy, annoyed bark.

"What?" he growled.

"It's me. Get your ass out of bed, and get dressed. I'm picking you up as soon as I can get off the freakin' 405. I need your help on something. Dress yourself up nice and be ready to go."

Van began to protest, but Jaycee hung up. She may not be a seasoned homicide detective, but she also wasn't dumb enough to make this next stop—wherever it was—by herself. On a hunch, her next call was to City Hall Office 402 and the aide to the City Council President. Someone who may help her find a person named Olive.

"Zander Butant," the voice stated.

"It's Jaycee Wilder, don't you hang up!"

Jaycee could hear a huffed response and the sound of metal chair legs forcefully scraping the tile floor. Zander was likely moving away from the earshot of someone.

"What the hell, Jaycee?" his voice was muffled and definitely irritated. "I'm not ready for a story…"

"Listen, Zander," she cut him off. "I need a favor. This isn't about the police or Zoe. I need you to tell me who Olive is in your sleazy world of naked coed dungeons and dragons."

An alarmed question followed. "What happened to Olive? Is she okay?"

Gotcha! Jaycee loved using a droplet of information to unleash a waterfall.

"She's okay, I promise. I need to talk to her. It's critically important, and I promise you not for TV."

Zander sighed loudly, relief mixed with sheer irascibility. "She's very private, Jaycee. She won't talk to you. I'm not sure she even comes out during the day, and trust me, you don't want to go looking for her at night."

"Let's begin with who is she?"

Zander groaned. "This didn't come from me, okay?"

"You have my word." Jaycee promised.

"Olive is sort of like the Queen. She's highly regarded as a dominatrix and only sees a small group of clientele. She runs her own club. It's a good one."

"You've been there?"

"Yes. I've never been alone with Olive, though. I only know *of* her. She is legendary in our circles." Jesus Christ!

Jaycee's mental puzzle pieces were moving, gathering to form a border. It was always easiest to work your way in. Olive was all the way in.

"How do I find her?" she asked.

"I honestly don't know," Zander told her. "She's there some nights, others not at all. Like I said, she's an appointment-only partner."

"You said she runs her own club? What do you mean? She owns it?"

Zander made a vague grunt. "Jaycee, seriously, I'm not tight with Olive. No one is. She's a businesswoman and runs a good place. That's all I know."

"So people work for her?" she asked, looking for a different route to the same destination. At times, that was necessary if an interview was growing stale.

"I guess so," he told her. "There are a few guys who bartend. And if you want something specific at her club, she can find someone to give it to you. Maybe they're her employees. I don't know; I really don't. Those aren't the kinds of conversations I've ever had there. Sorry."

"Thanks, Zander. One last thing. Where's her club?"

Zander Butant had had enough of Jaycee Wilder for the second time in nearly as many days. He just wanted her to go away.

"1500 Hollywood Boulevard. Lower level, you enter through the alley."

"What's the name?"

"Jaycee, it doesn't have a name. None of these clubs do."

Chapter Seventeen

"You're going to have to find a Starbucks. This is, like, the middle of the night for me, Jay Jay. You're messing with my REM cycle, big time!" Van looked like a bulky, fully pissed off James Dean with his metal-rimmed aviator sunglasses perched on the straight bridge of his nose.

Jaycee shut him up with a glare. "Don't be such a whiny bitch," she chastised him. "I don't give a shit what cycle you're in, when I call you should come running. It's called being in a relationship."

"Yeah, an *abusive* relationship," he muttered. They were crawling back toward downtown; Van slouched in the passenger seat—not yet lucid enough to drive—headed for Hollywood Boulevard and, hopefully, some useful information from an elusive dominatrix. Jaycee planned to use Van to get in the door, if anyone was there this time of day, and then corner her for information.

"This is important, Van. I need you to put your acting skills to work."

"What makes you think she'll talk to me?" Van had only vague instructions to pose as an alluring job-seeker.

"You're hot, and she's in the business of sex. Duh." Jaycee gave her boyfriend's muscled thigh a squeeze. "Just get me in the door. I'll take it from there."

"What are you going to ask her?" Van wanted to know.

"I got a tip. I think she may have inadvertently had contact with the killer. Or maybe one of the victims."

"Zoe?" he asked.

"No, not Zoe. Not the other two girls, either. There's been another attack. You need to shut your trap about that. Got it?"

Van lurched forward. His tired body twisted toward Jaycee like it had just received an electric shock. "Jaycee, call the police!"

She nodded. "They already know."

Van shifted back into the seat. "Jesus Christ," he sighed. "Why are you here with me, chasing down some obscure woman with a strange name and not at the scene with Ben? Something's not right here," he said, looking again at her profile. "Your news people don't know about this yet, do they?"

"Technically, no."

"Just you?"

"Yes, for now."

"Oh, Christ," Van groaned. "I don't like this," he told her. "Not one bit. *Law & Order--Special Victims Unit*, Season Two, Episode Four. Detective becomes obsessed with a homicidal maniac, loses her mind, needs professional help. Remember that one, Jay Jay? Sound familiar?"

"Please," she replied. "How about the episode where a reporter's boyfriend helps her expose a killer before he strikes again?"

* * * *

Jaycee kept her head low as she and Van crawled around overflowing trash barrels and empty cardboard boxes stacked waist high. They were halfway down an alley between Hollywood Boulevard and a narrow street that ran parallel to it. Squeezed to the side was a white Mercedes SUV with the vanity plate, OLV. They may have just gotten extraordinarily lucky.

"Sweet ride," Van pointed out. "Those run at least sixty-five grand. Olive must like some fine leather under her thighs."

"Don't be nasty," Jaycee said, huffing at his attempt at humor. "This is huge. Chances are good that she's here." They found a decaying door with a rusted knob. "Lovely place," she said, stopping to look around. Van knocked loudly.

Nothing.

"It's too early," he said. "These places don't come to life until the sun goes down. She probably left the car here last night."

"Try again," Jaycee insisted. "Louder."

Van sighed. "Fine!" He rapped the long metal door again with his knuckles. Again, nothing. "Happy? See, no one's here…"

"Shit," she interrupted, shoving Van aside. "Move!" Maneuvering around her boyfriend, Jaycee sprinkled the door with her own rapid-fire knocks. "Hello!" she bellowed. "Anyone in there?"

Van watched. Shaking his head, he marveled at how such pig-headed stubbornness had been poured into the body of his beautiful girlfriend. Her cheeks were bright pink while her blonde ponytail swayed between her shoulders. A determined and somewhat reckless display, but Van crossed his arms and allowed her a few more knocks. Finally, he pulled her away by the elbows.

"Jay Jay, there's no one inside. Come on, let's go."

"No!" she yelled back at him, yanking herself free from his grip and pelting the door again with her fists. Anger exploded deep inside her. She felt a desperate need to get through the door, almost like her feet were cemented to the threshold by a force she couldn't control. Jaycee was unable to move.

But then she had to because the door was opening from the inside. A square-shouldered Mexican woman with a tight perm was wearing a checkered apron and holding a clear plastic bottle with dark green liquid inside of it. She poked her head around the corner. Cleaning lady.

"*Quién está allí*," she asked. *Who's there?*

Jaycee reached for Van. Thrusting him ahead of her, she told him to tell her he was here to see Olive.

"*Hola*," he said, turning on his charm with a huge grin. Turning back to Jaycee, Van whispered, "That's all I know in Spanish!"

"*Hola*," Jaycee interjected with her own big friendly smile. She barely knew much more. "*Estoy buscando*…uh…Olive?" She hoped she just said they were looking for Olive.

The blocky woman squinted at the lovely couple. They seemed safe, certainly were not the *policia,* which she had strict instructions to keep away. Her boss did not take kindly to strangers soliciting her during the day, but the woman didn't want to turn anyone away if Olive was expecting them. She was torn.

Jaycee poked Van. "Tell her *por favor*," she whispered. "And be cute!"

"Uh, *por favor*," he said, in a sultry growl. He leaned his forearm against the doorway, exposing a rippled bicep beneath a soft gray Armani t-shirt. The woman's mouth dropped open as Van then lifted his shades away from his eyes, all crinkled and sparkly blue…just for her. Way better, in fact, than the morons on her favorite *telenovela* who kept their hair too long and kissed too many women.

She made her decision. If this man wanted to see Olive, she wouldn't be the one who kept him away. Maybe her boss would give her a raise in exchange for such a beautiful gift.

"*Bueno*," she told them, opening the heavy door to allow them entry into a large, square room. "*Allí*," she told them, pointing toward a dark hallway.

"I think she said back there," Jaycee hustled through the door, pushing Van ahead of her while adding several "*gracias*," over her shoulder. The woman quickly returned to her large cleaning cart and selected another spray bottle. "Tell her, *gracias*," she instructed Van.

"*Gracias, novia*," he added what he thought was a term of endearment.

"Don't be dirty, Van," Jaycee told him. "Be respectful."

"I thought I was," he snapped back, looking around him. "And, you're welcome. God, what a nasty-ass place," he grimaced, swiping at his nostrils in disgust. "Can you smell that?"

"Sweat and old cologne," she offered, gingerly stepping over a raised lump in the maroon rug. They looked around them. The room was huge, with shiny pink walls and a ceiling fractured by several metal track lighting units that featured multi-colored light bulbs. In the center was a hanging orb bedazzled by crystals to provide that obligatory disco-era vibe. The entire left side of the room was filled by a long, wooden bar with a wall of mirrors behind it and several stools in the front. It was fully stocked, but there were no glasses. Red solo cups were stacked on either side of a beer tap station. There was no attention paid to elegance here.

Van pointed to a series of plush, zebra print loungers pushed against another wall. "Welcome to the jungle," he joked. A few low ottomans with zig-zag designs were scattered about, along with several plastic chairs and round-topped tables to hold drinks. The décor was minimalistic yet fanciful, with bright swaths of electric blue and crimson red. An "Alice in Wonderland" sort of sensory overload.

Two hallways lead off the main room. One was entirely dark with only a red EXIT sign visible at the end. The other hallway was lit by a thin line of light from a partially open door on the right-hand side. Jaycee motioned to Van, and they quietly moved past closed, dark rooms and toward the sound of someone typing away on a keyboard.

"You go first," Jaycee pulled on Van's shirt before they entered the room. "If she's the one who's in there and sees me first she'll probably press some sort of panic button. You will throw her off."

"Is that good?" he asked.

"I think so," she told him. "Your only role now is to confirm she's Olive. If it's some guy in there, ask for Olive and tell him you're here about a job."

"This just feels wrong," he moaned. "How did you rope me into this?"

"Go!" she told him. "Come on, Mr. Hollywood Actor, show me whatcha got."

"I hate you," he said snidely. But Van more than held his own. He knocked on the door with a friendly, "Hello?"

A strong yet feminine voice confirmed her presence but immediately demanded to know who Van was. Jaycee held her breath outside the door, praying that Van could pull this off until she could take over.

"I'm here to see Olive," he said pleasantly. "My buddy sent me over; he said you might be hiring. I need some work at night. I'm an actor by day."

Jaycee winced. Too much information! Be cool, Van, she implored him silently. Let your body do the talking. Jaycee could detect a tinge of interest when she went on to ask Van what kind of work was he interested in.

"Oh, you know, whatever you need. I'm pretty flexible."

Jaycee cringed. This was weird listening to her boyfriend make sexual innuendo conversation with a mistress of the night. *Just give me confirmation, Van,* she thought. *Let me know it's her.*

"When could you start?" the woman asked. "I may have something available for you, but I'd need to know when you're available."

Come on, Van! Jaycee was on the balls of her feet, waiting for Van to deliver. *You can do this*, she cheered him on in her head. Get her name, Van, make sure it's her.

"Do you need to run it by Olive?"

Jaycee was still as stone, poised like a cobra waiting to strike. This was it.

She heard a chair move. The woman must have stood up. "I apologize," she said. "I am Olive, nice to meet you."

Perfect! Jaycee swept around the corner just as the two gripped hands over a messy, paper-filled work desk. Olive was a petite, small-boned woman with no makeup and a pile of dark hair dripping from a messy bun. She looked about twenty-five years old with a fake rack and a clean, scrubbed face. She had large expressive eyes and high cheekbones, exquisite in a Plain Jane sort of way. She wore black yoga pants and a t-shirt with a Brentwood School logo in the middle. Jaycee recognized that as one of the premiere private schools in L.A.

"Olive," she announced, walking into the room with an authority she was working hard to pull off and closing the door behind her. "I'm so sorry to startle you…I'm…"

The bitsy woman muttered a perturbed gasp but quickly recovered. She was not one for surprises.

"Save it," she replied stiffly, recognizing the blonde beauty despite the mousy baseball hat and loose hair. "I know who you are. I was wondering how long it would take one of you to find me."

Chapter Eighteen

"I've never been busier," Olive told them. She pointed to stacks of cash wrapped in slim bands. "This is last night's haul alone. It means longer office days for me, but I'm not complaining."

Olive had offered them coffee from the Keurig machine in the corner of her office. The room was well lit by an overhead light, and a lamp with a pastel flowered top. Lace curtains covered a slip of a window, keeping any natural light artificially tinged with soft colors. Olive's ornate wooden desk held a laptop, a smattering of bills, envelopes, and printouts organized around a desk calendar in the middle. Somehow, a whip-smart accountant was keeping her business on the right side of the law, and presumably, the IRS. A square leather deposit bag waited in the corner. The office held all the typical trappings of a business organizing its receivables and debt.

Once Jaycee assured her there was no camera in tow, she agreed to talk to them about the murders and what she suggested was an outrageous link to a sudden boom in business.

"It's created this whole new level of danger and appeal," she said, handing over two steaming ceramic mugs with kids' smiling faces on them and lopsided homemade handles. Jaycee's displayed the happy picture of a little girl with missing front teeth, while Van's showcased a little boy wearing reindeer pajamas and holding a candy cane. It was such an odd paradox; talking about sex for cash with sweet child faces looking on. Olive caught her in thought.

"They're mine," she confirmed. Jaycee commented on how lovely they were.

"Actually, I know the headmaster at The Brentwood School," Jaycee told her, pointing to the logo in the middle of Olive's chest. "It's a wonderful place. I did a story there last year about that new green playground they put in."

Olive nodded. "I remember that day. I thought you did a great job interviewing the kids. I do watch the news, you know. I assumed a reporter would find me eventually. Although I prefer privacy, I realize I have a reputation if someone is entrepreneurial enough. I won't even ask you to reveal to me who pointed you in my direction."

Jaycee smiled. "Thanks," she told her, prepared to ease her way into that disclosure, and the current state of Fiona, which was coma via medicine. "So, you must have seen the promos for the story tonight with Zoe Statler's family?"

Olive shifted back, giving the appearance of her thick, padded leather chair swallowing her whole. "I have," she told them, leaning against the comfortable back with a coffee mug in both hands. She took a delicate sip, pursing full lips that must be a huge part of her allure when they're properly glossed up. "I intend to watch."

"Olive," Jaycee began. "I know this is awkward for you, and there is new information I'm willing to share with you in exchange for your help. I realize you need to protect your…um…your livelihood."

Olive gave her a sardonic grin. "It's okay, Jaycee," she said. "You don't need to be sensitive with me. If you walk down this road, you need to have good shoes, yes?"

"I suppose so," Jaycee agreed.

Van coughed. Either he wanted to remind them he was still there, or he wanted to let them know he didn't want to be there.

"Should I go?" he asked, not sure which woman would direct him. "Do you want me to leave?"

"No," Jaycee said first.

"No," Olive said next.

Van sat back.

"Let me guess. Boyfriend?" she asked Jaycee.

"Yes, and reluctant co-conspirator. Sorry we lied to you. This is Van. I just figured you'd prefer meeting him first."

Olive chuckled. "Too bad, I thought this was my lucky day. Kidding, of course. I am well taken care of. My husband is in finance," she told them, confirming to Jaycee who her money wizard was. "He does my books for me, but he won't be caught dead here. He works days, I work nights, it fits for us."

"Wow," Jaycee couldn't help herself. "You're married, too? You don't look old enough to be someone's wife or mother."

"Thank you," Olive preened. "It is important to stay in shape. Yes, we've been married for over ten years now." Olive looked like an amused cat, thoroughly enjoying their shocked expressions. "True love is very different from physical gratification. I keep my worlds entirely separate, but I can't deny I make a very good living for my family."

"He must worry about your safety," Jaycee figured. "Especially now?"

Van worried about her, and she was a straight-laced TV reporter living in the real world. Olive was a night crawler, hooking up with perverts in fantasyland. How did her husband ever feel peace?

"He trusts me," she shrugged. "But he has insisted I have safety measures in place," Olive told her. "However, they are only so strong…"

Jaycee watched Olive take another sip of coffee. There was something there; she just needed to be patient. This was a woman quite used to controlling the pace of everything in her life.

"As I was telling you," Olive started. "Business is better than ever. These…" she placed her mug on the desk and opened her arms wide, "…these murders have brought out the kinkies in droves. They're like zombie junkies searching for a particularly potent batch of heroin. Once word spreads that it's out there, they all want it."

"That's just sick," Van muttered. Jaycee quickly shushed him, "Don't be rude."

"I'm not rude; it's sick, and you know it."

Olive was neither offended nor put off. "I agree, actually," she told them. "But, it is what it is. I've added more security, spread the word to my colleagues and friends, and shared my own personal information I have with them…" she trailed off, but Jaycee picked up on her thread.

"Would you be willing to tell me what that is? I assure you, I will not publically share it. You have my word," Jaycee told her earnestly.

Olive eyed her carefully. "Why do you care, then?" she asked Jaycee pointedly. "If I tell you something you can't put on television. Isn't it your job to do exactly that?"

She felt Van watching her. Olive's gaze was equally as intense. Jaycee never liked to lie. "I care about these girls," she stated simply. "Especially Zoe. But none of them deserved to die. You can understand that, right?"

"Of course," Olive quickly agreed. "But I've also heard media reports that put the blame squarely on the girls simply because they subscribed to a certain lifestyle. How do I know what I tell you won't be used to further discredit my industry?" Her eyes bore into Jaycee's, a display of strength and grit much larger than her stature.

"Olive," Jaycee began. "This isn't about your industry or their choices. I'm not interested in telling people they can't have naughty sex in the red room of pain. I'm trying to find a killer. Please, trust me. This is so far beyond my job or yours."

Olive folded her thin arms and thought it over. "I consider myself a businesswoman and right now, my business is thriving. However, I can't ignore that I am also the mother of a daughter. Young women are being hunted, and that's concerning."

"Thank you," Jaycee said.

"What do you want to know?" Olive asked.

"Do you know the victims?" Jaycee began. Start there, she thought, see where this goes.

"No," Olive told her. "But my clients don't share with me their personal information. Even though none of the attacks have happened at my club, I cannot say with any certainty that they haven't been here before."

"Did any of the girls look familiar to you?"

"Vaguely."

"Does your club allow everyone in or just the good-looking people?"

"I have a discerning clientele," Olive told her objectively. "My club is known for that. I have earned a reputation for providing excellent variety and services, *the* place to be if you fit a particular category. Male or female."

"How does someone get to you directly?" Jaycee wanted to know.

"Word of mouth," Olive told her. "I use a referral system from people I trust. Occasionally, I will entertain a new client if I feel him out and deem him willing to pay my price. An hour with me doesn't come cheap."

Jaycee noticed the huge diamond on her left finger, and the perfectly manicured red nails above the bling. She was expensive looking, for sure.

"Do you know him, Olive?" she asked. This must be why Fiona Cooper would send police her way.

The slim figure hunched. Van tensed. Jaycee moved to the edge of her seat. This could be pivotal.

"I think so," she told them, with no dramatic prelude. "He almost killed me. But then he decided not to. I haven't seen him since."

Chapter Nineteen

Van and Jaycee gaped, it was a huge bombshell, and yet Olive was cool like a ladybug perched on a dewy loop of freshly cut backyard grass: totally chill and matter-of-fact.

"Let me explain," she started. "I have regulars who come and go, and some of them prefer a more potent approach. This man calls himself Slade. He and I have had mutually enjoyable encounters several times, but he has a dark edge to him. Typically, I can quickly feel out a client's breaking point and we straddle it at times, but rarely cross it. I want them to leave satisfied and fulfilled, not fearful or hurt. This man, however, has no breaking point. Pain is as desirable to him as pleasure, both to receive and to give."

"So, he smacks you around?" Van asked. Leave it to Van to cut through the psychological verbiage and get right to the point. Spit it out, Olive! The asshole abuses women, and at times, kills them.

"Yes, but in this venue, that's not unacceptable behavior, Van," Olive corrected. "Against societal norms, yes, but that's why a place like this is appealing to certain people. What I'm saying is he takes equal joy in delivering both."

"Olive, does he know you own this place?" Olive was smart. She had power and authority. She was not a Throw Away Girl.

Olive tipped her head to consider the question. "I can't say for sure what the word on the street is about me. He does know I'm on a different level from the young ladies he would meet on the floor, and he's very generous. Even so, his last visit was extreme."

"I'd call trying to kill you pretty extreme!" Van blurted. "Why didn't you call the police?"

The women ignored him.

"What did he do to you?" Jaycee asked.

"He choked me," Olive replied. "Hard. To the point where I thought of my mother and my fate if I were to be judged in that moment. To be clear, I *never* think of my mother, and I don't believe in a hereafter."

"He freaked you out," Jaycee added.

"Yes," Olive nodded. "And that doesn't happen very often in my line of work. I don't like feeling like I'm not in control."

"Did he say anything to you? After he let go?"

"Not a word. He threw some money at me and left. I haven't seen him since, but I've also put the word out to my crew that he's not welcome to spend private time with me anymore. I won't prevent him from coming back to my club, but I'm fairly certain he's moved on. I have looked into his eyes, though, and I have no doubt he could kill."

Jaycee couldn't help but feel disgust building for Olive's money over murder approach. The mystique of a madman was fueling her cash flow, and she didn't want to fuck that up. Really, though, what would she expect from a woman who wanted to be Carol Brady and Jenna Jamison all rolled into one? Olive may be lining her pockets well but her life priorities were a hot mess!

"When was this?" Jaycee asked. "Recently?"

"Oh yes, just a few days ago, I think. It's hard for me to keep track of dates and times, given my work hours float from one day into the next."

Olive leaned forward, sweeping tendrils of her hair away from her elegant throat. "See here?" She directed their focus to faded blue and purple streaks that encircled her windpipe. "I've been wearing turtlenecks in public. In Los Angeles!"

"Can you describe him to me? What he looks like?" Jaycee asked.

Olive reclined into the chair again and appeared to give that some thought. It seemed strange to Jaycee that the face of a man she'd been intimate with and almost killed by wouldn't be an instant recall.

"Well, it's always dark so I don't know eye color or any distinguishing scars or marks. I do know that he doesn't have any tattoos or piercings that I could tell and I've seen every part of him."

Van cleared his throat. Jaycee shot him another look. "Is he tall? Muscular like Van or thin?"

Olive again considered that for a few seconds. She scanned Van from head to folded legs slowly and seductively. "He's tall, but not nearly as thick as you are, sugar," she winked at him. Jaycee narrowed her eyes, but this woman was a trained pro. She could make a zit-faced scrawny teenager feel like a stud.

"What about his hair," she continued.

"Longish," Olive told her. "Very dark, but it felt…" she rolled her fingers together trying to refresh the sensation in her memory. "…it felt almost synthetic."

"Like a wig?" Jaycee pushed.

"I'd say so. And sometimes he wears a hat. Like the one you have on. Not with a team's name or logo on it, just plain."

"Any accent? Does he sound southern, or foreign, or anything you'd recognize?"

"Solid question, Jaycee. You're good at your job; I can see that."

Patronizing, Jaycee thought but remained silent. "Hmmm, his voice," Olive weighed that question, strumming a long square fingernail against her pert nose. "We don't have long conversations, more like short commands or moans and shrieks."

Van stirred again, uncomfortable and anxious for this to end. Jaycee could feel the uneasiness coming off him like an electric pulse. It surprised her that a man who posed in his underwear or made out with actresses in front of a camera would be so affected by a waif of a woman who barely reached his shoulder. It was intangible. Olive had reach. She was a solid force field against a man's ego, a challenge despite being a sexual sure thing. That's why she was still alive.

"No, his voice is normal, I think. Like your average guy in L.A. I'm not trying to be vague. I realize this is not very helpful."

"No, it is. Now I have an idea that he's tall, moderately handsome, thin, wears a wig and doesn't have body art. That's more than I knew before I walked in here." She doubted it didn't sound sarcastic.

"I'm sorry I can't be of more help." Olive stood up. She was ready to see them out.

"Olive, there's one more thing," Jaycee remained in her seat. "I mentioned there's a development…"

"Yes?" Olive's right eyebrow arched up, a sign that she was intrigued. She sat back down.

"Do you know a woman named Fiona Cooper?"

Olive's plump lower lip slipped open, revealing a line of perfect lower teeth bleached to perfection. "Why do you ask?"

"She gave police your name. A detective passed it along to me, and I found you through another friend who likes to get his freak on at places like this. Fiona is in the hospital."

If Olive was upset, she didn't show it. "I'm surprised I hadn't heard that. I assume she was attacked?"

"Badly. Is she a client of yours?"

Olive nodded. "Sometimes. Fiona is a popular girl. She's a novice dominatrix, actually, very strong and physical. I've known her for many years, but I haven't seen her in awhile, she likes to club hop. It's unfortunate she ran into him."

Unfortunate? Jaycee got a flash of the willful body wrapped in tubes and fighting to survive. Yeah, it was unfortunate, all right. She felt a chill and wanted to get out of there. She'd had enough of this narcissistic slut. Far be it from her to tell someone how to support her family, but this woman was ice cold.

"This won't hit the news until the police release it," she told Olive stiffly. "I'm not going with it right now because she's in protective custody. You should be prepared for the police to come looking to talk to you."

"I know nothing more than what I've already told you."

"Still, Fiona named you."

Olive looked suddenly annoyed. The idea of having to talk to police was aggravating. "She was among the friends I alerted, yes," she confirmed to them. "But now do you understand what I mean?" Her face was animated. Jaycee saw the pathetic truth that Olive loved what she did for a living. She felt sorry for the rich kids tucked away at private school and the man back home who adored Olive even while he slept alone.

"She knew he was out there," Olive continued. "Fiona knew, but it only fueled her desires. It heightens the experience for us. Sexual bliss is closely intertwined with danger. It's like the ultimate aphrodisiac—"

165

"Yeah, I get it," Jaycee cut her off, holding one hand up and rising up from the chair. She was *so* not interested in another self-serving explanation of the grand allure of anonymous nooky dipped in murder. She thought of the palpable agony tearing apart the Statlers, and how they wanted to warn other parents about what their precious baby girls could be doing before the unthinkable happened to them, too. An altruistic truth-telling that, as it turns out, was all part of the game that was making Olive a very wealthy woman. Might as well shout it from the rooftops:

Hey, ladies, you'll either have an orgasm or get your throat slit. Come on in, and have at it!

"It's good for business and all that, you don't need to explain. Thanks, Olive, for your time and information. I appreciate it."

Van was up and headed toward the door in a flash. Olive walked around her desk to see them out. She stopped next to Jaycee.

"Here, you have a beautiful family," Jaycee told her genuinely, handing back the mug with the little girl. Olive smiled, gripping the warm cup with both hands. She looked down at her rhinestone flip flops, breaking eye contact.

Jaycee and Van were rounding the corner and headed back toward the door when Olive yelled for them to come back.

"I'm not sure this matters," she started, once they were back near her office. Jaycee nodded expectantly.

"Slade likes to use nicknames," Olive revealed.

"Like dirty nicknames?" Van asked. "The stuff you hear during phone sex?"

Again, both women ignored him. "What names?" Jaycee asked.

"Cutesy, mostly, but I've been called kitten and bitch all in the same encounter. Again, my own husband calls me silly names all the time. It probably means nothing…"

"Probably," Jaycee agreed, "but it's a start, right?"

"Right. Goodbye," Olive waved. "I'll be watching tonight."

"Stay safe, Olive," Jaycee said, quite certain she would never set eyes upon this woman ever again.

"You, too, Jaycee."

Chapter Twenty

"You're so quiet." Van shook Jaycee's knee as they drove him home.

"This is nuts; I think I'm on overload. And I feel like I need a shower. Thanks for coming with me. I know that was gross."

"It's L.A.; I'm used to gross."

"Even still," Jaycee glanced over at Van. "Kids and a husband at home and she's crawling around with creepers every night. I just don't get it."

"She's kinda hot," Van said. "In a Christina Ricci sort of way. Little bitty girl with big attitude, you know? She straight up scared me."

"That's what makes her so appealing to the losers who pay for it. It's like those disgusting fat-ass movie producers who have fine young things pawing at them on the red carpet," Jaycee went on. "It's all power and control. That's why he didn't kill her. He has respect for her."

"Still banged her up pretty good, though," Van reminded her.

Jaycee nodded. "That shows he's impulsive. He's been with her several times, so why hurt her now, but not before? Maybe he's not as in control of himself as he thinks he is."

"*Law & Order*, season eight, episode fourteen. Bipolar killer with personality disorder. One of his personalities likes to wine and dine good-looking women, but the other rapes and kills them. He told police he can't control which one shows up for the date."

"Good God," Jaycee scrunched her nose in disgust. "No, I don't think this guy is bipolar, but he is ramping up. He can't help himself. It would be useful if we could figure out the root of his misogyny. Why he hates these women so deeply."

"Maybe he's just crazy. Simple as that. Dude's insane."

"Certainly true," Jaycee agreed, wincing as a Maserati screeched by. She was particularly alert to noises these days. "But everyone has a touch of crazy and they don't go around butchering women. No, it's not as simple as that. I agree he's mentally unbalanced, but something triggered this. We have to figure that out. Somewhere in his life, this guy was turned off by a certain category of women…" Jaycee was thinking aloud, her thoughts percolating in a gummed-up blender loaded with supposition, speculation, and too few solid clues to gel it all together.

"So Zoe's story is ready to go? It's done?" Van startled her racing thoughts. She nodded. "Uh, hum," she mumbled.

"I'm sure Ben made it look pretty," Van commented.

"He did his thing, yes."

"Does he know about this new attack?" Van pressed.

"Why does that matter?" Jaycee asked.

Van huffed again at her refusal to acknowledge the inherent risk in getting wrapped up in the pursuit of a serial killer. "For real?"

"What now, Van?" she prompted impatiently. "What am I doing wrong now?"

"Jay Jay, I am more than merely your wingman used to infiltrate sex clubs and entice professional whores. I have occasional sparks of brilliance and right now, my spark is telling me you need some peeps watching out for you. After this airs tonight, your face is all over this story."

"It already has been. I'm not the only reporter covering the murders; everyone's on it."

Van rolled his palm over her kneecap, a gesture to calm the air. "What does your cop friend think they'll get out of Olive?"

Jaycee shrugged. "He's not sure. I'm supposed to put him on camera tomorrow. Not sure yet what we'll focus on, unless he's ready to release info on this new attack, or confirm the note at all the crime scenes. Maybe they'll be able to pull more out of Olive or Fiona to get a description or sketch. That may be useful."

"Do they think he'd try to get to that Fiona chick in the hospital if he found out she survived?" Van asked.

"I guess it's a possibility. They do that kind of stuff if a husband attacks a wife or a family member and the victim survives. They put the patient in a lockdown type of protective custody to keep the dangerous person away if he's not in custody yet. I'm assuming this is a similar type of situation, or they want to use Fiona to ID him. If they can ever catch him."

"Wouldn't a description be a waste of time? Given the guy wears a wig and even Olive couldn't really provide much."

"We run police sketches constantly. I'd say they're somewhat useful in burglaries or bank robberies, but that's only if anyone who recognizes him comes forward. I'm not sure sex club attendees will feel comfortable doing that."

They were rounding the corner into their gated condo complex. Bright sunshine bounced off pale white walls of the multi-storied luxury building and then swirled around the tinted windows of the lobby in arches of rainbow-colored light. It was expensive as hell, but Jaycee always felt a sense of pride when she pulled into her home. She'd earned this little slice of heaven for herself in one of the highest rent districts around. Not bad for a girl who came from not much.

She leaned over to kiss Van. "Thanks for your help, wingman." She nuzzled his neck, sprinkling light pecks with her lips across his throat. She inhaled deeply. Van smelled clean, so different from the raunchy stench inside Olive's cave.

He gripped her ponytail and pulled gently, wrapping the blonde strands around his fist. Van squeezed Jaycee into his chest. A charged stillness enveloped them both.

"Be careful, Jay Jay," he urged, pressing himself into her protectively. "I can't be there all the time. Your cop friend can't either."

For the first time in what had otherwise been a mostly physical connection, Jaycee felt roots plant themselves deep in her gut. "I will, promise."

Van pulled back. Using the edge of his finger, he slid it along her jaw and then placed it upon her lips. He reached around to the pile of mail he'd placed in the backseat. "Here, don't forget to open your mail." He handed off the short stack of envelopes and got out of the car. With a wave over his shoulder, he disappeared into the lobby of their building.

Jaycee stared at the closed doors. Van wanted her to be safe. Her boss did, too. Jaycee took to heart everything Barton had told her, but she had convinced herself this was a hunter targeting a very specific prey. There was no evidence he harbored any desire to harm women outside of the fetish playgrounds they frequented. No, there was no risk to the public at large. Nor had there been in Miami, and Philly, or anywhere else dead bodies had accumulated. They became cold cases driven by a man's singular hatred of women who fell below society's firm demarcation of good versus bad. At its core, this was a highly metaphysical superstructure of balance. The killer—if Jaycee was to believe had been behind more than one murder spree—was not willing to wait for action from a patient entity. He would act first. It was a terrifying logic, yet he believed punishment was his to disperse.

But only for the Throw Away Girls.

This man lived a life, she was sure of it. He wasn't breaking into homes and dismembering innocent people. No, he reserved his wrath for only a few. He likely had a job and maybe even a dog or children of his own. Sickness wasn't always pervasive enough to rot away a person's entire connection to his own humanity. At times, Jaycee had learned, it only consumed part of it. That's what was happening here. Jaycee was following his plan from a distance; she wasn't part of it. She was safe. As long as she didn't venture onto his battlefield, she was not a player in his game.

Right? Sure.

Jaycee tried to call Barton. Voicemail. She put together a list of questions she wanted updated. What was the status of forensics? Had they talked to Olive yet? Was she forthcoming? Did they have anything of use from the latest scene? Was Fiona still alive?

Beating sunshine warmed the side of her head through the window. Turning up the air conditioner, she turned inward, as she often did when telling a story, ordering her imagination to create him. Visualization was a skill she called upon often in her job. She saw her script before she wrote it, a series of images and backdrops intertwined with words and colors. She pictured a tall man with a handsome, yet hipster vibe. He could please a woman, and yet torture her. He was thin, though strong enough to wound and injure. She made him ordinary but special. She altered special and added striking. Was that it? She wondered if this man—seen only in her mind—would cause her to look twice if he passed her on the street, or if she'd notice him at all. It was a difficult exercise that yielded nothing but a blurry image of a poltergeist.

She sighed. Taking a sharp left, she pulled out of the parking lot and headed back toward the freeway. It was time to get back to work. Stuck at a red light behind a low-rider truck with booming Spanish rock music, she shuffled through her mail. One envelope held an invitation for the Governor's Red Dress Ball, an American Heart Association event she had MC'd in the past. She folded that back into its envelope and shoved it into her purse. She would have to deal with that; Clare would find a lack of response unacceptable. She reached for another slim, white envelope with the return address of a Los Angeles school. In it was a request for her to be part of the annual Reader's Day, a chance for community members to select a book of their choosing and share it with their young students. Jaycee saved that one, too. She enjoyed meeting little kids. None of them gave a shit she was on TV; they just liked the fact that someone was reading to them. Not every child had that privilege at home. The third envelope was a long-winded, hand-written letter from Los Angeles County Prisoner number 3346781, demanding she look into his case for he had been convicted by an unjust system.

That one became a mashed ball she tossed in the backseat.

Another was a notification from her TV station's parent company that it was almost time to enroll in the new quarter's benefit package. That, as well, was stuffed into her purse for later review.

Traffic moved along. Jaycee navigated ahead of the truck and settled into the middle lane of the freeway. She engaged her left knee to hold the wheel straight and plucked out the envelope that had been beneath her windshield wiper. As she tore it open, she figured it was probably just another anonymous news tip. They poured into the newsroom all the time, usually accompanied by printouts supporting or negating a particular topic, and directed occasionally to a specific reporter or to Clare. They opened all of it, but only followed up if the tip was worthy.

She fumbled with the glued lip of the envelope. It tore midway. Expecting it to contain a newspaper clipping or magazine article folded inside, Jaycee's breath caught when the image of her own face poked through the slit. Furiously, she ripped the envelope apart to reach its contents.

Goosebumps chilled her skin. *What the hell?* Her hands shook as she squared up a four-by-four photograph while taking occasional glances at the road.

Someone had snapped a shot of her at the beach! Her face was restful, mouth open. The shot was tight. Van's torso was planked next to hers, their hands touching atop the sand, the picture likely taken from a distance. Someone had been watching her.

She swallowed hard. If she wasn't in the throes of a big story, using insider information, and about to reveal even more about a killer on the loose, she'd consider this a coincidence. Some crazy guy letting her know he thought she was hot. But then she flipped the picture around and all hope of bad cosmic timing was lost. No, this was intentional, a killer's way of telling her to back off in bold red pen.

Jaycee Wilder-Throw Away Girl?

The penmanship was crisp and sharp, an irrefutable message that she was putting herself directly in his crosshairs.

So much for her theory of the battlefield. The killer was taking his fight straight to her.

Chapter Twenty-One

Jaycee stood inside the studio, ready for her live intro. Just behind her, on a sixty-five-inch plasma screen was a soft-edged picture of Zoe and her parents. The image had been beautifully altered by the graphics department and formatted to fit just below the heading: Remembering Zoe.

In her ear, she heard the producer cue the anchors to a two-shot, meaning they were both on the middle camera to start the newscast. They lead with breaking news: a shooting in Van Nuys, suspect still at large, and then a pedestrian struck and killed in Sherman Oaks. Jaycee was up next.

The station still employed production assistants. Although many of their competing stations had eliminated humans in favor of automatic cameras on the floor, ABC 12 opted for a more hands-on studio. Jaycee liked the older man behind her camera, with wild gray hair that poked out like a mop head. He was responsible for alerting her to stand-by, and to cue her when to go with her script. Truth was, after opening that envelope in her car, she considered the more people she could put around her right now to be protective armor.

She'd fiddled slightly with her story's lead, not fully able to focus, and was counting on the package she'd put together with Ben to leave a powerful statement with the viewers. And, likely, the killer. Jaycee was much more aware of that now, and it was difficult not to reveal another

Throw Away Girl lying in a hospital bed. It was like doing her job but only to the halfway mark.

The anchors both had a few lines to lead into Zoe's story. They recounted the status of the investigation, open, and reminded viewers of the other two recent murders at Los Angeles nightclubs. Finally, they tossed to Jaycee, and the interview viewers will see on only one station, TV's propensity for self-promotion at its finest.

"It's been an agonizing time for this family," Jaycee began, following the words on the teleprompter. "Not only have the Statlers lost a daughter, but they've also learned intimate and shocking information about her lifestyle. Their message tonight is for other parents to pay closer attention to the choices being made by their adult children—even if it's difficult to know the truth."

She leveled her reporter's gaze into the camera for a fraction of a second before her package rolled. She watched it on the monitor in the studio with a detached, critical eye. Was it resonating to others as it had to her? Was she too close to be objective? Was Barton right, and most people didn't give two shits about this subculture of immorality? She looked over at the anchors to gauge their interest. Most times, when she was live in the studio, they fiddled with their hair or scribbled on their scripts during her stories. They were both still, their attention fixed on the monitors built into the desks.

"Stand by for tag," the producer told her in her ear. She regained her game face and stared into the lens, taking steady, even breaths. This was it, time to drop Barton's big clue. Her final line in her story was delivered and the cameraman pointed a finger at her. She was back up live, but again, delivering only a fraction of what she'd learned.

"There are breaking developments in this investigation, tonight. A law enforcement source is now confirming exclusively to ABC 12 that the killer left behind a message at the scene of Zoe Statler's murder. (And the others, too.) We do not yet know what it says. (Yes, I do.) This is very much an active investigation, so stay tuned for developments." (Folks, the notes are legit, I just got one myself, how's that for a development?)

Jaycee added details about a scholarship program established in Zoe Statler's memory and referenced viewers to the station's website for more information. She signed off, waited to be cleared by the producer and then she unplugged her IFB and mic. Quietly, she left the studio and entered the newsroom to a flurry of applause.

"Great job, Jaycee!" her colleagues said. Clare motioned to her from inside the Fishbowl. She wanted to see her.

"Hey," Jaycee said, stepping through the open office door and plopping down into the chair across from Clare's desk. "You liked?"

"Great job, it looked solid. Ben did it justice."

"Always does," Jaycee told her.

"Anything come from today? When you had to step out?" Clare hadn't asked yet, she'd been locked in her office when Jaycee returned, but obviously wanted to know. Clare gave her reporters some latitude; she didn't micromanage their days as long as they produced quality work on air. She liked to trust her people.

Jaycee shook her head and was careful with her facial expressions. She wanted to remain free to pursue the story. Telling Clare about the note or the latest attack would result in Jaycee covering garden parties at the Women's Club. Clare would never put her back in the field on this if she felt she was in danger. No one was to know about the picture—and its implied threat—the killer had sent to her.

"No, dead end," Jaycee said firmly. "Nothing that does us any good."

"What's next?" Clare asked.

"Well, I'm putting my police contact on camera tomorrow. He's new in the department so this will garner him some useful exposure. I can push him. He may reveal another exclusive detail, and we need to be prepared for some sort of media event. I'm hearing they may be announcing a task force and may confirm the three deaths are connected."

"Okay," Clare nodded. "You're on it for the day. Let us know what you get so we can start to brand it. You schedule your cop interview, and then you and Ben can work around any presser they end up holding. From there, depending on what they say, you'll work that into your story."

"Yup, sounds good."

Clare studied her. She cocked her head and attempted to figure out what it was that she was missing. Jaycee was the most conscientious reporter she had on staff; she covered her bases and her ass. Something wasn't adding up here, and Clare couldn't help but think Jaycee was holding back.

"What are you not telling me?" she began.

"Huh? I'm not following." Jaycee stretched out her long legs and pulled at the fabric bunching around her thigh to keep from looking Clare in the eye. She knew she looked skittish and vacant, not her usual confident and ready to kick some ass. Clare was worried.

"Jay Jay," Clare began. "The best stories are the ones that make us feel like we're stepping over a landmine, but there's a lot to be said for staying safe when you leave my newsroom. I won't push you, but I have a bad feeling that you've been sneaking around."

"Clare," Jaycee protested. "I'm always safe. I have Ben—"

"Yeah, when you're here," Clare interrupted. "But if you want to pursue a killer on your own time, I'm not okay with that. You think I'm some Pollyanna airhead who thinks you took two hours off this morning to go to hot yoga class?"

"Oh, please." Jaycee tried to deflect, thinking it was exactly what she was trying to avoid, Clare threatening to pull her off the story. "I'm just doing some digging. You know, the kind of work that earns all those shiny gold statues you keep in your office." Jaycee good-naturedly pointed to the shelves holding many Emmy Awards earned by the staff at ABC 12 News. She wanted to break the tension and get the hell out of this office. There was something else she had to do, and this was as good a night as any.

Clare smacked her lips. She shifted her argument after making her point. "Fine, but don't think I'm not noticing you look like shit. You're getting too skinny, which tells me you're working this too hard and it's becoming personal. What's the golden rule for survival in the world of murder, mayhem, and deviant human behavior we like to call TV news?"

"Don't take it in. Let it roll off," Jaycee mumbled. She used to be so good at that. Clare had set her up well to stay solvent in a rough and tumble job. She felt some trepidation and guilt for not following her advice, but this was too important. The killer could already be picking out his next Throw Away Girl. For all she knew, the gravely injured Fiona could have slipped away, too. She fed Clare what she wanted to hear, but planned to do the exact opposite.

"Exactly!" Clare's eyes went wide. "I want you eating again. When I stop hearing from Spanx reps and start hearing from anorexia support groups, I'm coming after you, Jay Jay. I want crumbs at your desk. I want receipts from In-N-Out and the occasional ketchup stain on your shirt. Show me you're sustaining yourself on more than

Vitamin Water, sugar-free Tic-Tacs, and murdered bitches."

The two women looked at each other, the protégé and her mentor. Jaycee was the first to look away, even though Clare's cavalier reference to the girls stung. "I understand," she told her.

"I'm serious, Jay Jay. Get your interview tomorrow, move the story forward, but then I want you to take a break. Get your head straight. Those girls are dead, but you're very much alive. Remember that."

Jaycee almost protested, but Clare wasn't going to lose this battle. "This is not up for discussion," she told her firmly. "Get out of here, go home. See you tomorrow."

Jaycee nodded, feeling both frustrated that Clare would threaten to take her off the story, and thankful that someone besides Van and Ben finally cared about her. It had been a lonely, self-sufficient existence.

She stood up and headed for the door, turning back when Clare fired off one last request.

"And don't forget that stack of mail I gave you. You open that yet?"

Jaycee's stomach flipped. The lie felt big on her tongue. "Of course. Nothing out of the ordinary. I'll get back to everyone."

Everyone but the killer, that is.

Chapter Twenty-Two

Jaycee stared at the pile of jeans she'd thrown onto her bed, and then tossed them onto the floor one by one. She cursed herself for her uppity preference for designer threads. Dolce & Gabbana high-waisted jeans wouldn't fit in where she was going.

"Shit," she muttered. She couldn't risk appearing snobbish. Fingering a pair of faded black True Religion cut-offs with sloppy, frayed edges, she paired them with a striped gray and black t-shirt and analyzed the completed look atop her bed comforter. Stepping back, she nodded. That would do.

Her hair and face were next. Los Angeles floated upon a sea of tall, blonde women, so feasibly, Jaycee could hide in those waves just as she was. She opted for the opposite. Rolling her hair into a bun, she secured it with a few bobby pins and reached for the Halloween wig she'd worn last year when she'd gone to Van's work party as Teresa Giudice from *The Real Housewives of New Jersey*. It was thick, black, and wavy.

Perfect. Transformation almost complete.

She adjusted the curls until they fell like feathers aside each eyebrow. She added brown contacts to cover her blue eyes, and rimmed her eyes with fake eyelashes, and a boatload of her blackest-black Clinique mascara. Strawberry Red Chanel lipstick topped off the look. She was ready. Time to make the call.

Jaycee pushed out a hard breath through her gooey lips. She wasn't positive he'd answer, but she had to risk it. She needed his help. She placed the call from her landline. He wouldn't recognize that number. She needed every little trick in her reporter's book to make this work. Two rings. He answered before the third.

"Zander Butant."

"It's Jaycee, don't hang up."

An exasperated sigh filled her ear. "Seriously?" he quipped. "How the hell do you have my cell?"

"Yes, seriously, I have my sources, but then I'm gone, and I really don't think I'll need you after this. You have my word."

Zander sighed again. He was stuck between a rattlesnake and a great white shark. Which was worse? They were both deadly when provoked, right? This girl had the power to liquefy his political reputation into the scum that rides atop a pond full of buried secrets.

"What do you want? I assume you didn't find Olive?"

"Don't assume anything. This call isn't about her. I need your power of deduction; there's some top-down logic I'm trying to pursue."

"Don't be vague, Jaycee."

"You say none of these places have names?"

"They don't. Not the ones I go to anyway. I'm sure there are some with stupid, predictable names, but I don't go to those. Why?"

"Because I want to stake some out," she told him. "Just me, no camera."

Again, Zander sighed. This woman was exhausting. "I can't stress this enough. That is a very bad idea."

"Why?"

"A million reasons why! You don't go to these clubs just to watch. If you do that, you'll be asked to leave. And, there's a good chance someone might recognize you. Remember what I told you. You'd be surprised by the people who are there, and they don't enjoy being played."

"That's not my intention, and I'll be careful. No one will recognize me. I need to figure out what clubs along Hollywood Boulevard he hasn't killed in yet."

"Christ, Jaycee! How am I supposed to know that?"

"Simple, really. We already know where the three girls were killed. The club addresses have been released. I also know of another suspected place, so you tell me the ones that are left, and through our power of deduction, we'll know the clubs he hasn't been to. Or, at least, the ones he hasn't killed anyone at. So, Zander, where do all the beautiful people go when they want to rock each others' worlds?"

Zander wasn't happy about it, but he worked with Jaycee to form a list. She included Olive's place, though she knew intuitively that the killer wouldn't strike there, he held Olive in higher regard. She also crossed off the area of the most recent attack that left Fiona's face in disrepair. That left them with six. If she followed the assumption that a dog didn't shit where he ate, the killer would not return to the clubs he'd already murdered in. The attacks were coming more rapidly. It was just a hunch, but Jaycee felt she needed to do something.

"For a weeknight, all the action is on Hollywood Boulevard," Zander said. "That's convenient when you live and work in L.A., it's logistically easier, and may even be the reason he seems to focus there. That may be something to follow. He could be closer than you think."

Oh, he's close all right, Jaycee thought.

"Thank you, Zander. I appreciate all your help tonight."

"I'm involved now," he told her. "I feel responsible for your safety."

"Zander, hardly, I—"

"Let me finish. I won't be able to sleep tonight knowing I've sent another woman to a potentially dangerous place. I'm coming with you."

"The fuck you are!" she fired back.

"I am, and tough shit if you don't like it," he shot. "You called *me*, Jaycee. Remember that. You chose to involve me. I'm calling you on it."

Now it was Jaycee's turn to sigh. He'd surprised her, and it was not her style to allow someone else to be on top. "No."

"Then I'll call your news director. I'm sure Clare would be tickled to find out what her precious reporter is up to."

"She'd consider me enterprising," Jaycee ventured.

"More like reckless," Zander countered.

"You really suck, Zander, you know that?"

"Yes, we've already established that. Right back at you."

Jaycee shook her wigged head, feeling the soft hair flutter across her shoulder blades. She was cornered. "Fine. But don't you dare get in my way."

"So what do you do if you find what you're looking for?" he asked.

"You mean if I find him?"

"Yes," he told her.

Jaycee studied herself in the mirror. She looked like someone who would pursue men in seedy nightclubs. She could be a Throw Away Girl, with her come-hither lips and sexy, flowing hair. Even though he could be her worst nightmare, she wanted to be his.

"I'm not sure," she replied honestly. "But I'll come up with something."

"God help us," Zander barked. "Give me your address. I'll pick you up in a half-hour."

Chapter Twenty-Three

Zander was wearing dark jeans and a checkered button down shirt. He smelled like Christian Dior's Higher Energy. "Is that your power scent?" she asked, staring out the window of his BMW 328i as they zipped toward the city. The leather was smooth, the stereo chirped out Justin Timberlake, and the entire experience felt like a man using every cliché to score on his first date.

"Uh, I wouldn't talk. Who are you trying to be? Cher? Angelina? No, wait, don't tell me, Lindsay Lohan during her dark years?"

"I think she's still in rehab, actually, so you're not even funny. That's just cruel."

They drove on. Zander laid out some rules. He would enter first. Jaycee would follow five minutes later. They would not speak, or stand together. They must remain in the main room, and she would raise her right hand if she felt threatened or unsafe. Otherwise, Zander promised not to get in the way. He also suggested Jaycee not make a big deal out of spotting a celebrity or two.

"I've seen a bunch of Lakers at these clubs. They're tough to miss, actually. And a certain first baseman with a wife and triplets at home. It's protocol, Jaycee, don't tell your TV people about this. We all keep each others' secrets."

"I don't care about dirty celebrities," she quipped.

"Do you even know what he looks like?" he asked.

"Somewhat."

"What happens if he sees you first? Don't killers like to watch their stories on TV? He may get pissed that you're following him."

"Duh," Jaycee scoffed. "That's why I'm all decked out like this. And all this," she motioned to her dark head, down to her skimpy shorts, "is a Real Housewife from New Jersey. Most certainly *not* Cher."

He smiled at her. Jaycee noticed a dimple in his cheek. He really was a handsome, ambitious man, though this aspect of his personality would better fit a character on *House of Cards* than a real-life candidate who would face the press test. Anyone doing media on him could easily dig up his salacious sex preferences. If this proved worthy, Jaycee decided she would warn him to clean things up if he was serious about his future.

"Have you talked to the cops yet about Zoe?" she asked. She prepared for his dismissive answer.

"Under advice of counsel, I can't really say," he replied steadily. "Let's just say I'm hoping this stays between us."

Jaycee nodded. It would add a juicy angle to the story, but in her gut she knew he'd done nothing criminal, or even intentional. It wasn't his fault Zoe was dead. She wasn't the kind of reporter who exposed people simply for the sake of hurting them.

"If it comes out, it won't be from me. I promise you. You've more than earned your reprieve."

They drove on. It was near ten o'clock. Turning off the 405, they traveled east through Century City and West Hollywood. Jaycee thought of Van, and how horrified he'd be if he knew she was in a car with a fetish-freak to do some serial killer hunting. Her goal was to be home, safe, makeup- and wig-free, before his shift at the bar ended.

"The first place is close to Sunset. We're almost there."

Jaycee's neck started to sweat. Her feet squirmed in her espadrille heels. Bad choice, she thought. If she needed to run, these would break her ankles.

"Ah-hum," she said through closed lips. Her mouth tasted like old Gatorade.

"It's okay to be nervous," Zander told her. "I was the first time I went, too."

Jaycee glared at him. "Excuse me," she began. "I am not a first-timer like that."

"You are sort of," he argued. "First time at a place like this counts for something."

"I've already seen one," she retorted. "Just not at night."

Zander chuckled. "I rest my case."

The first club was similar to Olive's. It was set back, down an alley, so non-descript no one would know of it unless they were looking. Zander parallel-parked along the main road. "Five minutes," he reminded her. "It's fifty dollars at the door, do you have cash?"

"Yes," Jaycee confirmed. She'd pocketed a few hundred dollar bills before leaving.

"You know what to do if you need me?"

"Raise my hand," she confirmed. "Go, Zander. I'm good. We'll give it a half-hour or so and then move on."

Zander nodded. His mouth opened to speak again, but he chose against it. Jaycee's mind was set. All he could do now was hope she didn't get herself into trouble.

She watched him cross the street and enter the slim alleyway. He disappeared into the darkness. Jaycee felt very much alone and out of place. It was supremely unsettling. Her hands twitched in her lap. Her scalp itched beneath the ridiculous wig and her heart raced. "Good God," she muttered to herself. "Get a grip!"

She rallied, recounting her fearsome approach to uncovering the truth. Jaycee had braved the mean streets of South Central L.A., flagrantly marching toward hovels holding potential murder suspects and drug lords. She did what it took to get the story. She filed Right-To-Know requests and poured through government documents that uncovered dirty deals and backroom handshakes, tirelessly searching for the one nugget of evidence that would allow her to put high-level public officials on television. It was her job. Hell, it was her life!

"This is what you do," she whispered in the car, psyching herself up to leave the comfort of the soft leather. "Zoe, Fiona, and the others are why you are doing it. Get your head in the game."

Calming her breathing, Jaycee counted off another two minutes. Four more people had entered the alleyway after Zander, none of them together. Business was obviously brisk here, too. Olive wasn't the only benefactor. Such a sick world.

She stepped out of the BMW, keeping her eyes downcast and chin low to ensure the spiral curls covered most of her face as she walked across the street. She was certain she was unrecognizable. Fingering the bill in her pocket, she entered the alleyway. It was shadowy and littered with plastic water bottles, empty chip bags, and bright lipstick stained cigarette butts. A heavy door swung open just as Jaycee went to reach for its handle. She had to move quickly around a pack of men, sloppy drunk and obviously freshly sated. They laughed and slung arms around each other's necks, pleased with whatever they had just come from. Jaycee automatically felt her mouth turning down in disgust. She had to remind herself she was posing as a woman here for the same thing.

Turning the corner, she was met by a burly bouncer wearing a narrow leather vest. Tattoos were sprinkled across his chest, and each earlobe held a line of sparkly studs. He looked her up, and then down. When he held out his palm, she assumed she'd met the sexiness quotient. She placed her hundred dollar bill into his fleshy hand and accepted her fifty in return. He motioned her forward into the main space of the club. Jaycee swallowed hard. This was it. The killer could be right in front of her.

Club music assaulted her. Electric lights pulsed to the beat and the air took on a smoky quality even though smoking wasn't allowed inside. The breeze being pumped in was cool, yet quickly took on a thickness that was sticky and humid. In one corner was a pool table. Men in rolled-up sleeves leaned over to take their shots, as women—some bare-chested—encouraged them, massaging their asses and kissing their necks. They floated from one player to the next, mouthing, fondling, and touching whatever body they bumped along the way. Quite a few obscene gestures were made with both sticks and pool balls.

Free love.

"Sorry, baby," said a female voice to her right, as she and Jaycee bumped shoulders. Her soft fingers wrapped around Jaycee's forearm, as she gazed longingly into her face. She was a lovely young woman, a sensual mix of Asian and African American that must drive men wild. Or, maybe other women. Jaycee stepped away, following the edges of the room in a slow circle. As long as she stuck close to a wall, she could observe from the outside. Beyond the pool table was an empty hot tub with a sign posted: Due to Health Department, We No Longer Can Offer Hot Tub Services.

Nasty!

Bodies, dry as they were, entangled inside the square plastic bathtub, still making use of the space. Jaycee looked away and moved to her left. The back wall was covered in pornographic graffiti that was both garish and explicit.

194

Jaycee backed up beneath the pink light and scanned the room. "Bullpens" were advertised down one of the hallways, (what the hell were those?) while a sign on the other side noted: Coat/Wallet Check. Large glass bowls on wooden tables held an assortment of condoms and other paraphernalia, and a few sixty-inch plasma TVs flickered either ESPN or porno movies from their wall mounts.

She examined faces without being obtrusive. The women were mostly young and exquisite looking. They were typical Los Angeles beauties, trendy and sexual in both movement and dress. The men weren't nearly as high-end. She noticed many of them had beer bellies, and receding hairlines. A few were dressed as if they'd just come from the office: button-down shirts, loose ties, and suit pants. She was so focused she barely felt the tug on her wig.

"Excuse me," she began, before she remembered she was lucky he hadn't copped a more intimate feel.

"Black beauty," the man giggled, taking a strand of dark curl and running it through his lips. "You're sexy, momma," he growled, encircling her waist with one arm and pulling her into his chest. "Let's dance." Jaycee looked at him. He was her height, thickly built. Not at all what Olive described. She didn't want to waste precious time on this bonehead.

He was all hips and pelvic thrusts. Jaycee gave it a half-hearted attempt—in the spirit of appearing as if she actually meant to be there—and then twirled off into the anonymity of the crowd. His drunken eyes searched for her, but not for long, before he simply moved on to the next scantily clad female.

Men paired off with women. Women found other women, and a few men ended up with men. They wandered from the pool table to a lounge with scattered barstools and square tables, and then back into the middle of the room where dirty dancing took on an x-rated quality that even the lithe Kevin Bacon couldn't match. It was like watching animals in a mating frenzy. Jaycee tried not to become distracted. She again focused on faces and body types. There were so many people in the room she divided it into grids. Up and down and into rows, she scanned profiles, bodies, and hair. Was anyone wearing a baseball hat? Did his hair look fake? She shook off advances and shunned touches. As she rounded the corner of her final grid, back near the entrance, she felt a hand pull her sharply on the elbow.

"It's a quiet night," the man suggested. "Let's move on."

The sight of Zander grounded her. She felt like a buoy had just appeared for her to clutch as stormy seas threw her from one cresting wave to the next. She hadn't seen the killer. She'd only seen the lewdness in which he carried out his acts. These places were overflowing with Throw Away Girls; he could hunt here forever!

She felt hot and chilled at the same time. She nodded. Zander was right. The only thing she'd find here was a sexually transmitted disease.

"Okay," she agreed, allowing him to take her hand and lead her back into the night.

They weren't done yet.

Chapter Twenty-Four

His night was marred by the dreams. Spread-eagled, sweaty, and agitated, the man tossed his head from side to side, burdened by the memories that haunted his sleep. When he was overtired or ridden with anxiety, the dark hours of night filled with the carnival freaks from his past.

They were all there tonight.

He was back in the poverty-stricken southern town, riding his bike, perhaps around twelve years old. He felt his scrawny legs straddle the banana seat as each foot wrapped around rusty pegs that used to hold a pedal. He felt the air whip against his cheeks as he pedaled down to the cool waters of the lake. His quiet sanctuary when his mom and dad went at it hard.

Turning the corner around a gathering of mailboxes, he followed the dirt road, feeling the stress fall from his bony shoulders with the more distance he achieved. Home sweet home? More like a house of horrors.

Once the yelling started he knew what came next. A slap turned to a punch, fingernails became daggers, and one or both of them ended up bleeding, unconscious, or wailing at anyone still standing. The young boy played this macabre game with himself before stepping back inside the trailer after their daily dust up. Would he: 1. Discover his drunken mother splayed on the couch or huddled under the flea-ridden, booze-stained comforter on their bed? 2. Have to help his father off the back porch where he would have passed out with a burning cigarette between his fingers? Or,

3. Would they both be hanging from the shower curtain? He preferred 3 but most of the time ended up with 1 or 2.

It was a dreadful childhood, and he was smart enough to know it.

Intelligence ran on both sides of his family, but unfortunately so did bipolar disorder, alcoholism, and an uninhibited will to beat the shit out of each other. The boy couldn't remember when he had fallen out of love with his parents, but he sure knew when he first started to hate them.

He'd been eight. A straight-A student and good with a paint brush. His mother would put his projects on the fridge: a sunrise melting over a cotton plantation, city buildings stretching into a night sky twinkling with soft white stars, a grasshopper perched on a drooping palm frond. They never lasted long. His father would come home from work, pissed off, sore and thirsty, and then scoff at the pansy his wife was raising. By God, he was a football legend in this town—a giant among men—and his kid better stop dicking around with finger paints and get his shit on the field!

The boy hated sports. On a hot summer night in August, as humid dew hung like smoke on the freshly-cut grass of the practice field, the boy took off his helmet, handed it to the coach, and walked home. His hand was still twisting the brass door handle when the first open-palmed slap split his lip. The second broke his nose and the third punctured his eardrum. Well, he thought it did. His family didn't believe in doctors, so no one ever checked him out. All he knew was that he couldn't hear out of that ear for a solid six months.

A barrage of insults followed, to which the boy merely nodded and agreed. It did no good for him to argue. When the rage subsided or the numbing effect of the gin took over, his father would slink away to the bar downtown for a round of poker with his boys. His mother would tend to her son's wounds, and then to his other parts.

"Want momma make it better?" she'd slur, her hot breath laced with whiskey and the bologna sandwich she'd eaten for dinner. Her lips brushed over the purple mounds of his injuries and then made a wet and sloppy trip south, all while her only son's frail body shook—not with ecstasy—but the pressure of holding in his silent tears.

When he dreamt now as a man, he fast-forwarded through the years of his greatest suffering to the moment he exacted his finest revenge.

He was sixteen, finally as tall as his father and able to match him blow for blow. He planned their execution carefully. Late one night, once he'd tucked away enough cash to get him to the next state over, he dragged the water-logged charcoal grill to the back of the house near the propane tank. Emptying the black, oily water onto the tufts of grass below, he filled the bowl with lighter fluid. When he had achieved a wall of orange-yellow flames high enough to lick the black sky, he rolled the oval metal down a sloping hill to where the tank attached to the mobile home.

He found his black duffel bag, stowed away in the back of one of the cars his father had parked out near the rocky driveway, and didn't bother to wait for the show.

He was about a half-mile away when the mobile home that had been filled with abuse and sinfulness blew sky high.

* * * *

Shaking himself awake, the freaks retreated like fog back to their homes inside his memory. He felt surprisingly morose. It was almost time to go, to start over and begin a new journey above ground. This rat hole would serve one more purpose before it was torn apart, analyzed for evidence, and eventually, rented to someone new. Such was life, a perpetual circle of renewal.

He was constantly in motion, riding the circle at all times to find renewal and rebirth within the highest level of truth. His body remembered but his soul was cleansed. It felt glorious, exactly as it did when he walked away from death the first time, leaving two bodies and his past in ashes. His very first turn around the circle as he began his duty to extinguish lives that were not worthy. He was no serial killer cliché, with a mama complex and a taste for blood. No, his missionary murders were purpose-driven. Instead of hating his parents, he was grateful to them. He had rational appreciation for how he was raised. Like all good mentors, they helped develop him into the man he was: a visionary. He had an objective and a duty to clean up the garbage, to prevent another child from being born to the lowest levels of humans not fit to raise a goat.

He took the women. The builders of life. He threw them away before they could torment another innocent being.

Damn, he was good at it, too. Years ago, when he'd turned his back on the smoldering shithole his family called home, he was less concerned about what was left behind because nothing was at stake. It was easy, actually. He changed his name, established a brand new life, and went on to successfully stump a system that should have red-flagged him right out of the gate. His old, sad existence fire-hosed into the sewers of the south, the state fire marshal calling it an accident, and presuming the body of the offspring inside the home had been incinerated to dust.

Puttering around the room, the man's hands twisted with anticipation. He needed another hit. He was close to pulling up stakes with a clean break. It was always an exciting time, to anticipate what came next, the new faces he would see, the experiences he would have. It was thrilling to know his messages would be analyzed and his story written. Long after he was gone, he hoped others would be inspired by his good work here in Los Angeles and elsewhere. Perhaps, some of them even spurred to action. To properly cleanse away the next generation borne from Throw Away Girls, they all needed to work together.

He lingered at the pictures tacked to the wall. He wet a finger with his own saliva and then drew a line across the throat of a sultry-looking woman with dark skin and highlighted hair. She had transfixed him during a trip to the grocery store recently. He trailed her through the frozen food aisle, and into the pharmacy section, even bumping her elbow as he pretended to check out the shampoo. They smiled at each other. When she paid for her things, he quickly left his carriage behind and scooted along behind her on the sidewalk. He was not prepared with his gear, his expensive camera was tucked away at his house, and all he had was his cell phone. His work cell phone. He only occasionally used that to take pictures of his women, but she was so exquisite he couldn't help himself. When she stopped to tap gently on the glass door of a pet store, chirping softly to the baby huskies licking the glass on the other side, he snapped five quick shots on his phone. They would be blurry, and of poor quality, but he wanted them anyway.

She looked a bit like his mother had before the alcohol and beatings got to her. Slim and narrow through the waist, with strong legs and gently tapered ankles. The man noted a shiny diamond on her left finger. This woman was married. She went home to a decent and loving man. He smiled at her. She was safe.

The picture hanging to the right was of a blonde-haired beauty. The man's smile straightened out. She was beautiful, no doubt, but he didn't know yet if she was safe.

203

The media was watching; *she* was watching. The police were all on alert, as they had been elsewhere. Some of the more entrepreneurial types would go on to study him, analyze his kills, and wait for him to resurface. He saw them sitting in their small, square meeting rooms with white boards full of dates, names, and locations, spinning out hypothetical profiles. They'll examine the clues: A crime scene note left at murders in Los Angeles nightclubs, perhaps even the abduction of a well-known television reporter whose boyfriend just might be suspected of doing her harm. It would fuel speculation for years. The man could already see the story hitting *20/20* or *Dateline*, the perfect way to grow his audience.

Murder, Desire, and Disappearance, The Story of Jaycee Wilder.

Let them work this into a three-night miniseries for all he cared. He still reserved hope that the reporter would be safe, but he had learned to be cunning about his options. It wasn't his first choice to punish a woman for trying to do her job. She hadn't earned a death for the reasons he lived by. He had warned her.

Criminal psychiatrists would label him psychotic with limited empathy. That was okay, but it was not to cloud his judgment. Once a human being made peace with the part of himself that flirted with ideas and thoughts beyond the boundaries of soundness, he could not be beholden to regret or sorrow. Preparation besought success. After he set his beginning and endpoints, the man was perfectly content to fill the middle as he went along.

There were too many whores filling the streets and too few hunters. His spirit soared when he broke the bones beneath their skin, as he abused their delicate faces and toned bodies. He felt her watching from above, approving of his work, encouraging him to continue. She was always there. Sometimes she talked to him. Sometimes she touched him. He felt her. His mother lived in the shadowy rooms he filled with Throw Away Girls, like a foreman ensuring the job was carried out properly.

He rubbed his eyes and returned his gaze to the highlighted, dark-skinned woman with the wedding ring. There was another club he'd heard of. One he had yet to experience. He would not kill tonight, merely maim or maybe even provide a woman pleasure. He hadn't decided yet, but she would look like the grocery store wife. Another man's property about to become his. It was exciting that he could hold back. Sometimes. He was superior in every way.

Another arc in his circle.

He changed his damp clothes and sat down to prepare his look. Time was precious. There were a few last things to accomplish before he left his filthy room with women's pictures lining the walls, and each corner of the space loaded with evidence left behind by a killer.

Then he would get the fuck out of town.

Chapter Twenty-Five

"Turn up the heat," Jaycee requested, hugging her bare arms as they traveled down another few blocks toward the final club of the night.

"It's seventy-five degrees out, what the hell is wrong with you?" Zander demanded, though he got it. Jaycee was chilled to the bone, and it had nothing to do with the weather.

"Fine," he relented, twisting the dial toward red.

They were quiet as he parallel parked across the street. Fewer cars were out, and pedestrian traffic had slowed as it pushed midnight. They had canvassed every club on the list, save for this last one. Jaycee had been grinded upon, dry-humped, licked, slapped, and fondled against her will. She'd seen things an entire gallon of bleach couldn't wipe from her memory, but no one who had resembled the man Olive had described.

"I have to rally," she whispered, "give me a minute."

"Take your time," he told her. "Same drill as before. Give me a sign if you need me."

She nodded without looking at him; Zander wasn't enjoying this either.

Her scalp was on fire, like a million bees were buzzing beneath the wig. She couldn't wait to rip it off, to scrub herself free of the excess makeup and other peoples' DNA. Now that she had seen these clubs for herself, she completely understood why flakes of skin, blood, or prints that could be used as evidence could so easily be dismissed by even a novice public defender. The clubs were a contamination factory.

Taking a few quick gulps of air, she squared her shoulders and approached another rusty door down an alley. This time, the room was so packed she could barely get in. The smell almost knocked her over, a stagnant swill that mixed barn animal on a humid summer day with locker room sweat. She almost wretched right there.

There was no space. Jaycee hunched into herself, wishing for a hazmat suit as she shimmied around an assortment of hips pressing into her abdomen as men slid by, some of them with their zippers open and their jewels hanging out. She felt hands on her ass, sliding down her thigh, moving around to the front. She swallowed the urge to bash fingers and elbow faces, moving faster toward the edge of the room. Finally, after nearly slipping on what looked like an orange-tinged spray of cottage cheese on the floor, she righted herself and flattened her back against the wall. She gulped for air. The women were as aggressive as the men. Three of them began to circle around her like tigresses eyeing a fleshy carcass. She had to keep moving.

"Jesus Christ," she muttered, navigating over a heap of jeans and shoes stacked into a corner. She squinted at a small grouping of men toward the middle of the room. One, in particular, was tall and thin, with dark hair reminiscent of a boy band member. It fell from an unnatural part near his ear. He rocked slowly to the beat of the club music but kept his hands inside the pockets of his jeans. He watched women and men alike. He didn't touch anyone.

Jaycee stepped toward him, but angled herself strategically behind other people. When someone leaned left, she went right, keeping part of her body hidden at all times. She didn't want to catch his attention, and yet she needed to look into his eyes. Olive had seen evil in them. Would she?

Sweat ran in lazy lines over her cheeks and into her mouth. She licked at her lips, tasting salt and cosmetics. The group splintered. He was the only one left standing there. He began to turn. Jaycee countered to the left. She stayed hidden. She was about three feet away when another man said something that must have been funny. The tall man laughed. Jaycee was close enough to see a ridiculous gold grill in his mouth, and a thick scar on his right cheek. Olive would've remembered that.

He wasn't the killer.

Frustrated, and feeling like this was another dead end, Jaycee raised her right hand, her sign to Zander that she needed him. She'd had enough. The crowd closed back in. She was being squeezed into the middle, near a low catwalk. What the hell? She fell forward, grabbing onto the waist of the woman in front of her to prevent crashing down onto her face. The woman held her hands, thinking Jaycee was just another tryst. It took some effort to disentangle herself and then skirt around the line of women as they stepped onto the platform. What was this? Where

was Zander? She slunk back to a wall and squared herself
to its cool, cement blocks. Men filed in, some of them bare-
chested and sweaty from excitement. A few were swaying,
drunk and stupid, but many of them still seemed to know
where they were and what was about to happen. Jaycee
noticed them reaching for their wallets or inspecting a roll
of cash from a pocket to check how much remained.

The music changed. The lights came up slightly, but
the room was still hazy. Jaycee jutted her head forward to
encourage the tufts of her hair to cover more of her face. A
few people reached for her to encourage her to enter the
game, but she just shook her head and glued herself to her
wall. They moved on. A drag queen hit the runway first.
She was all endless legs and outrageous afro wig,
bombastic and campy.

"Okay, y'all!" she drawled. "I'm Big Momma, and I'm
here to tell ya'll that shit's about to get all crazy up in here.
Y'all ready to see some hot sluts up for grabs?"

The crowd roared. Men high-fived each other while the
women discarded clothes and stripped down to g-strings
and not much else. The women on stage glowed like
goddesses in a sea of mortals. No wonder men thought
these clubs were the portal to paradise. Almost everyone
looked good when they were all oiled up and the lights
were low. How does anyone have a normal relationship if
this is what they think lust is all about?

Jaycee assumed what came next. Pair by pair, the
boobs would bounce down the runway and men would bid

on them. Who needed a day job when you could rake it in like this? She raised her right arm again, pissed off that Zander hadn't come running the first time. Where was he? She preferred not leaving her wall, but she had to move back toward the exit. She doubted the killer would pick his next victim from this meat market sideshow.

One step at a time, she shuffled her right foot, followed by her left. She scooted behind people, or around them, and was nearly flush with the corner that would lead her home, angrily preparing to raise her arm a third time, *fuck you, Zander*, when she saw him.

She knew it. Her gut twisted and then her brain pounced on her respiratory system, reminding her to breathe.

"Okay, okay, okay," she whispered to herself. "Ground yourself, Jay Jay." Every reporter instinct she had worked so hard to develop was pinging. Alarms in her head told her she was looking at the killer. She squinted through the veil of her black wig, memorizing every bit of him.

Take a picture with your brain, she told herself. *Make it stick. It may be your only chance.*

She started high. Spiky black hair hung below a backwards baseball hat. No logo. He moved with a certain elegance, his long, straight back barely swayed with each footfall. Wiry arms poked from a plain t-shirt, no ink on either bicep or forearm. His ass was small but firm beneath dark pants. No belt. Skater-boy sneakers with no laces. He must have just entered the room. He moved with authority and purpose, barely glancing at the array of naked skin sauntering down the runway. No, he wanted to touch, not watch. Jaycee took off behind him. She kept, at least, five bodies between them but was careful to keep him in her sights. He moved toward the bar. Shit! Jaycee couldn't go there; it was nearly empty with the show going on. She hung back again, watching.

He ordered a drink and sipped it. Turn around, she encouraged softly. Just turn around, let me see your pretty face. The man talked to the bartender for at least a minute, and then casually sat down on a stool. Putting both feet on the lower rung, he powered the swivel top with the momentum of his thighs. It began to turn toward her. Slowly. She could begin to see his profile. *Focus*, she thought, her fingers clenched and released. *Memorize. See him. Remove his wig. Isolate his features.*

The man was almost facing her. She could make out a narrow face, slim nose, and—

"All right, you ready?" Zander's voice was like an ice cube down her back.

"Shut up!" she roared. Jaycee whipped around, pulling Zander deeper into the crowd. "Wait here," she ordered and left him amidst a few choice words and very strong rebuke.

Shit! The man had left the barstool. Her eyes scanned the room. Goddamn it, she thought. She raced toward the bar, snapping her fingers to get the bartender's attention. "Hey, hey!" she yelled. "That guy. Where'd he go?"

The bartender gave her a, "Oh, no you did not" smirk and shook his head. He wasn't her receptionist.

"Asshole," she spat. Jaycee sighed, turning in a semi-circle toward the back of the room she hadn't been able to see when she was caught in the crowd before. She walked toward another wall and flattened up against it to get a better view of the area without worrying about someone coming up behind her. The ridiculous flesh-for-sale event was still going on, and the newly formed couples were disappearing into the lounge to "get to know each other." The thin man was gone. She'd blown it.

She was about to find Zander again when a wispy girl swept by her on a bubble-gum scent. She had dark hair, streaked with highlights, and a high, annoying giggle. She skipped toward the back, but Jaycee only saw empty, dark corridors. On a whim, she followed the girl until she could make out individual rooms with swampy light emitted from partially open doors. Just like Olive's. Private rooms were available if group orgies weren't on everyone's menu. The girl screamed. Jaycee raced closer to the noise. She poked her head around the room closest to the noise, able to catch a glimpse of the girl as she shed her white, lacy tank top, and wound her body around a plain t-shirt and dark pants.

Jaycee's chin was nearly clipped off as the door shut with such force the sound stung her eardrums.

She raised a fist to knock, to slam on the door with all her might to save the next Throw Away Girl from a certain horror.

But *was* she certain? What if she was wrong? She couldn't do it alone. She was strong thanks to weights and a daily date with a treadmill, but could she defend herself against a killer?

No—Barton had already told her that. Her own ego told her that.

Jaycee pressed her back into yet another wall, staring at the door and trying to work up a quick plan. She stepped away to retrieve Zander. If they needed to break the door down, she couldn't front-kick her way in alone.

What if the girl needed her and she couldn't get back in time? Should she call Barton?

It was a no-win situation. Jaycee raced back to where she had left Zander. He was gone. "Shit!" she yelled. Doing a fast spin in a circle, she scanned the room for him, praying he hadn't left with anyone, or *God help him,* put in a bid on one of the women.

It took far too long. Minutes, in fact. Jaycee was about to give up when she spotted him chatting up a gorgeous black woman with frosted blonde hair. Typical man.

"Get your ass over here," she grabbed him. "What the fuck, I needed you!" she leveled her most irritated glance at the woman, who took the hint that it was best she not mess with this hellcat, and left. "Thanks for having my back, Z," she spat out, pulling him back toward the hallway and the room where the girl was probably being hacked to death limb by limb.

"Jaycee, stop!" Zander resisted her shove. "Where are we going? I am not going there with you. I hope you know I like you and all but I'm not interested in that kind of—"

"Oh, will you just shut up already! I'm not taking you back here for *me*, you stupid ass! I need your help. *He's* here. With a girl. And they went in there! We have to help her. We have to break in!"

Even as she said it, she could see Zander was weighing his options. He clearly wasn't down with her plan to barge in. He wanted to bargain. Like the politician he was, he wanted a better deal.

"Whoah, whoah, whoah! You need to think this through," he started, but Jaycee pushed him by the chest and marched him straight backwards into the wall behind them. His spine connected with a thud. As she was unleashing a torrent of reasons why they couldn't wait a moment longer to storm the castle, the castle released its prisoner back into the night. Zander gently twisted her by the shoulders.

"You mean that girl? He asked. "She doesn't look like she needs saving to me."

Jaycee watched the girl skip back into the main room, all limbs intact and functioning. This can't be.

She had been so sure. That was the killer. That was him!

Jaycee felt her body deflate. Riding high on stress and adrenaline, she was crashing. This was a mistake. She was making bad choices, and ill-contrived assumptions. She'd just made a monster out of an innocent man just looking for a good time with a willing partner.

"I'm so sorry," she gasped. "I'm so sorr—"

She trailed off. Zander was talking, but all she could hear was the sound of wind. That must be what validation sounds like.

The man was walking out of the room. As their eyes met, it became crystal clear.

She was staring into the eyes of a killer. And he was staring right back.

Chapter Twenty-Six

The media scrum was growing. Jaycee muscled her way to the front, just beyond the podium set up outside the police department. Ben was set up with the other photographers in the back, angled high to shoot over the heads of the reporters. Barton ensured her once the briefing had ended, she'd be granted the first question. That was something every reporter wanted. Her station wasn't taking the presser live though Jaycee was to have the story ready for the evening newscasts. She had spent the overnight hours conducting her own debriefing, and just as the sun cracked over the horizon, had almost convinced herself she was a paranoid loon.

Or was she.

The guy in the club—the picture on her car. Well, sure, that was all concerning, but what if it was some whack job with a sick crush on her looking for attention by attaching himself to the story? Or, maybe the photogs at work were trying to scare the shit out of her with a picture and a cryptic message. Ben wasn't the only one who thought she was too intense on this story. And, really, weren't the odds ridiculously long that the thin man with the cold eyes and baleful glare was anything more than another satisfied customer enjoying a tryst in a nightclub?

She looked around her and recognized Elaine Topsham in the row just behind Jaycee. Elaine was a feisty, middle-aged print reporter who sold her own stories to the highest bidder. She had written a piece recently that had been featured in an offbeat city mailer called Angel City. It called out the nightclub killer as a coward and wimp. Surely, he'd find more reason to trail her to the beach, right? Maybe she had gotten a note, too.

"Hi, Elaine," she touched her elbow.

"Hi, Jaycee," she greeted her back. "Your Statler interview was excellent. Ben did a great job, too. He has such an empathetic eye."

"Oh, I know," Jaycee smiled. "Thanks, I do my best work with him. Quick question for you. Have you gotten any weird calls, or letters, from someone pretending to be this guy?"

"You mean the nightclub killer?"

"Yeah," Jaycee nodded. "I'm just wondering because I'd heard that from some of the other reporters covering this story." She was lying. Elaine was quick to respond.

"Really?" she asked. "I hadn't heard that at all. Who?"

"I don't really remember who exactly, I just recall a few girls talking about it." Jaycee detached as delicately as she could. Elaine denied any contact—weird or otherwise—with anyone purporting to be the killer. "But let him try," she said, raising one finely waxed eyebrow. "I have a Doberman and a Magnum. He won't survive either."

Jaycee smiled nervously. She certainly didn't want to give Elaine too much to think about. Just then, the press was given a two-minute warning. Photographers readied their cameras to roll, and reporters stared at the mirrored front doors of the department for any sign of activity. Once the door swung open eight uniformed officers divided into two groups of four to stand on either side of the podium, flanking the chief. Jaycee knew many of them, particularly the man third to last on the right. Detective Barton looked sharp, like he fit in. Jaycee repressed a small grin.

"Good afternoon," the chief began. A good partner in the media allowed his opening line to provide a quick mic check to ensure audio levels are acceptable. The chief let a few seconds pass for photographers to adjust the knobs on their cameras. He'd done this enough to be a friend to technology.

"Today, we're announcing the activation of our Homicide Special Section, or HSS, to look into the nightclub murders. As you know, three young women have been found dead at three different, yet similar locations, all along Hollywood Boulevard. We have spoken to witnesses, analyzed all crime scenes, and are pursuing tips and possible leads. As is always the case, we are mindful not to release any information that could compromise our investigation. However, we can confirm to you the presence of a message left behind at all three crime scenes."

Jaycee felt a couple of fingers jab her back, subtle acknowledgments from her colleagues standing behind her that she had scored the exclusive on that already. She met Barton's eyes. He held her gaze and nodded slightly. She nodded back. Would they confirm the attack on Fiona? Was that next? Jaycee knew they would withhold something of value from the public if that one piece of information could narrow down a suspect pool. If they had someone they could question, and he truly was the killer, only he would know of a fourth Throw Away Girl. It was a useful investigative tool, but only if they had a suspect to interrogate. Plus, they had to balance what they released to the media, with what could tip off the killer. Even though the goal was to stop the murders, they didn't want to scare him away before they could bring him in.

"At this point, we would also appreciate your help in getting a message out to our neighbors. To everyone who frequents these particular nightclubs, we ask you do so with caution. We ask you to be aware of your surroundings at all times. We ask you to report to us, anonymously if you prefer, anyone that appears suspicious, out of place, or dangerous. We will utilize extra patrols on the streets during the evening and overnight hours."

The chief went on to announce a tip line, and a website link. He never mentioned Fiona or got into the status of forensics. As he was closing his remarks, Jaycee shot her hand up. She wanted the first question. As the chief folded his notes on the podium, Barton gave her another nod. She'd go first.

"I can take some questions, but there will be aspects of the investigation I cannot comment on." He scanned the front row. Jaycee stretched on her toes. She was taller than most and used that to her advantage. The chief caught her eye immediately.

"Jaycee," he said. She took a breath. The question must be important, but it won't be as precious to her as putting Barton on camera after the presser. This would simply show she was taking the lead on this story. For herself and for ABC 12.

"Chief, can you confirm the status of forensics? Are you able to link DNA or prints, or anything specific to each murder scene? Are you ready to call this a serial killer case? What does the message say?"

It was a not-so-veiled trick every reporter used. A smattering of questions rolled up into one. The chief was adept at the art of deflecting the inquiry regurgitation. Jaycee knew he would answer perhaps one, possibly two of her questions, but never all.

"As far as lab evidence goes, we are still waiting for results. That will, obviously, be a primary goal as we move toward prosecution, and we intend to vigorously pursue any and all DNA profile links or possible links. I can't comment beyond that for now. As to your second question, we must work with what we have—not what we wish we had—as far as attaching a label to these murders. I'm willing to confirm three murders, at three similar locations, with a note left behind at each. I cannot tell you what that note says because it could compromise our investigation. Beyond that, it does us no good to call it anything other than what it is. Another point I'd like to make," the chief held up a finger for emphasis. "By assembling this task force, made up of officers with a wide background and collective breadth of criminal experience, we will now be automatically alerted when any other L.A.P.D. detective or officer calls in a homicide involving a female near or in suspect areas."

Interesting, Jaycee thought, isn't that the very definition of pursuing a serial killer? She appreciated being mindful of the investigation, but being vague for the sake of being vague was unproductive, and it always annoyed her.

"Jeff Halloway?" he pointed to the reporter from the Los Angeles Times standing three people over. He also pursued the forensic aspect of the investigation.

"Chief, just for clarity purposes. Even if you eventually find a DNA link to these scenes, it will not be useful unless you can match it to a known criminal in either your citywide database or the federal one, correct?"

It was the frustration that accompanied even the most pristine print, blood droplet, or skin flake.

"On the surface, true," the chief began. "But if we have probable cause to bring someone in, and can obtain a sample, it makes it highly effective to have lab results waiting. From there, we could have a match."

"But, chief," Halloway pressed, "that's only if you have a suspect. What I'm asking is, you may not have a known criminal on the loose here in Los Angeles. He may be an unknown, as far as the system goes."

The chief nodded. "One step at a time, Jeff. Let's find a person of interest first and then worry about the match. Sara Vasquez, you're up next."

The reporter from the CBS affiliate asked for more specificity about the clubs. "Chief, can you further describe the nature of these nightclubs. They aren't your typical clubs, are they? Far as I can tell, many of them don't even have a name."

"Correct. They appeal to a particular clientele, though none are operating illegally."

"They're sex clubs, right, chief?"

"Again, we have no proof of illegal activity."

Sara pressed her luck, firing off another question just as the chief pointed at the reporter waiting behind her. "What about security cameras in the area? Have they been useful?"

The chief acquiesced. "I'd rather not comment on that just yet, it's part of the investigation."

At that point, Jaycee detached from the reporters and went to get Ben. He needed to be ready to move when the presser adjourned and they had access to Barton. There would be nothing else of note to come from this. The chief fielded about six more questions before he indicated he was done, but would report back to them if anything developed. The reporters wandered away, yapping into cell phones or jotting down notes onto iPads and notebooks. A few pedestrians had stopped to listen to the event. Jaycee looked them over with a critical eye. She especially watched the men. She couldn't help it. Would he dare show up? Was he at work or did he sleep the day away after partying all night? Did he please his Throw Away Girls when he wasn't killing them? What did he look like without the wig and black eyeliner? Would she recognize him again? If, that was him at all.

His face was in shadows, and yet Jaycee could see it if she closed her eyes. Yes. Yes, she would recognize him again. Her gut wouldn't let it go.

"...Around the corner or something?"

She heard something, words, yet couldn't connect. She was still in the club, staring into the eyes of the man who stole breath, blood, and lives from innocent women. She was lost and irritated at her own unwillingness to believe in herself. Her instincts were always rock solid.

"Yo, space cadet, why you trippin'?" Ben's elbow nudged hers. "I asked if you want to meet him around the corner?"

She gripped Ben's forearm. A flesh on flesh connection she used to bring her back to the moment. "Shut up, man," she told him lightly. "I'm concentrating here. You're messing with my flow."

"Uh, huh," Ben swallowed. He watched her flit around. Jaycee did not *flit*. She was distracted and skittish when she was usually collected and razor sharp. He was concerned.

"Do you want him on a lav?" he asked, ready to disconnect the stick holding the mic flag with the ABC 12 logo for a smaller lavalier, a less obvious microphone that fit on a lapel. "Clean up the shot."

"Yeah," she confirmed. "We have the mic flag from the podium. Use the lav for Barton."

"What does this guy have for you?"

"I'm not sure yet. I've had some offline conversations with him. He may give us something solid."

"Do we know him?" Ben asked. His fingers worked quickly to have the mic ready in time.

"No. He's new."

He watched her. She was running a finger over her knuckles, but her gaze was miles away. "Girlfriend," he began.

"Yeah."

"Is Vansome still rocking your world?"

Jaycee coughed. "Seriously? That's what you're thinking about right now? My sex life?"

"I'm just trying to figure out why you're buggin' out right now. If Vansome is doing his thing, then you shouldn't have all this nervous energy bouncing off you right now. You're either sexually frustrated and trust me; I get that one, sista, or this case is fucking with you. Van's hotness quotient alone makes me think it's more likely it's the dead 'hoes' that have you all worked up."

Ben knew her so well. She couldn't hide from him.

"I saw you running out yesterday," he told her. God, was that only yesterday that she'd seen Fiona splayed out in a hospital bed, ambushed Olive for information, and then opened a personalized warning telling her to back off? It felt like she'd lived a lifetime since then. It occurred to her that she could have a developing case of PTSD.

"Since you didn't bring me back a half-skim, no whip vanilla latte, I'm assuming it wasn't a trip to Starbucks or Pinkberry?"

"Just a little snooping, that's all," she tried to keep it light. She wasn't ready to tell Ben about the things she'd seen and done without him. For this story, they couldn't be the team they usually were. She had to walk this path alone. For now. She turned to smile at him and almost flinched. Her soft-faced friend had gone rigid. His eyes were dead serious and boring into her.

"Cut the shit, Jay Jay," he growled. "You're making yourself a problem. This could get ugly."

She shook her head. "No, Ben. You don't understand…"

Like a veil, his expression changed. Jaycee stared at the lilt in his eyes; his shiny smile restored as he turned to greet Detective Barton, who was muttering something about being sorry for keeping them waiting.

"…Right, Jay Jay?"

She sputtered out something that sounded like she agreed with whatever he'd just said. She watched him make small talk with Barton. "I'm, like, a stylist and photographer, so I'm going to straighten your collar here, Detective, so you're all nice and pretty on TV."

Barton allowed Ben to adjust his collar and winked at Jaycee. "Does he do this to you, too?" he asked good-naturedly.

"Oh, I do worse to her," Ben laughed. "But she's used to it. Aren't you, Jay Bird?"

Her cue to giggle or give some cutesy response. She tried but it sounded like a horse neighing. The men looked at her strangely.

"You okay?" Barton asked.

"Yup, I'm good. Sorry, just, uh, a little tired."

Granted she hadn't slept a minute since returning from her sex club tour, but Jaycee had never used that excuse in her entire life. What the hell was happening? Ben threw his camera up onto his tripod and set the shot. Barton narrowed his eyes at her and mouthed, "Are you okay?"

She nodded dismissively, shuffling around to the left edge of the camera lens so when Barton looked at her, his profile would be nicely angled in the shot. "Ben, you all set?" She fumbled for the fortitude she usually had in the moment right before an important interview. She felt weak.

"Locked and loaded, fire away."

"Detective Barton," she started. "You are assigned to this task force. What are your first priorities in the investigation?"

A total softball but Jaycee wanted to warm him up. This was their first on-camera interview, and she wasn't sure how he'd come off. His answers were quipped, timed out well to fit into the context of a sound bite. It confirmed to Jaycee that he'd done this many times before. She lead him a bit further and then turned off course.

"Do you suspect a serial killer?"

"We can't confirm that just yet, but it is one of the angles of our investigation."

"Is there any evidence to suggest other women have been attacked? Not killed, but hurt in any way?" Jaycee could ask. Where Barton went with this would let her know if she was to get another exclusive.

"I can only say at this time we believe there could be at least one more victim, possibly more. Our newly formed task force will be in constant communication with each other and law enforcement across the state. If something suspicious pops up, we'll all know about it."

Jaycee nodded, but she was stuck on two words. *Possibly more?* Jaycee wasn't expecting that, nor was Ben, apparently, because she heard him grunt behind her. But was it a red herring to throw off the killer? Make him think he wasn't the only wolf hunting in the forest? Force him to do something that would smoke him out?

"Can you confirm the death of a fourth woman?" she prompted.

"No, we can't. I will only say we believe there could be an additional victim or victims. I can't confirm conditions or locations. The task force will be following these new leads, and we hope the public will not hesitate to report anything of a suspicious nature to the police immediately."

Jaycee turned back to Ben. "I'm good," she told him. "Grab some cutaways now."

Ben disconnected the camera from its tripod and began to circle them to roll at different angles. That video would help pad the story during editing. Remembering the mic was hot, Jaycee was careful to keep their chit chat on topic.

"Does the chief know I'm going with this tonight?" she asked.

"I cleared it. He's okay with the occasional exclusive and told me I'd picked the right reporter to give it to." Barton declined to tell Jaycee that his fragile new job was riding on his ability to work the reporter to his advantage. If she went with something that made the department look bad, his ass was ash. He was still watching her. "Something's wrong with you."

Jaycee stared pointedly at the tiny black mic still clipped to his lapel. Not now. He got the hint.

"I'll touch base with you before this airs tonight to make sure nothing else is developing. Watch for it at five and six. A shorter version will probably air at 11 o'clock. Welcome to Los Angeles, Detective, I hope I see you on future cases." She kept it very impersonal and cool. She wanted to be discreet, but both Ben and Barton considered it weird and totally unlike her usual demeanor. She could feel them staring at her.

"If you're all set, can you give me a minute?" she asked Ben.

"Yeah, sure," he said, grabbing his gear under one arm and hooking the camera's strap around the other shoulder. "Meet you in the car. Detective, take care." He reached for his hand to shake. Barton offered his left, as he did that first time to Jaycee. If Ben was surprised, he hid it well. Jaycee watched him walk back around to the front of the department and trot across the street to the Explorer.

"Thank you—" she began, but Barton was quicker.

"What happened to you?" he demanded.

"It's nothing, honestly," she wanted to assure him she was okay. She was up for this. Watching her friend walk away made her second guess her gut. He wasn't being sinister; he was worried about her. Christ, everyone was worried about her.

"All right, it's not *nothing*. I talked to Olive," she told him. "I did try to get you on the phone, but all I got was voicemail. I found her right there at her club. She told me…stuff."

"Don't worry, you're not betraying her confidence. I know the same stuff you do. I just wanted you to hear it on your own."

Jaycee nodded. "She was attacked, too, you know."

"Multiple victims, Jaycee. Remember what I just told you."

"Oh my God," Jaycee's eyes went wide. His comment clicked. "You're counting Olive as another victim. But she won't press charges. You know that, right? She's rolling in some serious cash right now and thinks it's because of him. In a good way."

"We are aware. She was forthcoming with us, but there will never be any evidence beyond her word against his. Anything of a forensic nature is long gone. She knows she won't be linked to this unless she pursues justice."

Jaycee blinked a few times. "Any update on Fiona?"

"She's doing quite well today. She is stable and breathing on her own. One lung had collapsed, but it's returning to full strength. It'll be a long road. Her face will be a work in progress for some time."

It made Jaycee queasy. Fiona's injuries were horrific. "I won't release her name, obviously."

"I know that," Barton interjected. "I trust you."

His eyes were kind and clear. Jaycee noticed how his cheekbones were visible now, tighter and more defined. "How do you do this?" she asked him before she could stop herself. "How do you shut this off? It's all I can think about."

He looked at her earnestly. "Jaycee, listen to me now." He stepped closer to her. He smelled like coffee and Chapstick, not a hint of stale alcohol seeped out of his skin. "I have had years of training to do this. You've had days. Maybe this was a mistake—"

"No!" she blurted. "Not a mistake. I'm in this. What I'm asking is, how do you keep your brain from thinking every single tall skinny guy is a serial killer? God, I'm looking at one of my best friends and wondering if he's skilled with a knife! I stare at random men who pass me on the street. I wonder if someone is hiding under my bed with a machete…"

Barton shook her down. He knew fear when he saw it. Jaycee was holding something back; it had just gotten personal. "He contacted you, didn't he?"

It wasn't a condemnation. It wasn't even posed in an angry voice. They both knew it could happen. Now, it had. Time to deal with it. Jaycee realized that she was wrong to keep it to herself. In case something ever happened to her, at least, one person needed to know the full story. She chuckled wryly at herself for being such a novice police investigator.

"I'm a total reporter," she began. "Always protecting the story, the integrity of the source, which in this case, is me." She met his eyes. "Yes, maybe he contacted me, or someone at work is screwing around with me. But there's more."

"More?" Barton shook his head. "God, I'm afraid to ask."

"I went looking for him," she said slowly, but clearly. She placed both palms up to stop him from interrupting her, which he seemed poised to do. "Wait, just hear me out. I took precautions. I disguised myself and was very careful. But…"

"But?"

"But I feel like I saw him, and he saw me, too. Like, through my stupid wig and bad makeup. I think he saw the real me and I'm pretty sure he doesn't like me. And then there's the possibility I'm flat out wrong and the guy I saw wasn't him at all. See, I'm all twisted up in here." She tapped her forehead.

Barton shuffled in place, agitated yet impressed with her enterprising grit. If the story wasn't coming to her, she was going to it, an aggressive yet inherently slippery trait that could either pay off big or send her sliding into some deep shit.

"You went to a club? I assume you were working off Olive's description of him?" Barton asked, pressing his eyebrows together with his left pointer finger. "What she told you he looked like."

"Exactly, although she was pretty vague. Full disclosure, I went to several clubs. All equally disgusting, but it happened at the last club we hit."

"Who's we?"

"Ugh," Jaycee moaned, regretting her careless response. She didn't want to admit she'd involved another civilian who could've been in danger. "Do I have to tell you that?"

Barton looked pointedly into her eyes.

"All right, all right. Zander was with me," Jaycee forged on to avoid Barton's response. "Listen, I swear the guy I saw last night was wearing a black wig, just like Olive told me. But there's also stuff about him that doesn't fit," she shook her head, trying to think it out. From her periphery, she saw Ben pull the Explorer up to the sidewalk, and Elaine walk over to his open window. What was that?

"What do you mean?" Barton asked, drawing her attention back to him.

"For starters, no Throw Away Girl turned up at that club, right?"

"Correct," Barton stated. "But that's assuming the man you saw is really him. You already admitted you realize that's highly unlikely."

"Theoretically, a low chance of probability, yes, but not impossible. I don't know, Barton, his eyes were…" she searched for a word. "…Evil. The way he looked at me made me feel like he was hurting me without even touching me. I know that sounds all messed up."

"He was with someone?"

"Yes, in a private room, which is where all the murders go down. Only this woman came out skipping. Literally, skipping away. I thought he was escalating, killing more often, more violently, like he did in other cities just before it stopped. It doesn't fit, you know?"

"Or maybe it does," Barton said. "He didn't kill Olive either. We have no idea how long he's been visiting these clubs without doing anything more than enjoying himself. One year? Five? And who's to say he doesn't have a larger plan. Maybe he doesn't kill women on nights he eats pizza. Perhaps he talked to his mom on the phone last night and doesn't like to hurt a woman on nights he talks to his mom. We can't possibly interpret his thoughts, only his actions.

You're right, he didn't kill anyone last night, and we don't know when he'll hunt again. Only that it's likely that he will. If not here, somewhere else."

They stood there together for a few seconds. Jaycee had enough to move the story forward for the evening newscasts. "You're on this now as much as I am," she said to Barton. "He'll see your face, too."

"That's my job," he replied calmly. "We go where the bad guys are."

"Your job nearly killed you once already," she reminded him, feeling a sense of responsibility for what she was about to do: publically showcase a once-damaged detective.

"Jaycee," he began. "That was a long time ago. I'm…fine, now."

Suddenly, she felt cold. With the Los Angeles sun blaring around them, Jaycee felt goosebumps break out along her bare arms. She wrapped her hands around her elbows, rubbing her skin for warmth. "Stress can cause a person to not be fine."

"Right back at you," he warned. "I want to know how he contacted you."

She nodded. "*Possibly* contacted me," she corrected. "I would say I irritated him with the Statler interview, but his warning—if it really came from him—arrived before that aired."

"On the phone?"

"No, via delivery. He took a picture of us on the beach and attached a sweet little message. My boyfriend and I, together, last weekend. He tucked it into an envelope and left it on my car at work. But here's the thing: it could be the guys at work messing with me. They know I get stuff left on my car all the time. Stupid stuff, from dudes, like business cards, or date requests. That kind of thing."

"On your car? At work?" Barton shook his head, obviously not yet willing to dismiss it as a joke. "When did you get it?"

"Monday, early, just before I met you at the hospital."

Barton's mouth was pulled tight. "That's concerning."

"Well, yeah, concerning for me, too. Because if it's not a joke, it obviously means this lunatic knows what car I drive and where I go on the weekends."

Barton jutted his chin out in thought. "All right, let's break this down a bit. You were on the beach Saturday, right? Did you tell anyone else where you were going? Invite anyone? Put it out on social media?"

"Seriously, you think I tweet about going to the beach?"

"This is LA, Jaycee, celebrities tweet about taking a piss around here. Then they post a picture of it on Facebook."

"I'm not a celebrity by California standards," she reminded him. "I'm just a reporter, and no, I did not tell anyone…" she took a quick breath on a thought. She had called Ben to ask him to come along. Did she tell anyone else in the newsroom? She couldn't recall. And, did she tell anyone what beach they were going to? She did confirm to her neighbor in the elevator that they were going to Venice, right? She remembered him asking because he preferred Manhattan Beach. What about the clerk at the convenience store they stopped at? Did she tell him, too? Good lord, there were limitless possibilities, and if the killer slipped out of a wig and into a normal life during the day, he could be anyone, anywhere. It was a wholly terrifying fact. "God, I probably told a lot more people than I realized."

"Is there a doorman at your condo?" Barton asked.

"No," Jaycee shook her head. "Just a keycard to enter the building and a separate key for my unit." She met his sharp look. "You think he's coming to my…my…home?"

Barton dodged. "You need to keep the envelope; there's potential evidence we can pull from it. At the very least, I want to see it. I want the picture, too."

Jaycee's breath caught. She'd missed that entirely! Barton was right. The envelope could hold DNA. Did she even save the envelope? She squinted. Barton was looking at her with growing concern. "Tell me you saved the goddamn envelope. Tell me I'm about to get really lucky."

She shook her head. "Shit!" she exclaimed. "I tore the friggin' thing apart. It was right after I talked to Olive and dropped Van off at home. It's in my car. In about a hundred pieces."

"Put it all in a bag."

She nodded. "If I get that for you, I need something in return."

"Jaycee, your safety is something I won't bargain with…"

"Barton, please!" she implored him with her eyes. "Please don't tell my boss. She'll snatch me off this story so fast I can already smell the basement she'll lock me in until it's over. Consider me an unofficial member of your task force. I'm working this, too."

Barton dodged again. "Why did you drop Van off at home? Where had he been?"

"With me. You're the one who told me not to go alone."

"I did," he nodded wryly. "So, let me get this straight. You have now involved two additional civilians? Not including Olive."

"I'm sorry, I'm a good reporter but a novice detective. But they won't say anything, I made them promise me. And don't forget you told me about Olive in the first place."

"Hmm, I know," Barton quipped. "Did you tell anyone else where you were going? Did you tell anyone about Fiona?"

Jaycee shook her head. "Of course not! Just the ones you already know about. But neither of them will make that public knowledge."

Barton's face was drawn. He was processing data quickly. "What are you thinking?" she asked.

"That the killer knows your next move before you make it."

Jaycee went from cold to frozen. Her teeth chattered. "I don't understand how."

"So, this is all using the scenario that the picture on your car actually did come from the killer, yes?"

"Yes," she nodded.

"So, your station was promoting the story, which was the connection I warned you about before. He's watching TV, and may isolate and fixate on your reporting. But before your interview with the Statlers even aired, he followed you to the beach. That means he knows where you live and what car you drive. He snapped a picture and sent you a warning. He's telling you he doesn't *want* to hurt you."

"In that scenario, I agree, even though it's only mildly reassuring. He's obviously annoyed with my reporting. There's no evidence any other reporter is being targeted, I asked around, and let me remind you we anticipated this, no?"

"We knew it was a possibility. But Jaycee, here's the thing..." he trailed off.

"What are you suggesting? Just say it?"

"He's telling you to back off, giving you a chance to stop looking for him."

Chills rippled through her again. "Because if I don't..." she halted herself on the horrifying thought.

"He may be coming for you."

Barton's statement hit her like a Mack truck. The killer was close.

Shockingly close.

Chapter Twenty-Seven

"Hey man, you losing weight? You look good." A patrolman placed a hand on Barton's shoulder as they took the stairs together up to their floor. "How's the case moving?" he asked. "Didn't see the presser, did it go okay?"

"Presser was good, but this case is slow and tedious. These are the days I really miss stupid criminals. This guy's got a brain, and a barrel full of fuzzy forensics to hide in."

"I hear ya, man. The crackheads and juice monkeys make our lives so much easier. Good luck."

The muscle-bound cop bounced by Barton, taking two steps at a time while he followed up behind him. Back when he was drinking, he would have tripped the fucker, pissed off that he was young and strong, and looking to take him down a notch.

Not anymore.

Now, Barton channeled all his anger and self-loathing and heaved himself up the final stairs with a flourish. Sweat trickled down his cheek. He hastily wiped it away and marched toward his office. His right eyebrow buzzed below a dull headache.

His office phone revealed several messages: Two television reporters and three print writers requesting interviews about the nightclub murders. His contact at the lab had also called to warn of yet another delay, *typical*, and his ex-wife asked about his plans for the weekend and if he'd like to watch Mason's soccer game. Solid progress there. He allowed himself the tiniest of smiles, but then refocused on his work. He needed to find a killer, had multiple agencies to deal with, a reputation to rebuild, a department watching his every move, and a time crunch. Throw in this bonus: Some whacked-out guy may have Jaycee in his cross-hairs.

Taking a long sip of his cream-filled coffee that didn't hold a candle to the Dunkin Donuts back east, Barton swallowed his rage. He hated criminals who fucked with the cops. It infuriated him. Now, he was fucking with Jaycee. This goddamn message was his way of expressing his purpose. He wasn't just killing, he was killing with a reason, but he was willing to take her down if she threw up a roadblock. Barton sighed heavily and scanned his desk. Typically, it was a disaster, a scattered playground for a reckless and distracted mind.

Not anymore.

Part of his makeover included a resolve to better organize his thoughts, both at work and as a father. He vowed to be present and aware. He was in the habit now of making straight lines of his notepaper and computer printouts. All his thoughts represented in neat piles that included sporadic notes attached to the bottom of pages he was using as a timeline of events. He separated forensic information into columns, denoting each with sticky tabs that stated Primary Transfer of DNA, and Secondary Transfer of DNA. The former indicated a direct exchange from a person to an item, though there were many factors that determined how much DNA was left. The latter was the buzz kill. Secondary transfers made via an intermediary, and in the case of the nightclub girls, there were likely too many "middlemen" to count. It would really hinder prosecution. The suspect was like an octopus, slimy and far-reaching. Close quarters invited sweat, saliva, and other fluids to intermingle and thus, completely fucked up a crime scene. Even Olive's limited information about the suspect's physicality was almost useless. He'd hurt Olive, and yet pleasured her, too. He'd killed and let live. He knew the media was following him, and yet appeared to fixate specifically on one reporter. None of the departments in other cities with unsolved homicides of this type had mentioned that little nugget.

Jaycee was special.

Barton exhaled sharply. Their relationship was skirting the danger zone. Light from the window adjacent to his desk reflected off the dark screen of his cell phone. He tilted his head, realizing he was waiting for Jaycee's name to pop up. She promised to search around for the remnants of the envelope and get back to him right away with any information. He used both hands to grip the bones around his eye socket. His right hand was an awkward fit, and any relief the light massage gave his pounding head made his hand ache with exertion. Saliva built in his mouth, and his stomach rolled. These were the moments when alcohol took it all away.

Not anymore.

His eyes moved back to his phone.

Call me, Jaycee.

Barton took an elbow and swept his neat paper columns into disarray. This was bullshit! He had to get through to her. She needed to back off for a while, take a break from this case and get the hell off this lunatic's radar screen. She was fast becoming the second coming of the ponytailed little girl, his to save or to lose. He had to move. He had to protect.

Jaycee Wilder was one tough chick, but she was getting rattled. Barton knew the risks of becoming a bad guy's collateral damage; it was part of his job. He couldn't escape the totality of the damage done to him in that ghastly Cambridge apartment that smelled like the belly of hell, but he could learn from it. It could make him stronger. He'd failed once, turning to liquid comfort instead of doing the hardcore work on himself. He'd preferred numbness over self-discovery. He'd taken the coward's way out.

Not anymore.

Sometimes doing the right thing felt like shit. He reached for the small frame holding Mason's picture, first with his right hand—a lingering habit his body still fought him on—before adjusting to his left to get a better grip on the glass that protected his smiling face. There was nothing he wouldn't do for his kid. He hoped if one day he wasn't around; there were enough good people left in this world to do it for him.

Like he would do now for Jaycee. His mouth twitched as he punched up the number for ABC 12 News. Didn't anyone love this girl? Wasn't there anyone in her corner pulling her out of the ring when her eye swelled shut? Jesus Christ. He quickly hung up and tapped out another series of numbers, anticipating the cool cadence of the voice that would pick up. The voice that still made his heart ping.

"Debra Wentworth."

His lips turned down. Deb had dropped him entirely. To him, her maiden name sounded like a curse word. "It's me," he stated.

"You okay?" Deb immediately expected trouble. He couldn't blame her; she had endured exactly that.

"Yeah, yeah, just need a dose of your sensibility." Deb was the most level-headed woman he'd ever known. Of course, the fact that she had divorced him only confirmed that he had so badly fucked up. They both knew she was always right.

"Workin' a case here," he started.

"Yes, I know, the nightclub girls. I assume that's the case you mean?" Although they never discussed his day to day activities any longer, Deb had an awareness of what was going on in the world. Coverage of the nightclub murders was hard to miss.

"Yeah, that's the one. You got a minute?"

Deb confirmed that she was between patients and could talk. Back when she was a cop's wife, these were the moments she waited for. When the brief cracks that opened in her hardened spouse would temporarily let her in. It was warm inside, loving and safe. She had learned to absorb it and save it for later, because just as quickly, he would shove her out again.

"There's a reporter working this," he said.

"Lots of them from what I have seen," Deb stated.

"Well, true, but there's one, in particular, I've been working with."

Deb knew that cops viewed the media like double-sided tape, it could keep your shit from spilling out in public, or it could let go and reveal the cellulite on your ass. "You're sharing info," she suggested.

"Yes, and this one gives as good as she gets. Bcfore you ask, no, I'm not doing anything that would risk my job here."

Deb sighed. "I didn't say that, James." She tried very hard not to remind him of all she'd done to revive his life and career. To do so would be cruel and she had never developed a taste for that, no matter how deeply he had hurt her.

"Sorry," he bit back more, choosing not to rehash everything that had gone unspoken. *Keep it simple, chump*, he reminded himself. *This is not about you.* "I need your perspective on something. I'm too close."

"Is this reporter a woman?" Deb asked wisely. Only an ex-wife could get away with that.

"Uh-huh," he grunted. He was about to explain, but Deb was too quick. She always had been uncanny in how she read him.

"I'm thinking you either want to screw her or protect her," she said, and then added a clarifier. "You're a single guy now, so I'm adjusting my James Barton radar to include the first part. It's only natural."

Barton smiled into the phone. God, he missed her. He closed his eyes and pictured her face. The way her bottom lip curled sideways when she laughed. That one crooked tooth that defied three years of braces and nightly headgear when she was a teenager. The way her nose crinkled when she told their son how much she loved him. Deb was dear. Deb had rounded out all his sharp edges.

Not anymore.

He fought through a sudden ache in his windpipe, found his voice again, and exchanged Deb's face for Jaycee's in his mind. Back to reality.

"I'm afraid..." he admitted, feeling a pulse of enlightenment flow through him rather than the murky current he was used to. Honesty was a powerful thing. For too long, he'd covered it with a toxic salve. "I'm afraid of losing her, too..." the release was so intense he felt like he had just coughed up a wad of charred steak.

"James, listen to me," Deb was firm. He felt her hand reach through the phone and grab his chin like she used to when she wanted his eyes on her. "You're the most intuitive cop I've ever met. If you're clean and sober right

246

now, and something is eating at your gut, listen to it, James. Listen to yourself. Something spoke to you inside that apartment in Cambridge. You were almost there; you had almost saved that little girl by doing what your gut told you to do. It's not your fault. It never was your fault. You did what no one else would even consider doing because your gut was talking. Listen to it."

James was still. He didn't even feel his chin dip to cradle the phone lower, closer to his heart. It still beat for her. Alcohol had made that too squishy to feel.

Not anymore.

He knew what he had to do. Deb was right. If no one else was going to step up and take care of Jaycee, he would. It was exactly what his gut was telling him to do.

* * * *

Clare Chatworth answered on the second ring with a voice that was already as barbed as an electric fence.

"Ms. Chatworth," he started.

"Please, call me Clare," she interrupted. "I don't do the Ms. bullshit."

"Okay, Clare. Hello, it's Detective James Barton, L.A.P.D. I apologize if this is out of the ordinary for you."

"I'm the news director of the number one station in Los Angeles, Detective, you think I do ordinary? What can I help you with?"

Barton chuckled. What a firecracker this one was. "Well, I've had the pleasure of speaking off the record with one of your reporters recently."

"This about the nightclub murders?" Clare was quick, always braced for a complaint or concern.

"Yes," Barton confirmed.

"Then you're talking about Jaycee. She told me about you. She was at the presser today, and it's not my style to apologize for my reporters being aggressive, Detective, it's how we stay out front…"

"No, no, that's not it," Barton corrected. Good lord, this woman was a viper. "She was there, yes, but I'd like your help on something. Jaycee has been a total professional. What I'm more interested in is her history at the station. She must get her fair share of interest?" Barton thought about the weirdness of random men leaving notes on her car. "Are you aware of any stalkers, odd notes, threatening viewer behavior? Anyone on staff with a criminal record?"

"Uh, *no*, to that one," Clare said incredulously. "I don't hire thugs, Barton. What's this about? Why are you asking personal questions about Jaycee?"

Barton spun a quick story he hoped would satisfy Clare's sharp mind. "Well, given the nature of this investigation, I'm just mindful of the reporters covering it, their safety and all."

Clare spurted out an agreement, signaling to Barton that was the right tactic to take. "Detective, I couldn't agree more. Thank you for your concern. So, to your questions, yeah, of course, on the stalker, creeper stuff but even my ugly-as-shit personalities get the same kind of attention. It's a TV thing."

Barton couldn't knock down a guttural laugh. "Sorry," Clare barked out. "I'm honest. Anyway, Jaycee has a file with the police, but so does everyone else here. I would say there's been nothing unusual as of late, and certainly nothing of the caliber you're talking about, or connected to the nightclub girls at all. You should know that Jaycee insists on staying on the story."

"Yes, I'm aware of that," Barton told her. He considered the note and the vague possibility that someone else with an ax to grind could use this high-profile case to air his own grievances with Jaycee. Scare her. "What about someone else she may have done a story on recently, perhaps that person had suffered legal issues as a result. Say, someone in a bad marriage, or involved in a restraining order violation, child custody issue? Someone who sees Jaycee as having messed things up for him. Or, could there be anyone Jaycee works with who may have a particularly strong interest in her?" Barton rubbed his palm over his scarred finger. It was throbbing like hell, as it did when blood pumped faster through his body. He was thinking hard, trying to flush out anything useful. He wouldn't break his promise not to reveal the picture and the note, but maybe Clare had something important to add.

Clare made a sound that indicated she was thinking about that. A few seconds passed and she answered in the negative. "No," she said firmly. "The nature of our business keeps us all tightly connected. We're working for the common good, on a deadline, so the producers, camera guys, and engineers are as important as the talent. There's no idolatry here, if that's what you mean, and Jaycee is about as real as they come. She is friends with everyone. And while she may report on people behaving badly, that's what we do. Generally speaking, if we cover some asshole caught smacking his wife around or threatening to burn the house down, he comes after us as a whole, not the reporter covering his story."

Barton thought through Clare's assessment. It was mostly what he expected to hear, save for one line that made his brain ting. *Friends with everyone.* Clare said Jaycee was friends with everyone, but who was everyone? He thought of wise Deb. *Listen to your gut, James.*

"You know the boyfriend at all?" he probed.

"You mean the stud she keeps in her stable? No, not well. Jaycee doesn't talk about men much. I do know she moved in with him not too long ago, and they work opposite schedules. He's not the type to pop in to work with roses, if that matters, but Jaycee seems happy with him."

He shifted gears.

"If you send her out on a story, who goes with her?" Barton wanted to know who was in her direct line of defense.

"Well, it depends," she explained. "If I need her to go live, she'll be with her photographer, but also my truck operators, and occasionally a field producer. I'd trust every last one of them with my life; they're all hard-core employees and good people. Especially Ben."

"Ben?" Barton sat up straight, further disturbing the lines of paper on his desk. The guy who'd adjusted his mic during their interview.

"Sorry, yeah, I should've been more clear. It's just that when I think of Jaycee I think of Ben, kind of like they're joined at the hip and sharing one brain. Ben Roderick is Jaycee's primary photographer. They work together almost every day and between you and me they're the best team I got. Trust me, if Jaycee is with Ben—and I intend to make damn sure she is—then she's perfectly safe. I've already spoken to Jaycee about this case. She's making it personal, and I don't like it. Detective, do you know something about Jaycee you're not spilling?"

Barton sighed. He tapped his middle finger against the desk, trying to create another sensation in his hand to distract him from the stubborn ache that never went away. He thought back to a case he'd worked in Boston a few years back. A female reporter stalked by a bug-eyed fan staking out her live shots and making her nervous. The guy was harmless, but Barton had hauled him in for questioning. He'd revealed that he would never approach the reporter while at work, he just liked to watch her do her job.

Maybe Jaycee was safest while she was working. He couldn't, in good conscience, take that away from her.

Listen to your gut, James. Something wasn't right, but it was too shadowy to nail down. Christ, his gut needed to speak up!

"No," he lied, feeling a stab of regret. "It's just a unique case, and I agree that Jaycee is highly invested. I'm just learning all my players. Before I let you go, Clare, do me another favor?"

"What?"

"Let me know if anything comes up," he passed along his cell phone number. "Anything that makes you concerned in any way about Jaycee, or this story."

"I will. She'll be with Ben for now. He would never let anything happen to her. But Detective…"

"Yes?"

Clare released a gulp of frustration. "Here's the thing. Ben is leaving. I knew he wouldn't be with me very long, he's just too damn good. He's taking a job with the BBC, heading to Costa Rica for the next year to work on a documentary about the rain forest or some stupid shit."

"Oh, no," Barton said. "When?"

"Soon. He also asked me not to tell Jaycee while she was so involved in the nightclub story. He is worried about causing her any more stress and wants to tell her himself."

"I promise I won't say anything. Just keep her with him as long as you can, Clare. That's all we can do for now."

They hung up and promised to keep in touch. *All we can do for now* wasn't sitting well with his gut. It gave him

252

a bad feeling that Jaycee's security team was losing an important member.

Chapter Twenty-Eight

"I smell chlorine and jock strap," Ben hissed as they stepped into the elevator near the information desk. Once the doors closed, Jaycee hit the number six, the ICU floor.

"Why do you punish me so?" Ben said, his voice muffled by the edge of his sweatshirt cuff covering his nose and mouth. The baseball hat she'd made him wear revealed only a thin strip of flesh. She preferred not to risk anyone recognizing Ben either.

"Don't be such a diva," she said firmly. "This is totally on the down low. There's another girl here. Another victim. Police are waiting for her to wake up so they can interview her. That's why they haven't released it publicly yet. She could be pivotal to the investigation."

"So, a fourth nightclub skank?" Ben rolled his eyes as Jaycee glared at him incredulously. "What?" he drawled.

"They're not all skanks," she clarified. Ben shrugged.

"Sure, they're fine upstanding young ladies who sip wine at their book clubs and volunteer at the animal shelter. That is, when they're not getting laid by strangers. Gotcha." He stuffed his nose into his sleeve. "I'm opting for the clean linen scent of my laundry detergent. Hospitals and I decided long ago we aren't compatible."

Ben was an overly dramatic witch whenever they had to cover something related to a medical building. She pulled the brim of her own baseball hat lower. This visit was to be incognito.

"Suck it up."

"Suck *you* up," he sneered back. "I can't take you seriously when you look like that girl pitcher from *The Bad News Bears*. She was a little ball-buster, too."

"Don't talk to anyone," she warned, in no mood for his frivolous banter. "You're not supposed to be here, and technically neither am I."

"Hence the ball-buster baseball hat," Ben said.

"Exactly," she told him. "And this does not go home to Clare, understand? She is not to know of this. Any of it." Jaycee stared into Ben's eyes until he nodded.

"Fine, okay," he told her with exasperation. "If I told her half the shit you pull in the field, she'd take all your Emmys and smack you upside the head with them."

"Ever thought this is exactly why I have those Emmys?"

"Whatevs, Jay Bird. Lead the way." Ben motioned to the hallway just beyond the open elevator doors. The sixth floor showcased a large sign notifying visitors they were entering the Intensive Care Unit, and instructions to call the nurse's desk for entry. Jaycee picked up the phone and pressed the red button next to it.

"Fiona Cooper," she stated. "It's her cousin."

"Cousin?" Ben whispered into her back as the doors automatically swung open to grant them entrance to the floor. "Is that hospital code for *nosy reporter*?"

"Shhh," she snapped. "Keep your mouth shut. The answers we're looking for might be right over there," she pointed to room number 601. "Has she woken up?" Jaycee asked the nurse sitting at a computer behind the desk in the middle of the ICU. The same nurse who had just buzzed them into the secure area.

"A few times. She's asking for her daughter."

Jaycee nodded. Poor little kid waiting for her mommy to come home. "Can we go in? He's also a relative." She motioned to Ben, who looked curiously around the busy floor.

"Keep it brief," the nurse replied.

"Of course, just for a minute."

Jaycee stepped into room 601 and peered over at the limp body in the bed. She took a seat next to it on a plastic chair. Ben hung back near the door. "Come here," Jaycee motioned. "You should see what he's been doing to these girls. That's why I'm trying so hard to tell their stories."

"Not my scene, jellybean," Ben whispered, pulling the brim of the baseball hat low over his eyes. He stayed near the hallway. "I only venture into this sick world from behind my camera."

Jaycee sighed. Ben hated the sight of blood and gore unless it was dimmed down by the black and white of his camera's viewfinder. He wouldn't even glance at an accident scene until he had his eye to the viewfinder. Just another gentle personality quirk that made her love him more.

"Fine, stay over there, you wimp."

Jaycee touched a finger to Fiona's still wrist. Just below her palm was the name Bella, tattooed in sweeping calligraphy. Likely, her daughter. Carefully, she laid her arm under the metal bar of the bed and reached for Fiona's swollen hand. The tips of her fingers looked like several fat blueberries were stuffed under her skin. Her torso was covered with those sticky monitors attached to a spider's web of wires.

"Fiona," she said softly. "Can you hear me?"

The woman's dry, cracked lips twitched and released a faint groan. She was trying to talk. Jaycee moved her fingers between the still ones on the bed, gripping Fiona's hand in her own.

"My name is Jaycee; I'm a friend. I'm trying to find the man who did this to you."

Fiona's right foot kicked out below the sheet followed by a subtle shift of one finger inside Jaycee's grip. Her head lolled.

"I talked to Olive," she whispered. She didn't need Ben overhearing more of her undercover escapades. He was irritated enough with her already. "I know what he looks like," she moved her torso over the bar to where Fiona's good ear was nestled against the pillow. The other was still wrapped in bandages. Jaycee could feel her pulse quicken, just speaking of the monster was fearsome. "I tried to find him."

Fiona's knee bobbed, and then fell. Gurgling sounds clogged her throat.

"I need help," Jaycee continued to talk into the wounded head. She held the now trembling hand. "He's after me, too," she confessed, surprising even herself. "Help me stop him, Fiona."

With supreme effort, Fiona rolled her head all the way to the other side of the bed. Only a small portion of her face was exposed, and her remaining eye was gummy with moisture that globbed her eyelashes. She squeezed the lids together in a clumsy blink. Then, she did it again.

Jaycee shifted until her face was directly in front of the eye. "Wake up. Talk to me." Jaycee was regrettably insistent, she didn't want to upset this poor woman, but desperately needed her information.

The strength of Fiona's soul was suddenly staggering. Jaycee watched her as she cleared the final hurdle of her subconscious and opened that one eye wide. The pupil was huge and black, but the iris was ocean blue. Jaycee could see how beautiful she had been.

"Hi," Jaycee smiled at her, feeling her chin quiver with emotion. One fat tear rolled over her nostril and became an opaque splat on the bone-white sheet. It was so inappropriate to feel this emotionally connected to another victim, and yet Jaycee simply couldn't help it.

The lips pursed. Jaycee recognized that as the movement her own mouth made when she speaks her name. The "j" sound that began behind the teeth.

"J..Juh...Jay..."

"Yes, I'm Jaycee, and I need your help. We have to stop him." She pulsed her fingers in rapid bursts, trying to metaphysically transfer her own energy directly into

Fiona's damaged skin and broken bones. "Tell me what I need to know."

"B...bbb...aa...ddd." Hard consonants bucked and skipped from her mouth, like the Tin Man in the *Wizard of Oz* before he got the oil can.

"Yes, bad. Very bad man, Fiona, he hurt you. He's hurt others. Tell me who he is."

The eye fluttered shut. Jaycee felt shame for putting her through this, yet couldn't stop herself. Justice trumped forgiveness.

Fiona's eye burst back open, like her internal pep squad had just rallied. She squeezed Jaycee's hand and nodded. She was ready to talk.

From the doorway, Ben cleared his throat. It wasn't a large or unusual sound, but it broke the momentum like a bucketful of icy cold water. Fiona's head thumped back onto the pillow; her eye strained to find the source of the male noise. It appeared to disturb her, her mouth clenched as the fogginess of her state prevented her from latching on to the discovery. She began to mumble a new batch of sounds.

"Nooooo..." she growled and hissed. "Ggggg...eeee......ttttt!! A...w...aaa..."

"Fiona," Jaycee tried to redirect her, she gripped her arm to get her attention back. "Fiona, the man. We need to find the bad man."

She jerked from Jaycee's grasp and wrapped her fingers like claws around the blanket, pulling at its edges in obvious desperation as her medicated brain sent flight signals to her extremities. Her heels slipped on the sheets as they pushed backwards. The strides she'd just made forming words were eviscerated into tense gurgles.

"Get the nurse!" Jaycee instructed Ben, who looked on in horror.

"What the hell did you do to her, Jay Bird?"

"Me?" she replied incredulously. "It's not me! Go get the goddamn nurse!"

Ben darted to the nurse's station to alert someone of Fiona's agitation. A pretty black nurse with strong biceps, a heavy Caribbean accent, and smiley faced scrubs raced over. She politely yet firmly instructed Jaycee to move. She found a thin plastic tube with clear liquid inside on the metal tray nearby the bed and then made quick time to clean the tip with a fast swipe of an alcohol swab. She connected the tip of the tube to one of the open IV connections along Fiona's arm. She pushed the vial down to distribute the liquid into her vein. About twenty seconds later, the thrashing slowed and then stopped. Fiona was still again.

"Don't blame ya'self," the nurse lightly tapped Jaycee's shoulder. "She has 'ta frights."

"The frights?" Jaycee asked, puzzled.

"Sometin' spooked her," the nurse clarified. "We just send her back to sleep. Let it pass."

"Oh," Jaycee nodded. "I thought it was him." She motioned toward Ben. "He's very scary."

Ben smirked. His eyes went large to signal to Jaycee that they needed to scram.

"Poor girl's got 'ta bad dreams," the nurse said, as she clicked her tongue in sympathy. "I read to her at night. Happy stories. Chase away 'ta demon."

They stared at the body in the bed. The medicine seemed to paralyze her. Jaycee felt both sadness and disappointment. She'd been close. Fiona had almost delivered another clue.

They left the ICU and pressed the L circle in the elevator for the lobby.

"Thanks a lot," Jaycee told Ben. "I was there. I was on the verge of some good shit. You really do have a way with straight women."

"I give them a fright," he mocked, taking on the swaying verse of the nurse's accent.

"You give me a fright all the time," Jaycee sighed. The trip had been both upsetting and a waste of time. Yet again, she'd come up short.

Chapter Twenty-Nine

The six o'clock newscast began with a potentially potent wildfire that had just broken out in some brushland along coastal Ventura County. The area was still recovering from another massive charring, and weather conditions weren't promising. It was hot and dry, with Santa Ana winds expected to gust at fifty miles per hour over the next several days. Crews were on high alert.

Jaycee waited for her cue. She was toward the end of the A block, on standby in the studio. Finally, the anchors got to her intro. The producer in the booth told her to standby.

"Tonight, a stepped-up police effort to find whoever's responsible for the brutal deaths of three women in Los Angeles nightclubs. Our Jaycee Wilder has been working this story and joins us now live with exclusive information, Jaycee?"

Jorge Pelloni tossed to her with an expectant expression. Jaycee nodded into the camera and began the story she and Ben had prepared.

"That's right, Jorge, while we know of three murders, police are not ruling out the possibility of more victims." Short and sweet, right to the point.

"Package is up," the producer said into her earpiece. Jaycee listened to her own voice tell the viewers of the formation of a task force. The first sound bite was from the chief during the presser. Jaycee added an audio track clearly stating the exclusive nature of Barton's interview.

She watched the monitor, waiting for him to appear in the story. He looked good. Jaycee squinted at the frame, pleased that his face came through so nicely on camera. Barton was professional and able as he confirmed the likelihood of additional victims. She hoped his haters were watching him battle back with grace.

"Stand by," said her producer. Jaycee readied her face for her tag. Once she heard the outcue of Barton's final sound bite, she began. "Police are not releasing the identities of other potential victims, nor will they say if there have been additional notes left behind. The task force will be sharing resources with other departments in the event of a similar crime occurring outside of its jurisdiction. Jorge?"

Jaycee waited. This was Jorge's cue to ask a question. All he had to do was read it from the teleprompter; she'd already scripted it out. "So, Jaycee," he began, all buttoned up and earnest as he pretended to care about loose women killed in clubs he wouldn't allow his Pekinese to piss on. "It's not as though police can shut down these nightclubs; they remain free to operate as normal?"

"Exactly, right, Jorge," Jaycee nodded. "Because of that, the task force is also issuing a plea to anyone who frequents these particular nightclubs. Be alert, be careful, and report anything or anyone of note right away. Live in the studio, Jaycee Wilder, ABC 12 News."

The anchors moved on to a two-shot to tease the stories coming up next. A series of commercials followed.

Jaycee unhooked the mic from the collar of her dress and walked back into the newsroom. She could see Ben in Clare's office. What was that?

The newsroom was emptying out. The night crews had already dispersed to work on their stories, and the late show producers were busy putting together the rundowns for their newscasts. No one really acknowledged her exclusive. She twisted her mouth as she plunked down into a chair. Her nose for news had always been impeccable. Maybe Barton was right. Even though the families of these girls would carry on in utter devastation, the public at large had already written them off as salacious and unsavory. Sure, it was fodder for discussion during cocktails on a Saturday night, but for most people with nine-to-five jobs, a mortgage, and daycare bills, this class of society was forgettable.

They truly were Throw Away Girls.

Jaycee's mood was darkening. All the care and effort she'd put into her coverage. For what? Even Clare seemed so preoccupied with Ben she wondered if she'd even watched her story. Whatever! Fuck them all. She buckled down at her computer and angrily dashed off a list of questions for Barton. She wanted him back on camera to discuss a few more things. Up next: Did the method of death match for each victim? Could police predict size or height of the suspect? How about the angle from which the killer delivered his blows? All questions she would ask Barton the next time she saw him. She printed out the sheet and logged off her computer. Packing up her bag, she found her car keys and got up to leave.

"Hold it right there, care bear," Ben said. He and Clare were closing in on her. She hid the sheet of questions behind her back.

"What's up? I was just heading home. Is there something going on?" Jaycee always extended her shift if there was breaking news to cover.

"No," Clare began. "We're set here. Your story was excellent. There are obvious follow-ups for us to pursue."

Huh? *For us to pursue?*

"That would be for *me* to pursue, correct?" Jaycee could feel her head begin to pound. She was pissed. All this work, for what?

Clare and Ben looked uncomfortable, as if she had a giant zit on her nose, but neither wanted to point it out. "What's going on with you two?"

"You're not going to like this, but I won't take any bullshit." Clare was already expecting a fight.

"Clare, no," Jaycee was prepared to battle to the death to stay on this story. She glared at Ben, already blaming him for telling Clare what she'd been up to. He shook his head like, "Don't blame me."

"Please don't take me off this! Come on! Give me a few more days at least. Why would you punish me for being aggressive on a big story? I don't get it! I'm pushing my source…"

"Jaycee, listen." Clare stepped closer and interrupted her protest. "It's not that. Your work is everything I expect it to be. I would do this anytime a story got too hot for any of my reporters, not just you. I am demanding we—collectively—take some precautions."

Jaycee twisted her head. She hadn't revealed the note left on her car, nor did Clare know about her visit with Olive, her trip to the nightclubs with Zander or—if Ben didn't spill the beans—to the hospital to see Fiona. Either time. So why was she suddenly taking precautions?

Barton!

"Don't even…" she started, her voice deep and hostile. "He called you, didn't he?"

Clare wasn't about to pit her reporter against a detective. She bowed out as gracefully as possible. "I'd be a shitty boss if I didn't take your safety seriously. Like I said, I'd do it for any of you. Even this guy if I had to." She elbowed Ben to lighten the moment. He pretended to double over in pain. Jaycee wasn't playing.

"Is this a question of my job being at stake?" she said, her face reddening.

"That's up to you," Clare told her.

Jaycee nodded. This was hardball. She worked the angles in her head. She wanted a compromise. "If I agree to cool it, will you agree to let me go with one more story? When it's ready to be told?" Jaycee wanted Fiona on camera. Barton had brought her in for that purpose. If the surviving Throw Away Girl was to go on television, he wanted it to be with Jaycee. She wouldn't give that up. Not without a showdown.

Clare mulled it over. "So, you agree to back off with covering this every day? I want you back in the rotation tomorrow covering other stories. You okay with that?"

"No," Jaycee told her. "But it doesn't sound like I have a choice."

"There's one more thing," Clare continued. She looked behind her for Ben to step in.

"Your chariot awaits," he said with a flourish. "I'm Ben, and I'll be your driver this evening, M'Lady." The freckles on his nose crinkled as he tried to look like an upper crust servant. It broke the tension.

"Good lord," Jaycee sighed. "For how long?"

"For now," Clare told her, sliding her hand down Jaycee's arm. "Only 'cause I care about your scrawny ass making it home safely. I won't risk you. Him…" she popped Ben lightly on the arm again. "…I'd hand over with an apple in his mouth, but not you."

Jaycee crumpled the paper behind her back into a ball and tossed it into the trash. Blowing by Ben, she told him she'd be waiting in his Explorer. Clare sighed in relief, making her way back to her office. "What the hell am I going to do without you," she tossed back over her shoulder. "Fucking Costa Rica, really?"

"Love you, too, Big C," Ben grinned. He bent over and plucked out the paper from atop an Oreo cookie wrapper. His eyes skimmed the contents. Damn girl was obsessed.

* * * *

"Go grab a drink, I'm going to change." Jaycee threw her purse onto the kitchen counter and sauntered into her bedroom to climb out of her work clothes. She walked past the guest bedroom and pulled the door shut. Just in case.

"You need to spruce this place up, Jay Bird," Ben yelled, as he opened and shut kitchen cabinets. "Don't you know Sherwin Williams' "Hello Yellow" is the hot new trend in kitchen paint? This is too drab to properly display your style and fabulousness."

"I'm too tired to be fabulous." Jaycee appeared in the living room in Victoria's Secret pajama pants and a tank top. "And this is total crap." She flopped down onto the sectional, moving magazines and newspapers onto the coffee table and out of her way.

"What, your kitchen? It's a bit dull, but I wouldn't go all the way to crap."

"No, Ben, not my kitchen. What's crap is the fact that Clare thinks I need a babysitter."

"Oh, can it, you little wench. She cares about you. Can't you see that?"

"I feel like I'm being kept from doing my job. Why put me on the I-Team, and then as I'm doing exactly what I need to do to tell a story, bench me?" Jaycee wound her hair into a bun and secured it with an elastic. "If I were a dude we wouldn't be in this position."

"If you were a dude, I'd be trying to get you drunk and take advantage of your weakened state." Ben retrieved two

268

wine glasses from the cabinet above the stove. "Red or white?"

"Don't care," she said.

Ben popped the cork on a good Merlot and poured. He filled both glasses and sauntered over to the couch. "Here," he handed the glass to Jaycee.

"Thanks," she muttered. Her eyes stared out at the darkening skies. The nightlights of Los Angeles were just beginning to twinkle to life. "If Clare puts Derek back on this story I'm going to lose my shit," Jaycee said through a tightly drawn mouth.

"Don't worry," Ben joked. "Derek's been trying to expose a Hispanic crime ring funneling in fake Cartier watches. I had to edit a tease for it last week. He's accounted for."

"Lord," Jaycee sighed. "Fake watches." She shook her head in disbelief. "So, we'd rather expose skinny teenagers tucking fake watches into their assholes and crossing the border than a killer slashing away at innocent women?"

"Hey, don't discriminate against teenagers or assholes. Both have an audience, Jay Bird. This is L.A., after all."

She smirked at him. Swallowing a full mouth of wine, Jaycee leaned her head against the plush backing of her Pottery Barn couch. She looked around her. Her beautiful condo, furnished with high-end pieces and stylish touches, was a source of pride. She'd worked hard for the nicer things in life, moving her way up the ladder by being aggressive and hard charging in the field. The Los Angeles

TV market was a sweatshop and Jaycee had sharpened her claws to cling to the top. Why was that suddenly a bad thing? Why would Barton shun her? Her mind spun in a fast circle fueled by disappointment and frustration.

"Don't hate me if I'm not in the mood tonight. I'm tired, Ben. How 'bout we call it a day." It wasn't often Jaycee didn't enjoy the light-hearted banter with her friend, and she had never asked him to leave before. "I'm sorry."

"I'm supposed to hang with you until Van the Man comes home," Ben told her. "Clare's orders."

"Clare's orders can go fuck themselves."

"Ouch," Ben reared back. "Float like a butterfly but sting like a bee."

Jaycee felt the red wine untying knots in her tongue. Stuff she would normally tuck away was about to break out. Ben was usually the one she dumped on, sharing her deepest thoughts about life, family, and the horrors of their job. She told the stories of death, desperation, and grueling human suffering every day while Ben took pictures of it. They had a kinship most people would never understand. Inexplicably, Jaycee's eyes grew misty.

"I have only a few people in this world, Ben," she made it sound like a confession. "When something really great happens, I tell you. And now, Van. I've jumped cities so often I don't even remember my old addresses. I don't have time for silly girlfriends who only want to shop and bitch about how fat they are."

"Neither do I," he sniffed.

"What I mean is that I pour my heart into my work. And it backfired." She listlessly threw one arm over her forehead. "Trusting Barton was a mistake. I've never been screwed by a source like this before."

Ben pursed his lips in thought. "Actually, Jay Bird, maybe he's doing you a solid here."

"In what way?" she asked, peeking out at him through her elbow.

"Saving your skinny butt, for one!" he exclaimed. "Maybe he and Clare pulled you off to save your life. She's not fucking around here; she's straight up worried about your safety. Could care less about mine, but whatevs, I'm good with that. And Elaine is asking questions, too. You should know I had to talk her down from calling Clare herself."

"What are you talking about?" Jaycee's ire was piqued. "Elaine Topsham? Worried about me? Why in the world?" she asked, not seeing the concern she had caused with their conversation about the killer contacting reporters.

"She said you asked her some weird questions about being contacted by the killer."

"Elaine told you that?" Realization sunk in. Of course! That's why she had been sticking her hawk neck into Ben's window after the presser. Tattling on a colleague! What the hell was going on with the media in Los Angeles? Why was everyone turning on her?

"Everyone else can cover this story and then leave it at work," he began.

"Really, Ben!" she jumped off the couch. "Because I care about these girls, I'm a loose cannon suddenly?" Her eyes blazed with anger tinged with the sting of a hard truth. "Is that what everyone's saying? That I can't do my job because I'm emotionally attached to this story? Because I worked my ass off for an exclusive, I'm some deranged wingnut who needs to be shut away for my own good?"

"Jaycee, calm down…"

"Fuck you, Ben! Fuck you! I can take care of myself; I've been doing it a very long time. I don't need you, or Barton, or Clare, or Elaine to hold my hand. I'm a smart, tough reporter, and I've done nothing more than anyone else to cover a story!"

"He wants you to back off," Ben said softly, slipping his hands down her shoulders.

"Yeah, I know, he won. Barton won." Jaycee tried to wriggle away. She didn't want to be touched.

"No," he held her tightly, his long fingers digging into the flesh connecting her bicep to her armpit. "Not Barton." His eyes were clouded and throwing off an oddly feral glow in Jaycee's dusky living room.

"The killer. The killer wants you to back off. You need to shut the fuck up for once and listen!"

Chapter Thirty

She needed space to breathe and to free herself from a physical grip. She couldn't bear hands on her. Jaycee moved swiftly down the hallway toward her bedroom. How did Ben know? Who told her? It must've been Barton. She shook her head in rage. Both he and her boss were labeling her a reactionary novice, a risk to both herself and the investigation. It was both humiliating and more irritating than a third-degree burn.

"You can't see it, Jay Jay, you're too close." Ben was following her, his long legs closing the distance. She could feel his heat on her back. She thrust her arms at him to keep him away.

"I was doing my job!"

"You were putting yourself on a chopping block!" he sputtered. "You're throwing away your future for a bunch of whores!"

Jaycee squared her shoulders and turned so fast Ben's torso bumped her and then bounced off. He was markedly stunned and stepped back.

"Don't you dare call them whores," she growled at him, her voice low with intensity. "They had parents, Ben. Families. They had lives. That girl in the hospital? Fiona? She loves her daughter so much her name is tattooed on her wrist. Did you know that?" In spite of trying to clamp her teeth together, Jaycee's lower lip quivered with emotion. "Did you know these *whores* were doing exactly what the men were doing? It's not fair! Why aren't they getting ripped apart by some psycho? Huh? Why are these women targeted for liking the same shit the *m*...*"

He flew at her. Jaycee swallowed the rest of her tirade as she became cemented by shock. His body hurled her shoulders back into the door of the guest room she had pulled shut. The stupid lock had never worked properly. It gave under the strain of her body and popped the door wide open. She saw Ben's eyes move behind her. They scanned left and then moved slowly right. His mouth fell open as utter consternation jolted the heat of the moment. Jaycee braced for the condemnation.

She slumped into the wood of the paneled door. Ben stumbled by her and into the heart of the room. He did a slow circle in place, awed by what was revealed.

"Olivia Pope," he whistled, "Olivia Pope done moved into your guest room, Jay Bird. I haven't seen this much crazy since *Scandal* went on hiatus."

Jaycee's mouth turned down. She moved defensively toward the corkboard on the wall opposite the bed and placed her body in front of the pictures, newspaper clippings, arrows, post-it notes, and marker scribbles that— to the average person—might resemble a kindergartner's foray into the haphazard art of mural design. To Jaycee, the diagrams, question marks, photos, dates, and names all made perfect sense.

"You've been a very busy girl."

Jaycee nodded. In an effort to keep up with all branches of this case, she'd moved it into her home.

Pictures of the Throw Away Girls were tacked on the wall next to articles about their murders and then sprinkled with hand-written notes she'd added sporadically whenever a new thought or question entered her mind.

"You see?" she asked him softly.

"See what? I see quite a lot here."

"No, Ben," Jaycee went to stand next to him. She pointed to a picture of Zoe she'd cut from the *L.A. Times*. "I want you to see *them*."

She took his arm and pulled him over to the wall. She gripped Ben's finger in her own and then traced the picture with their hands. "Zoe Statler. She was nominated for teacher of the year. Her dad still paid her bills."

Jaycee moved their joined hands over to the picture of Sara Walsh. "Sarah Walsh," she said softly. "She loved animals. If she'd gotten better grades in high school, she may have become a vet."

Their fingers moved south. Jaycee stopped on another small square picture. "Mackenzie Drew," she drew a sharp, sad breath. "Her friends called her Mac Attack."

Jaycee turned Ben's hand until his palm rested on her heart. "And you've already met Fiona," she told him. "Her daughter's name is Bella. She's wondering where her mom has gone."

Ben's jaw was set but his body had turned soft against hers. Gone was the wild anger that had forced its way into Jaycee's investigative shrine.

"Now do you see? They aren't just whores, Ben. They were people. And they deserve justice. That's what I was trying to give them."

Despite working side by side for years, in cramped live trucks and edit bays, their bodies were closer than they'd ever been before, their breath mingled below sorrowful features. Theirs was a friendship that had just been scraped raw. Would it survive?

Jaycee waited. She could not gauge what his reaction would be; she'd just seen a side of Ben that rocked her to the core. He could say the same about her.

In a long, fluid sweep of his arms, Ben wrapped her so tightly against him Jaycee's air squeezed out of her. She inhaled. He smelled of cedar and birthday cake. A homey warmth enveloped her. With her friend Ben, she was always safe.

Ben placed his chin atop her head nestled into his chest. He swayed gently in the moment.

"Jay Bird," he said against her hair.

"Yeah?"

"No matter what happens, I want you to know one thing."

"Okay," she said, her lips brushing the buttons of his striped Vineyard Vines perma-press shirt.

"You are the only woman I've ever loved. And I'm sorry."

She cocked her head beneath him.

"About everything."

Chapter Thirty-One

Hot air. Blinding pain. Sluggish limbs.

Van rolled from a fetal position but his temple connected with something hard and unforgiving. Liquid poured from his face in hard fast trickles that stung his eyes and tasted like thick sea salt. His legs pushed to extend but slid on cold concrete. His arms wouldn't budge.

Where am I, he thought. *What the hell happened?*

Van blinked through devastating pain behind his eyes. He wanted to rub them, clear away the grit and get a look at his surroundings. His brain ordered his arms to move. The handcuffs that linked him to a leaky radiator had no slack. The metal rattled. The subtle noise sounded like a tornado was howling through his injured body. And it was freaking hot in there!

Van maneuvered his head from its side, to its back, rolling his neck and trying like hell to think through a torturous veil of agony that sliced across his forehead. Warmish water trickled out at a steady pace.

Blood? Oh, God.

Breathe! In, out, and then do it again.

Strangely, his high school football coach was in his ear. Van faded back in time to listen to his grizzly-faced mentor. In his mind, Van was down on a bad play. The snap went sideways, and Van's elbow went with it. He was in pain; it was bad. On two arthritic knees, his coach snapped and popped into a crouch, so he was on level ground with his star center. He stared into his eyes through the grates of his helmet.

"Van, you just breathe now. In and out. And then you do it again."

Okay, coach, Van muttered in his head. *I'm okay. I wanna go back in.*

His eyes flew open; the football field vaporized into a foreign room, but he breathed. In and out. And he thought. *Come on, Van,* he told himself. *Think hard! Remember what happened.*

In a hot room. No air. Head wound.

Van recalled leaving work. It was late; he was closing the bar, the last employee to head home for the night. His shift had been normal, nothing out of the ordinary except for a nagging worry about Jaycee and the nightclub case. She wasn't herself. Van was concerned.

He turned to the left. A scuffling sound surprised him. He tried to holler out.

Sudden blackness. His coach was back in his face.

"Breathe, son, you stay with me now. Help is on the way, you just breathe. In, out, and then you do it again."

"I got this coach," Van tried to tell him.

He was still breathing, just like coach told him to, but he was getting dizzy, and could only imagine how much blood was leaking through his head.

Van shrieked like a caged tiger. It exhausted him. He cracked one eye. The overhead light was muted as it cut through one thin window. Otherwise, the room was sooty and obscure. He could see a dirty bed with no sheets and dark, oblong stains on the white mattress. On the other wall was a low desk with a mirror mounted to its back. A messy mix of tubes, crumpled Kleenex, and makeup jars littered the top. He looked down at his splayed legs. They felt dead. Van could see his pale blue work shirt had turned completely red. Every bit of him was dripping out; his energy was low, and his head foggy. All he wanted to do was go to sleep.

"Van," his coach was back. He shook his head. Why wasn't the game over yet? "Come on, kid, you breathe, in and out. Do it again. Stay with me, here, you're gonna be just fine. It's second and four, Van, come on, son, we need a first down!"

Just breathe. In and out. Do it again. *Okay,* Van thought, *I'm okay.* He suddenly realized there was a lump below his left haunch squared against the last rungs of the radiator.

His cell phone!

Reach, he told himself. *Reach those fingers around the metal cuff and grab the phone.* Van felt blindly along the ribbing of his jeans, seeking out the sliver of fabric at the top of his back pocket. Where was it!

He found it. Van coaxed two fingers down into what felt like an endless hole until his finger brushed the top of the square phone. He summoned strength. Goddamn it, he was struggling to breath, his air so shallow it made his lungs burn with hunger. Van wouldn't have been surprised if someone told him that was what dying felt like.

Coach's hands were on his head, pushing him up. "Van," he said, "we need you, the team needs you, *she* needs you…"

Van's eyes went wide. His fingers retreated into fists. She needs you.

She!

Jaycee! Oh my God. Of course, this was all about her, it always had been. Jaycee was in danger. Jaycee is next!

His eyes so badly wanted to close. No. He fought the exhaustion.

She needed him. His voice surprised him. He cried her name.

"Jaycee!"

"She needs you, son, just breathe. In and out, and then do it again," his coach wasn't letting him ride the blackout.

"Be still, Van," coach said. "Listen to your heart. It will always tell you what to do."

Suddenly, Van saw it like a movie was playing behind his eyes. Rewind. Look closely. Just before the crushing blow to his head in the empty parking lot, Van saw a flash of brown in the dull streetlight. Two brown boat shoes. Clean, neat, just-out-of-the-box brown leather.

"I know who," he slurred, on the border between unconscious and coherent.

The small room was silent around him. No yelling, no shouting, it was all peaceful and clear. He saw her smile, that beguiling grin that made his stomach clench. He went to her, to tuck a strand of blonde hair behind her ear. He kissed her soft cheek. It took the pain away. Too much pain.

"Shoes," he whispered to himself. "I know the shoes." Sperry Top-siders. Neat and perfect just like he was.

Oh God, he had to get to Jaycee. Warn her. Now!

"The shoes," he choked. "I know who did this...you have to find him…I know who the killer is…"

Van looked beyond the worn gray walls, piled high with cement blocks, and into another realm. He teetered between the two worlds. He saw his coach walking back to the locker room; his job here was done. The fans stirred in the stands, waiting for the big play, the hurl down the field that would win the game. Van was there, but he was so far away. He had to see this through first. Just one more play. He could do it. She needed him.

With every last speck of energy he dug from within himself, he spat out a name. No one was there to hear it.

He repeated it once as tears streaked down his cheeks. He needed to get to Jaycee before he lost her for good.

To him!

But he couldn't. He was just too tired. His fingers went still; he stopped reaching for that silly cell phone tucked way too deep.

The game was over, and Van just wanted to go home.

Chapter Thirty-Two

Her dreams were vivid and cartoonish. Overblown faces with distorted voices chased Jaycee until the chirpy burst of her cell phone cut through the disturbing jangle. Her head felt heavy like it did the morning after a liquor-fueled argument with Van. She reached for her cell but did not recognize the number. She was afraid not to answer. If someone was calling her this early, it must be important.

"Jaycee Wilder," she stated, trying to sound alert.

"Get up girl," came the response. "Shit's going down!"

Huh? The voice sounded just like Ben's. A series of sharp knocks on her door followed. Jaycee shot out of bed and raced toward the hallway. What the hell was going on? It dawned on her that the space beside her in bed was empty. The third bedroom she passed on the way to the door, also empty, and the couch was unfilled, too.

Where was Van?

The pounding on the door resumed.

"Coming!" she yelled out. Taking a quick look through the peephole, she confirmed it was Ben and let him in. He was all freshly pressed with cargo shorts and a wrinkle-free navy blue polo t-shirt. If she felt like crap, he looked fresh as a garden daisy.

"What's wrong? What are you doing here?" she squinted at him.

"We gotta roll, darlin', something's shaking over on Hollywood. Consider it your last hurrah, and move your ass before Clare changes her mind and sends Derek, the dunce."

Jaycee latched onto a few keywords. Hollywood. Clare. Derek.

"Another attack?"

"I dunno know for sure. I just know we have to fly."

"Okay," Jaycee mumbled. She scrambled back to her bedroom to get dressed, her thoughts on overdrive. Another girl in a club? Is the girl dead? How come no one called her? She plucked her cell phone off the messy bed and confirmed there had been no calls, and no messages.

"Ben, no one called me!" she yelled out to the living room where Ben was waiting.

"I know. Clare called me instead," he hollered to her. "Remember, I'm technically your bodyguard, and she wants me with you on the scene. Consider me your own personal Kevin Costner, and you're my badass Whitney Houston, God rest her soul."

Jaycee poked her head around the corner just as Ben kissed two fingers and then put them up to the sky.

"Almost ready," she told him. Stepping into a pair of freshly dry-cleaned black pants, Jaycee threw on a green sleeveless Ann Taylor shirt, added a thin chain around her neck and two small silver hoop earrings. She threw her oversized Kate Spade bag over her shoulder, confirmed her makeup pouch was tucked inside and hustled back to the living room while running a brush through her hair. It was still ruffled from her pillow, but smooth enough to tuck behind her ears.

Nagging questions jostled her hastened departure. Why would Clare have such an abrupt change of heart? Where the hell was Barton's tip? Why hadn't anyone called her directly?

"Come on, Jay Bird," Ben threw an arm around her shoulder to lead her out the door. "We gotta fly! Don't want to get scooped on this."

* * * *

"What phone did you call me from?" Jaycee asked once they were settled into his Explorer, and she was applying makeup in the visor mirror.

"This old junker," he told her, holding up a cell phone she'd never seen before. "Dropped my work phone into my koi pond. Don't tell Clare but the fish are using too much data." He was oddly sarcastic for such an early hour and a potentially grisly story to cover. Jaycee thrust her mascara wand back into its tube and grabbed her phone again. She scrolled through Twitter and Facebook, certain she'd find a breaking news alert somewhere. Social media was eerily quiet.

"What exactly did Clare tell you," she asked, turning toward Ben.

"That I needed to get you up and out A-SAP. Potential nightclub skan—" he caught himself. "Sorry, I mean victim." Ben looked over at her sheepishly. "See, I am

284

becoming a more evolved person. I will refrain from using the word skank to describe loose women."

"Much appreciated," Jaycee nodded.

"Then she told me the address, and I came to get you. They're waiting for us to confirm something's happening before they go blabbing all over the place. So keep this shit off your Twit-Book, for now." Twit-Book was their shortened version of Twitter and Facebook. Furiously fast posts were how they typically attacked breaking news in the field.

"And that, my little ladybug, is all I know."

"Okay," she looked back down at her phone. "No Twit-Booking. For now. There's nothing yet anyway. Not a single post anywhere."

Jaycee did a quick recount of her expedited exit from her condo and the irregular absence of Van. This day was off to a very weird start.

"Van didn't come home last night," she said absently.

"Really?" Ben glanced at her. "Did he have an early audition or something?"

Jaycee shook her head. "No, not that I know of." Rarely, Van would throw back a few too many after work and end up sleeping in the club's office on the musty futon, but he always called to let her know.

"Did you call him?"

"No."

"Why?"

She shrugged. "If he's too busy to let me know where he is, then I'm too busy to worry about tracking him down." In truth, she was more worried than busy. She'd give it a while longer. Then she'd rip his balls off. Van knew better than to stay out all night long without telling her first.

Her fingers punched up her contacts. James Barton. She looked at his name, stone-faced and hurt. She thought they were a team. Maybe he really was just a broken cop from Boston who made promises he couldn't keep. She'd tried to lift him up. His loss. She would not call him. She'd tell the story without him.

This one last time.

With no traffic this early, they breezed along. They were approaching the rougher section of Hollywood Boulevard. Drunks in baggy clothes weaved around stop signs and over curbs, still on the hunt for a place to sleep off whatever they poisoned their bodies with the night before. Jaycee recognized the slip of an alley between two familiar-looking dark green buildings. One of the gross clubs she'd blown fifty bucks at the other night. "What's the address?" she asked Ben impatiently.

"Next block, on the right," he told her. "Almost there."

Jaycee expected police lights, yellow crime tape holding them back from the new scene, maybe even an ambulance hauling away the tattered remains of the latest Throw Away Girl. Instead, Ben lead them to another narrow alleyway bathed only in natural light supplied by the rising sun.

"Ben," she said expectantly, her stomach muscles clenched. "There's no one here; this can't be right." She felt nervous, but not truly fearful, not with Kevin Costner by her side.

"Jay Bird, come on!" Ben was already baling out of the rig and charging toward a creepy stairwell that looked like it might take them directly to the devil himself. Jaycee hesitated only a fraction of a second before her reporter's innate, sometimes reckless curiosity took over and had her scrambling out of her seatbelt. Nervous energy percolated through her as she mumbled nonsensical bursts of words her brain often used to settle itself down in precarious situations. Ben called her Mrs. Rainman.

"First I'm a ladybug," she rambled to herself, "then a Jay Bird. Jesus Christ, Ben, don't you know you can't mix a predator with a ..." her mouth slammed shut.

Olive.

I've been called kitten and bitch in the same encounter.

Nicknames.

The killer calls his girls nicknames.

Oh my God! Jaycee called up her wall of evidence: Questions, random thoughts, and notes she had attached to pictures of dead girls. Her burning need to find him before he found her.

Ben was yelling at her to hurry up. Her head swiveled in the direction of the scary stairs. She felt like the rope in a schoolyard tug-of-war contest, pulled between her own unwillingness to trust her gut, and the very real possibility she was losing her mind.

Sweet Ben? Her cherished gay friend who had seen her naked and barely flinched, who cut the edges off his bologna sandwiches just in case she wanted a bite. No! It couldn't be Ben.

A tall, thin man. Wears a black wig. No accent. No tattoos.

"Jaycee, get your ass over here. Now!"

She shook the crazy away and silenced her frantic mental clutter. In this moment, she would make a choice. She would trust. This case had her spinning from the beginning. She was all messed up. Dead wrong at every turn.

Shit! "I'm coming!" she called out. Jaycee reached around to shut the SUV'S door, and glanced into the back of the rig. Ben had taken his camera but forgotten the portable unit they sometimes used to go live from a scene when the truck couldn't get there. They might need it if this turned out to be something big and they broke into morning programming with breaking news. This could be huge! She was only sabotaging herself with this bizarre speculation. Ben was her partner, her trusted right-hand man in the trenches. They were a team, goddamn it, and it was their time to break this story despite getting dumped off it by both Clare and Barton.

Well, fuck them. Jaycee Wilder would get the goddamn story on her own, like she always had. And Ben would help her.

With a final decision made, Jaycee hoisted the TVU backpack around her shoulder and took her first step down into the stairwell.

Chapter Thirty-Three

The door to a basement apartment stood ajar. Jaycee peeked in. This was no nightclub and Ben had disappeared. Stuffy, humid air wrapped around her legs like a clammy hand as she stepped over the threshold. Eyes narrowed and adjusting to the soupy light of the small room; Jaycee's nose twitched as something kicked off a wicked stench. A good reporter perfected the art of breathing through the mouth to block out disgusting scents. She'd never forget the rancid essence of a hoarder found rotting inside a decrepit home. She hadn't eaten for two days after that. Or, the way the air was flavored by spilled gas at a car crash scene.

This was different. This room smelled like death.

She tried to back out of the threshold, this was gross but obviously not the scene of some suspected crime. She needed to find Ben. Where was the club? Where was the victim? Where was—

A vicious force struck between her shoulder blades and sent her stumbling forward hunched over and out of control. Her legs pumped wildly to keep up with the sudden momentum. Instinctively, Jaycee wrapped her tongue around her top teeth to protect them as she tumbled, head first, onto the rock-hard floor of the room, the TVU backpack spinning away into the open space. Her chest hit first, followed by a hard, fast meeting between concrete and the bone behind her chin.

She recoiled. There was no way to tell where the pain started; it enclosed her entire body.

So much for Kevin Costner! Where the hell was Ben? Jaycee carefully arched her back and got on all fours, taking one knee and using it to propel herself upward. She had to be alert and upright to face whoever or whatever had just attacked.

Just as she found the strength to stand, Jaycee perceived movement below the tiniest window she'd ever seen. Yes, something was moving on the floor. She tried desperately to make out a shape. Was it a rat? A street dog rummaging through scraps? Her heart lurched as the movement became more pronounced.

Was that…a *leg?* Really? A leg? Yes, she confirmed a long, jean-clad leg was bent. As it straightened, a low moan escaped from its owner. It sounded deep and guttural, not at all feminine, though she couldn't ignore the possibility that she was feet from the latest Throw Away Girl.

She had to act. She had to help!

She wasn't a reporter anymore; Jaycee now sought only to rescue, to save this poor soul. She bit back ghastly needles of discomfort that assaulted her own body to stretch out a hand.

"I'm here to help you," she called out. The crumpled leg did not move. Jaycee inched forward, her palms up. The light shifted, and her stomach went soft. The leg was atop a wide circle of red. Blood! She raced to the leg attached to a torso splayed sideways over an old-fashioned radiator shedding off curls of white paint. This was no Throw Away Girl. This was a man. A strong, thick man who was bleeding out. His red shirt was soaking wet and stretched across broad pectoral muscles.

God, she thought. If someone could take this guy down, I'm in serious trouble!

She had to get out. Jaycee knew this man needed immediate medical attention to survive. Her cell phone was locked in Ben's Explorer, of no help to her now.

Where the hell was Ben?

She tried searching for the source of the blood. He had thick hair that made it impossible to root out a gash, but the trajectory of the blood told her it had started up top. As she inspected closer, she noticed product held together waves of dark brown hair toward the back of his head that had been spared from the gore. She leaned down and gave it a sniff. Expensive-smelling. Both she and Van blew through hair product at an embarrassing pace. This dude obviously liked his style held.

Her mind told her to turn away from him, and his hair, and run. Fast! Get out of there and make the damn phone call.

Find Ben!

Still, she stayed. Her body—or perhaps her heart—prevented her from leaving. Something about this damaged man had a lock on her logic.

She couldn't leave him.

His eyes were tightly shut. She tried to make out his nose and mouth, but rivers of blood distorted it all. She looked at his neck. Was he wearing a necklace? A cross?

No. Nothing.

Shit!

She felt guilty doing it, but Jaycee forced herself to turn away. As she did, her eyes lowered and peered just to the left of the open collar on his red shirt. She noticed embroidery, a swoop of writing in a fancy loop-dee-loop pattern.

She squinted at the script. The fabric around it was blue. Light blue, just like the shirt Van wore to work that she ribbed him for because it matched his eyes. My baby blue boy, she would giggle as she sprinkled kisses across his supple lips.

My baby...blue...boy.

Oh God! Jaycee dropped to her knees, not aware of the slapping sound her kneecaps made against the cold floor.

Van!

The heavy door to the apartment slammed shut. The nightclub killer stood against the wall, a bemused expression coloring his boyish face.

Chapter Thirty-Four

"Ben, thank God, help me! It's Van! He's hurt. He's really hurt…" Jaycee's throat felt scalded as she clambered to her feet and pointed down at her battered boyfriend. Tears broke from her eyes. Even as she pleaded for his help, Jaycee did not go to her friend. Just as her body would not allow her to leave the broken creature on the floor, it also would not carry her to the enemy. Deep inside her, she knew.

"I think it's time we had a little chat," he told her, his voice peculiarly altered, the flirty lilt replaced by a flat malevolence. Jaycee gaped at the astonishing transformation. Ben was not here to save her, or Van. The tender face she loved had morphed into a beast she did not recognize.

Jaycee stared. Try as she might, there were no words to support her scuttled thoughts. Her mussed mind was overwhelmed by sadness.

"Let's begin with a proper introduction," he said tartly, walking toward her. Jaycee shrunk back, putting herself between Ben and Van.

"From this moment forward, complete honesty, I promise." He crossed his heart with a pointer finger. "I'm Samuel Greene, and it's my pleasure to finally meet you. I've been a fan for years." He threw out a prim hand, his face full of teeth and giddiness. It was too much for her to take. Jaycee tested her hand, squeezed it into a fist.

And then she smacked him in the face as hard as she could, landing a direct hit on his nose. Blood slipped out one nostril. Ben grunted in surprise and cupped his face as he bent over his knees to catch the trickle of red. Jaycee scrambled around him, falling on her hip, a grimacing tweak she felt all the way to her bone.

She rose, tripped again, as her hand reached wildly for the door knob. She heard a groan behind her. Ben was up and moving; his heavy steps fell just behind her. Her neck snapped backwards. A torturous burst of pain stabbed the base of her skull over to her shoulder blade. Her hand rushed to her hair to search for his fingers, aching to stab his flesh with a fingernail, force him to release her. She connected with his wrist, but her wiry friend was too strong. He stood above her. Drops of his blood splattered onto her face, into her mouth, and down her throat. She gagged on the salty liquid, felt vomit tickle her tonsils, and promptly passed out.

* * * *

"Hi," he said once her eyes slit open again.

She sat up. They were still in the muggy apartment, but the lighting was changing. A golden glow of daylight poured through the small window. With horror, she could now clearly see the extent of Van's blood loss, and the threat of a new wound. Ben was holding a slim knife next to Van's wrist. Its blade rested just above his bulging artery.

"Let's try this again, shall we?" he began. "I'm Samuel Greene. It's nice to meet you."

Jaycee glared at him. She refused to play his game.

"What are you doing, Ben? What the *fuck* are you doing?" Jaycee's voice was hushed with revulsion.

He sighed. "Being honest with you here, Jay Jay, just like I promised. My real name is Samuel Greene, not nearly as cool as Ben Roderick, but true nonetheless."

"Sure, and my real name is Mother Theresa," Jaycee coughed back at him. "Being perfectly *honest* with you, I don't give a shit what you call yourself. You're a monster!"

"As I was saying," he said, clicking his tongue to chide her for acting up. "Now pay attention, Jay Jay, this is the story of my life! You've only been asking for it as long as I've known you. All nosy and bossy pants, snooping around in my business. So, here goes." He paused for effect.

"It may sound a bit cliché, but I am the product of abusive parents. I learned at a very young age that if I didn't take care of myself, no one else would…"

It was true. Her nature was to ask questions and learn what made people tick. She had practically begged him to confide more of what he had described as a rough start. It was all a smokescreen, an excuse. She wouldn't have it. She interrupted his march down memory lane.

"I had shitty parents, too, a lot of people do. Fortunately, most of us are still able to grow up, keep our real names, and have an honorable life that doesn't involve kidnapping your best friend, assaulting her boyfriend, and murder…" she could barely believe what she was saying. "And murder innocent women. Don't you dare blame your actions on mommy and daddy issues!"

"No, no, you're not listening! I'm not blaming, I'm *explaining*," he treated her as he would a moronic toddler put in a timeout. Van stirred. Jaycee felt relief that he was still alive. But for how much longer? She attempted to hurry him along.

"I will only listen to you if you get away from him. Put the knife away, Ben, and then I'll listen."

Ben ignored her entirely. She became acutely aware he had waited a long time to share his depraved truth. He would not be rushed.

"I'm grateful, actually," he continued. "Maybe if they'd been even a smidge better than they were, I'd never be as intelligent and driven as I am today."

He was mad, the worst kind of psychopath: one with an enormous ego. She prodded him. "Where are your parents now? My, they'd be so proud."

"They've been dead for a long time."

"Well, sorry about that, but…" she trailed off. "Don't tell me. Your doing?"

"Yes, my doing. But they deserved it!" He was defensive. "They were trash, Jay Jay, total white trash, complete with a broken-down trailer and rusted-out cars in the yard. They were what we would call a hot mess."

With nary a shred of remorse or a lick of self-loathing, he went on to describe his life. His earlier years spent traveling through various cities, stopping to take art classes and learn photography, maybe kill a couple of women if the urge arose.

"I have always been artsy; my father hated that. He wanted Tom Brady but got Neil Patrick Harris." Ben sucked his lips in. "He would slap me silly simply because I preferred a paint brush over a football."

"I'm truly sorry that happened to you." Jaycee offered.

"Anyway, TV news was an obvious, creative choice for me. And," he looked at her sheepishly, "a chance to keep tabs on how my cases were being investigated."

Jaycee looked away. He was everything Barton had warned her about and more.

"I enjoyed working with you, Jay Bird. You are truly great at what you do. We made good TV together, and I'll miss it."

She shook her head. Unbelievable. He obviously felt human connections like affection and admiration, yet was undaunted by them. He may like her, but he'll kill her anyway.

"I take pictures of beautiful women I see in the world," he made an eerie, thick sound. "I appreciate a good-looking woman, you know, I admire their angles and curves."

"But you don't kill them all?" she asked, determined to uncover more of his motivation. "Only the Throw Away Girls. Why?"

Ben smiled at her with a ghoulish, Freddy Krueger snarl. "More on that in a minute," he said, reminding her of their anchors just before a commercial.

"I have another question, then," she would try to flush him out.

"Hit me."

"Are there more? More than just here in L.A." She recalled the research she'd done; the bodies of wasted women discovered in other cities, all of them punished with a violent demise.

"More pictures? Yes, many more. I use both fancy cameras and my simple work cell phone. That's why I had to ditch it."

Jaycee scanned the walls. Dozens of pictures displayed the faces of random women. It made her sick to think of him taking pictures of strangers on his work phone. He had two lives going at the same time, right next to her.

"Fancy pictures, Ben, but I meant are there more victims? How many girls have you killed in this shape-shifting life of yours?"

His eyes looked to the ceiling. He appeared to do some math in his head. It made Jaycee shudder. There were more. She knew it. Barton knew it. How many stories had she done in her career that ended with the phrase...*police are looking at the potential of more victims.*

"A few more," he stated flatly. "Although I don't really keep track. They're just worthless pigs, anyway. Trust me, none of them have been worth the massive amount of coverage you've done on them. My other stations put the sluts' murders in the B block, Jay Bird. You made the whores the lead. It was becoming a problem."

It's all your fault.

Jaycee exhaled loudly through her nostrils. Too much. Simply too much to take. She slumped into herself, peering into the darkness, unable to help Van and knowing in that moment, intuitively, that she was all alone. Whatever twisted tournament he had brought her to, she was the only player on the court. Disbelief felt like a chunk of concrete on her heart. She had been a fool. For all this time, she had been a complete and total trusting idiot. Ben was sick. Insane. Her best friend was holding her hostage and her boyfriend was dying. She wanted to run, but he'd only catch her again. She looked at him with hooded eyes.

She was going to die here.

"I thought you were my friend, Ben. My very best friend. What happened to you?"

"That's what I'm trying to explain," he said sharply. He was getting annoyed with her; the knife pushed into Van's skin. Jaycee instinctively sat up. The air felt electric; his body chemistry was changing. Her eyes begged him to stop.

"Okay, then. Explain. But please spare me from the 'poor me, I was an unloved child bit.'" She risked a hard jab. Ben laughed at her but pulled back on the knife.

Jaycee exhaled. She'd bought some time.

"Sorta kinda," he said, amused. "I just want this to come together for you. For you to see what and who I am. You've earned it, for sure, all your hard investigative work. Your snooping and digging should end in a just reward, right? But I want you to understand why I had to adapt, make things happen in my own way." Ben's expression grew fervid. "I did everything in my power to prevent this from happening." He seemed genuinely pensive about that.

Jaycee nodded. "You put the warning on my car," she told him.

"Well, yeah!" His eyes flashed. "You and that stupid cop with a stumpy hand! Now, normally, I admit I am in awe of your wily ways of uncovering a story. The police have perspective, right? It's just a job to them, nothing more than a bad paycheck and some flimsy forensics. But you, Jay Bird," he cocked his head and gave her an atta-girl smile. "You were getting too close to the whores; you cared about the trashy, useless girls." Ben's hand shook with disappointment and a bubbling rage.

"No reporter had ever come looking for me like that. Your trip to City Hall to shakedown poor Zander," he clucked his tongue. "I tried to stop you. It was the investigative wallpaper that finally sealed it for me. You weren't going to stop until you had me by the balls."

All at once, it slid into place for her. Devastation was complete and utterly ruthless. She was being punished for being too good, for approaching her job as she always had, seeking justice for the slighted.

"You saw me that night," she couldn't look at him. "In that club not far from here."

"I saw the Italian mobster mistress version of you, yes."

"I was trying to disguise myself."

"I would recognize you in a monkey suit."

Jaycee gulped and looked around her. Women who resembled Fiona, Zoe, Sarah, Mackenzie, and even herself smiled with frozen faces plastered on the walls. "We interviewed Zoe's parents, Ben."

"Again, not by choice," he clarified. "And really, I could've done without the field trip to the ICU, too. All that energy and medicine poured into saving her pathetic life. You just know she has no health insurance." He sniffed gently like an elitist psycho.

Fiona had recognized him. Even in her drugged-out, numbed condition, her tormented soul felt fear.

"Anyway," he continued, his satisfaction growing that finally, she would know everything he'd done to avoid having to hurt her. "Usually, I can slip out of town when the fuzz closes in, and start over somewhere else. As you know, folks in our business are fickle, we get bored when the blood dries up. Once I stop, the media back off and move on. The forensics come back clogged and useless. Cops call it cold and shuffle the case to the bottom drawers of their desks. That's how it works. How it's *always* worked. Until now. Until you, Jay Bird."

"The police," she sputtered, shaking her head, repulsed and suddenly very weak. "They have your prints, Ben! Forensics are slow, but they're solid. They'll find you!"

He shook his head. She wasn't getting it. "I don't exist," he said calmly. "I am a rumor, a ghost story, a bad dream. I'm like the shifting sand on a beach, Jay Jay. I am here, but I'm not."

"You have records, Ben. You have paychecks and bank accounts, you can't just expunge your life every few years."

"Oh, but I can. I do. I talk my way into jobs based on my charm and talent, not a detailed bio. Sometimes I tell people all my shit burned up in a house fire. My names change, and I move around. I don't put down roots and leave nothing behind. It's like chasing a shadow. As for Barton," he smirked at her. "Your 'source' who is one sip away from the unemployment line or a straight jacket, yes, he may have my DNA, but they have a gazillion other splats to work through first. Honey, I am a product of an overextended system."

He puffed out with such pride Jaycee got chills. "Why L.A., why now?" she was trying to follow the route of a killer, a strange, loping journey of dolefulness and decay.

He shrugged. "The timing is like semantics; you don't really need to get lost in the importance of that. I picked L.A. because I hadn't lived here yet. I landed the job with you, shot some decent shit, had a few laughs, and the rest is history. But, please know this," Ben lifted the blade from

303

Van's wrist. Its steely sharpness bobbed up and down, carelessly nicking Van's forearm. Tiny pricks grew red and oozed new blood. Jaycee began to tremble.

"I couldn't stop even if I wanted to. I don't have a choice, it's like a calling. My life's work. Keep haulin' ass like a heat-seeking missile. Only, I chase Throw Away Girls. Unfortunately, they're a plentiful target."

Jaycee wiped at her face with her shoulder. Her entire body ached with the effort of putting everything in order. "Ben, you promised you'd be honest with me. Full disclosure?"

"I am being honest."

"Have you forgotten you're gay? That trip to Mexico with Blake?"

Ben nodded. "Follow me here," he told her. "But in the spirit of true honesty, will you admit something to me first? Will you admit that you are a bit hard on men? I picked up on that right away. You're not even nice to Van. Poor guy," he tapped at his chest with the knife. "Anyway, I needed to make myself unthreatening to you, gain your trust. I mean, I get it, you were basically abandoned by your own father so that gives you an excuse, but do you agree with my psychological assessment?"

She shrugged her shoulders. "You didn't answer my question."

"Am I gay?" he repeated, but she got the point. Another lie.

"Blake?" she spat at him. The sweet boyfriend with whom he'd taken an imaginary trip to Mexico.

"Just a name, Jay Jay, a random name to feed your curiosity and give me some space to get my work done. And a good cover for that gash on my face. That was from Zoe. She was like a bear cub, trying to be all tough and scary. Even at the end."

Jaycee's stomach rolled at her name. "By work, you mean murder."

"Yes, but only to stop the cycle!" His face became hot and diseased. He was suddenly angry again.

Jaycee sensed a vulnerability. She pressed it, trying to make him squirm.

"Who are the Throw Away Girls, Ben?"

She felt her cheeks flush as Ben grew more agitated. He sunk the knife into the surface of Van's wrist, mobilized by a seething hatred for someone in his life who had hurt him deeply. Propelled by revenge, Jaycee figured. She could sense a ruthless need to scourge the force that had ruined him.

His parents, she circled back around to the beginning. He said they were dead.

Start there.

Ben heaved a release of building rage inside him. Jaycee knew it was risky to push him into battle with a specter from his past, but she had to keep him talking. If he was talking, they were still alive.

"Tell me about them," she coaxed. "Your parents."

"Okay, Dr. Phil, but please understand I have planned for everything that's happening." He looked around and with a sweeping gesture, adjusted his statement. "Well, this here was an improv, but only because you gave me no choice." He looked pleased with himself for being able to think on his feet.

"How did your parents hurt you, Ben?"

"In every way possible," he said without hesitation. "But here's the thing, Jay Jay. I have learned to love my parents for providing a clear vision of my life's purpose. Because my mother sexually abused me when I was just a skinny little kid desperate for love, I knew what I needed to do. Everything happens for a reason, right?"

Jaycee's reporter experience was gluing his real story together. She slid that information right into the center of the report she was editing in her head. Reporters always started with the lead.

Ben's mother was the lead.

"Your mom was a Throw Away Girl."

"Oh, for sure!" Ben rumbled. "The original Throw Away Girl."

"How did you kill her?"

"That's not important," he dismissed the question.

"Every girl you find in a dark sex club, in every city you live in. They are all her." Jaycee's eyes glistened with the emptiness of his existence. He was just a scared kid pissed off that no one had ever loved him.

"Aren't they?"

Ben wasn't keen on any sort of emotional release. He shared his facts as though they were pathetic elements of someone else's problem. "Yes."

She knew it.

"And no," he went on, surprising her. "I admit that when I slaughter a pig, I do often pretend it's her. That gives me a temporary justice, but it's fleeting." Ben's slim nose crinkled as he tried to explain his motivation. "Consider it like being a CIA agent. I know how to defeat the enemy, but I have to be all secret and weird about it." His free hand twisted like a wizard giving a demonstration.

"I have to lie and move around a lot because the enemy is like a well-funded terrorist organization, always building the next generation of warriors. It's my job to find them before that happens."

Jaycee strained out a hoarse question. "You eliminate the Throw Away Girls before they can become your mother…"

Ben nodded enthusiastically. "Ding, ding, ding!" he raised his hand. "We have a winner! More accurately, Jay Jay," he tempered himself slightly. "Before they can become a mother at all. Any woman who seeks pleasure in the sick, fucked-up jungles of cheap sex and unnatural physical love can't be allowed to breed. So, I take them out before they can."

It was like a delirious version of ethnic cleansing. Ben visualized himself a biblical figure on a mission of purity.

That's how he justified his vile acts and why he would
never stop.

"That's why you leave a message behind," she said.
Barton had told her how killers sometimes use a note or
message to explain themselves.

"Pretty much," he confirmed. "That's it. That's the
whole story. I'm sorry for all of this, but…"

Jaycee nodded. She understood. "But you can't help
it," she said sorrowfully. "We're just collateral damage."
She looked at Van, who was now entirely still, his leg had
stopped moving, and round dots of blood had coagulated
along his forearm.

"Why him?" she pleaded for one more answer before
he killed them both. "Why would you hurt Van? Why not
just come after me?"

"It's like the last sound bite on a really good story," he
told her. "The one that ties it all together for the viewers.
Van will be playing the most critical role of his entire
career."

Her heart was broken. She could see the story Ben
would leave behind. The apartment full of evidence left
behind by a killer. The macabre pictures on the wall. The
man who had lured his girlfriend to her death, because she
was getting too close to uncovering the truth about his
murderous alter-ego.

Ben was telling the story of his life, but he swapped in
Van to take the heat.

"Because you saw my room," she whispered. "You went after Van last night."

Jaycee had expedited this. She'd forced him into acting faster and closer to home. She'd set up her own boyfriend. Van would be called a killer while Ben would move on to the next city, the next set of Throw Away Girls.

"I'm paid up here for months," he spared her from confirming her suspicion. "Perhaps someone may get around to cleaning this hovel and renting it again, or not. If they do and feel inclined to report it—you never know these days with people not wanting to get involved in such things—your buddy Barton or someone on his useless task force will get the call." Ben reached behind Van to undo the cuffs that pinned his arms to the radiator. Van didn't move.

"The big guy here is the nightclub killer. You're his final victim. Tragic murder-suicide, we cover them all the time. The cell in his back pocket is dead. There will be no dramatic final calls for help. Eventually, Barton will follow all the clues I have laid out here and make the connection. That fancy forensic stuff you mentioned? It will solve this crime by identifying the female remains as yours. Case closed. Barton will probably uncork a bottle of good scotch to celebrate his successful sleuthing."

Jaycee was breathing in short, rapid bursts. "But I thought you said I wasn't a Throw Away Girl? The picture? The message? You can't kill me, Ben, I'm nothing like your mother!"

"No, Jay Jay. You're not. That's why I'm not going to touch a hair on your pretty little head. Nature will take its course. Because you are not a Throw Away Girl, you will rush to your boyfriend's side and try to comfort him in his final moments. You will not follow me out the door. You can then bang away on it to your heart's content. No one will hear you and even if they do, they'll assume you're some crackhead having a bad reaction. I will slip away while you remain locked in here. Clare will look for you, but not for me. I've resigned. Clare believes I'm moving on to the next big adventure in my stellar career." He kissed his mouth and blew it away. "Poof," he breathed. "I will fade away into thin air. Effective immediately."

With a calculated dip of his arm, Ben sliced just deep enough into Van's wrist to split the top of his artery open. Without immediate pressure, what little blood he had left would gush out. Van would be dead in seconds.

Jaycee gaped. She counted off.

One.

She could tackle Ben. She was still strong enough to at least try.

Two.

Van moaned. She couldn't leave him.

Three.

Ben walked briskly to the door. Every step carried him farther away. Jaycee stood up. She could still take him down.

Four.

Her heart made the decision, just as it had the first time she had the choice to leave his side.

Five.

Jaycee tore off the Hermes belt she was wearing and wrapped it around Van's wrist.

Six.

Ben shut the door. He was gone.

Chapter Thirty-Five

She ignored the clank of the door shutting. Jaycee's only thought was to stop the bleeding and figure out a way out of this hot box of a room. She tightened the belt, wrapped it three times around Van's wrist and then secured it through the last tiny notch. She stared. The flow of blood became a trickle.

Yes!

She talked to him as she worked the room in short, positive bleeps of hope. *We'll get out of here. I'm working on it. Hang in there.* She inspected every corner. Looked up and then down, behind the pictures on the walls, beyond the cement prison. There had to be another way out!

A square of sunlight warmed her wrist. Jaycee followed it to its source. The window. The smallest she'd ever seen, at least, fifteen feet above the floor. Ben had figured it was impossible to reach.

Or was it?

Jaycee ran to the ramshackle desk. Its legs whined as she pushed it until it was just below the glass panel. If it held, it gave her an extra three feet of height. She could jump from there to grasp the window ledge. If she could somehow get herself up that high, she might be able to squeeze through the bitsy dormer.

Van moaned. She had to try. He'd die if she didn't do something.

They'd both die.

She climbed atop the desk, testing it. It was wobbly beneath her weight. Dangerously unsturdy. She bent her knees and tried to calculate how much force she'd need to reach the slim wooden lip of the window. She fought through a wave of dizziness that buckled one leg. Angling her head was making her see double. She leapt up. The tips of her fingernails scraped the dusty ledge but did not land it. She fell back down with a thud that ripped through her injured body.

Shit!

Focus! She admonished herself. She was a smart, strong girl. She could do this! She crouched low again but was distracted by Van's gurgle. He was struggling to breathe. Time was running out. He was dying. She jumped down from the desk and knelt beside him; her eyes flew wildly across the room. There had to be another way!

She could see the heap of fabric that held the TVU backpack she'd thrown when Ben kicked her. He'd left his camera inside the room, too.

Stupid, Ben. In his haste to leave her to rot, he'd left his gear behind. A stupid mistake she had to capitalize on!

She had an idea. About a year ago, Clare insisted all her talent learn how to use the backpack unit. It was relatively new technology and a huge boon for crews out in the field. They could even go live from a moving vehicle! They grumbled and complained, asking why on-air talent needed to know this, but everyone including Jaycee, suffered through the tutorial and then had to prove they could do it on their own.

The TVU unit funneled live images straight back to Master Control inside the newsroom at ABC 12. An operator was on duty twenty-four hours a day to deal with programming and satellite coordinates that brought in video from all over the world. If she could get Ben's backpack to fire, she could potentially send back live video to ABC 12! They would find them! They would save Van!

She scampered to the unit, pulling back tabs and plastic pockets to find the power button. She had blown off the lesson, barely paid attention. Ben always took care of this part; she'd never even watched. Goddamn it! Jaycee thrust her knuckles against her eyes desperate to remember the mandatory demonstration run by a tech guy with a droll voice and tortoise shell glasses. She'd played on her phone the entire time.

First, find the 'on' button, he'd instructed them.

Okay! She pressed a small knob below a flap held together by a strip of Velcro. The unit powered up and crunched a series of startup commands. Yes! She did it. What's next. Remember what tortoise shell told you.

Watch for the viability of your air cards.

Air cards? What the hell did that mean? She shook her head. Focus! Okay, air cards. Ben said they were the same thing as a gazillion cell phone lines. Jaycee thought back to their last live hit with the backpack. They were at a park, right near a swingset. A child was approached and assaulted by a stranger. Jaycee was live for the five o'clock news. Ben powered up the backpack for a closer shot than the live truck's cables could provide. With the backpack, they could get right near the monkey bars.

She saw red in the monitor. Shit! Red was bad, Ben told her red meant the unit was searching for a cell tower. She had to move the unit.

The window!

Yes, she had to get it to the window. If Jaycee could get a shot of their surroundings back to the newsroom, help would be minutes away. She could still save Van.

Jaycee lugged the backpack over to connect to Ben's camera. Thank God she knew where to plug the wires. She'd seen Ben do it a dozen times; he had been fascinated by the tidy backpack's capability to produce a live shot.

We only need one green, Jay Bird, I think that'll be enough. Just one of these little dots here needs to turn green for us.

She prayed for green. Climbing back onto the desk, Jaycee angled the camera toward the window and watched the backpack chug along. One green dot became two, and then three. Green means go. The signal was good!

Jaycee grinned to herself. Dizzy, weak, yet determined, she bent low again. This time, the weight of Ben's camera was almost enough to buckle both legs. She took deep, labored breaths to steady and center herself for what came next. She needed all her strength, courage, and hope to pull this off.

315

She had to get the video of her location back to master control. It was her only chance out. She had no idea how to produce audio. The video had to tell it all.

She wrestled with the camera. Activating it required a switch flipped and a button pushed. She did both. The camera whirled to life. Thank God for Ben's propensity to constantly recharge his equipment's batteries. He made it a point to have ready-to-go gear at all times.

Jaycee activated her quad muscles. She had to extend the camera above her shoulders, shatter the glass, and then aim out the window. Immediately, her shoulders shook with fatigue that rendered them almost useless. She faltered and lowered the camera to catch her breath.

Jaycee bit back a wave of nausea, fighting through a sheen of stinging sweat that burned her eyes. She huddled low and then shot upward, angling the camera's lens at the window to stab at the pane. It shattered into thin shards that rained down onto her head.

Yes! She'd broken through the window. Now, to climb high enough to get the shot.

Jaycee pulled the backpack beneath her and stepped on it. She'd gained more height, but was it enough? Defeat wasn't considered. She had to try.

Ben's camera had a long, leather strap he used to carry it when he needed both hands-free. Jaycee looped it around her, shifting the weight of the camera to her back hip. If the added height could give her a better shot at the windowpane, she could grab on and swing the camera out.

Salty liquid poured down her cheeks. Her vision began to swim; the wall seemed to expand and contract like it was breathing. She touched it to remind herself it was solid as her skin broke out in chilled goose bumps. Feverish and punchy, but there was no more pain, she had lost feeling to weariness. Her body couldn't support both. Maybe this was God's way of telling her she had done enough, and it was okay to let go.

Maybe…

Bullshit!

Since when did Jaycee Wilder just let go? She heaved herself back. She crouched again and pushed off strong. The first attempt failed. Jaycee crashed down onto the rickety desk. She rose again.

Come on, she willed her legs. They felt paralyzed, as though they belonged to someone else.

Get up!

She saw them then, ethereal wisps of light standing together like a line of soldiers. The Throw Away Girls; they'd come to her. She had to do it. For Van and for them.

She brushed back dripping strands of hair and wiped her eyes to better see the window.

Okay, she told them. I'll do it.

What happened next felt like a time warp; events whirled by her too fast and then excruciatingly slow. She had a vague sense of her fingers clutching, and then wrenching herself up and out. Blinding agony tore through her side as Jaycee thrust the camera through the tiny window and then followed it headfirst. She hoisted her body through the shattered glass but then became stuck. Half-way in, half-way out, she was a grotesque mound of flesh caught in the middle.

Fearless, she hit buttons and switches on the camera. She cheered herself through blood and pain. Maybe, just maybe, someone was watching.

Even if no one got there in time to save them, the evidence was still fresh enough to clear Van. By climbing out the window and trying to alert her colleagues to her whereabouts, she had done as much as she could for the man she loved.

That was all that mattered now.

Jaycee felt her heart beat hot and rapid, and then slow into a tired murmur.

Her last thought was not of Ben. It was of Van. The burden of the investigation, her friend's betrayal, the dead girls, all of that was finally released. It was not hers to carry any longer.

She slipped into soft darkness and closed her eyes.

Satisfaction danced on her lips.

Chapter Thirty-Six

Clare reached into her black Michael Kors purse and unzipped a small side pocket where she hid her medications. Her hands bobbled the childproof top of her Lorazepam even though she'd told the fucking pharmacist she didn't have a child to proof it from. She took two small round pills guaranteed to quell the bottle rocket exploding in her gut. Then she thrust her meaty hand back into the pocket and blindly felt her way around small bottles and long lipsticks until she found that signature squat container that held her beloved Advil. She popped out four. Then she sat back and waited for all that toxic garbage to start working.

She felt horrible about Jaycee. Taking her best street reporter off her story was like telling a scientist who had just cured cancer that he couldn't share his recipe.

It sucked. What sucked even more was Ben's abrupt resignation. He was gone. Costa Rica-bound earlier than thought. His Explorer left in the parking lot of LAX. She'd get to that later.

Clare had arrived to work tired and worried. She was grateful the only thing going on this morning was a follow-up on the fires in Ventura County. No breaking news but the day was still young. Her morning anchors were a half-hour into their show with two reporters out live on the perimeter of the blaze.

And then everything changed. Through the fishbowl, Clare could see the master control operator dash toward her

319

door. The wiry man slid on the thin rug but immediately sprung back up. Clare hoisted herself from her desk and rushed to him.

"Donnie, what's wrong? Are you okay?" she noticed a spray of coffee decorating the front of his t-shirt.

"Can't...breathe..." he bent at the waist to catch his breath.

"Donnie! Tell me what the fuck is happening!" she shouted at the nervous man. When he was ready, Donnie McCabe, the station's most loyal employee who kept everything humming from the darkness of Master Control, delivered news as powerful as a clap of thunder that shook the ground beneath them.

"I've got a signal..." he started, blowing out bits of spittle that collected around his lips. "From Ben's backpack."

Clare winced. Odd. Impossible.

"That can't be; Ben is on a plane. He was supposed to leave his rig at LAX. I was going to send someone out to pick it up later today."

"Well, someone is using his backpack, Clare. It's up live!"

She didn't ask if he was mixing up the signals. Donnie didn't miss a thing. He kept video feeds straight if they were coming from Van Nuys, New York, or Tokyo. He was that dependable. If Ben's backpack was firing, then Ben's backpack was goddamn firing!

Holy shit!

She grabbed her cell phone and moved like a sprinter out of the gate, flattening everything in her path on a direct route to Master Control. "Show me, Donnie," she wheezed. "Show me watcha got."

They entered the guts of the station. Behind a wall of small TVs all marked with numbers and letters was a room of wires gone wild. Colored piping connected to cables, tape decks, and computer screens. Images spat out from a myriad of locations. Clare saw one reporter standing in front of what appeared to be city skyline. Another shot was piped in from a golf course somewhere.

A third TV in that line labeled TVU #5 showed white haze interrupted by burps of black and white. The connection was there, but it was breaking up as lines crisscrossed over a tenuous signal.

"Ben's backpack," he panted. "TVU #5."

Clare nodded. "I see it. Come on, baby, tell me where you are." Clare coaxed the TV to provide an image they could lock onto. The shot was scrambled.

"Do you think someone stole Ben's rig?" Donnie pondered.

"Hmpf," Clare muttered. "Don't think your typical meth-head thief would figure out how to fire this up." She thought. "No, someone has a vague understanding of how to use this."

The shot jumped. The camera was in motion. Donnie and Clare braced, their hands clutched the round edges of the control board. They saw a street. Cars passing by.

Buildings and dumpsters shot skyward from a rodent's low perspective.

"It's on the ground," Clare said. "The camera is on the ground."

Donnie nodded. The camera bounced again to reveal more buildings that looked like a giant's labyrinth poking up from below. The shot tilted sideways. Clare and Donnie peered closer to the TV mounted on the wall. A dirty hand thudded against the sandy ground.

They both yelped in surprise.

The camera skirted to the left. Blonde hair splayed out on the ground, tinged with streaks of red.

"Holy mother of God!" Clare sucked in the words. Her finger hovered on her cell phone, twitching as she tried to find Barton's contact info. As she was ready to make the call, her assignment editor appeared in the door.

"Clare, something's going on. Got a call from some dude on Hollywood about a girl hanging out a window. Who do you want me to send? Both morning reporters are already out on that fire."

Clare stared at him. Ben's backpack was firing. A blonde woman was hanging from a window on Hollywood Boulevard.

Goddamn it! "What's the address," she asked her assignment editor, her voice shaky and brusque.

"Uh, 5152 Hollywood Boulevard."

She punched up the number and made the call. Barton answered on the first ring.

"5152 Hollywood Boulevard," she said slowly, as she tried to catch her breath. "Get there. Fast."

Chapter Thirty-Seven

Barton's heart pounded in his ears. He raced through three red lights, just ahead of a screeching ambulance. He accelerated through another stop sign before pulling off to the side of the road. He searched wildly for a window holding a body, a TV camera, anything that would reveal what the hell was going on. Clare said Ben was gone but his camera was there, and it had revealed a troubling situation.

He flew out of his car and moved north on foot. He could hear sirens approaching and saw a couple of vagrants standing near what looked like an apartment building. Heads drooped down they were staring at something low. On the ground.

A basement window!

He raced toward them and pushed both skinny men in sloppy clothes out of the way. He saw her and almost choked. A battered woman with blonde hair bent aside a TV camera, her torso and legs unseen behind her.

Red lights reflected off slivers of the shattered window. He blinked. This woman had burst through solid glass! Her hair was matted over her face, but Barton could see the beautifully sharp cheekbones and tawny forehead. He knew her eyes were blue even though their lids were closed. He knew her mouth when it laughed and more recently, when it had been pursed in worry.

He was too late. Just like the ponytailed little girl in Cambridge, he was too late to save her.

Jaycee's finger twitched. Barton's chest seized. She was still alive! He gently brushed back her hair and whispered into the shell of her ear. "You're okay, kiddo, you're okay. I'm going to get you out of here."

She mumbled something. It sounded like a name. Or a vehicle.

"Vvv…" she tried so hard to push it out. She wanted him to know something important. "…a…n."

Van.

Cops banged on the door inside the apartment. Barton heard them using a battering ram to get through. The tires on the ambulance crunched into the dirt behind him. Voices filled the room below the window. Barton heard them say someone was on the floor. He couldn't move. He had to stay with her. He couldn't let her go.

Barton inspected her head. He could see nicks and cuts but none appeared life-threatening. Her hands mottled with crusted blood sprouted purplish mounds atop her skin. The edges of the window were tight around her, but she was so thin she could easily slip back down. What was holding her in place?

Then, he saw it. A gaping wound just below her ear. Jaycee must have sliced it open on a razor-sharp sliver of glass. It was pumping out sheets of red. He took his left hand, *his good hand*, and tried to close it around the cut. His fingers were too thick to fit between Jaycee's skin and the unyielding metal of the narrow window frame.

No! The EMTs were attending to her, too. The angle was too awkward. No one could properly hold her neck closed to move her out of the window. If they jostled her, they'd lose her. There had to be a way. Barton swiped his right hand over his mouth in frustration. He looked at it. The disgustingly shredded flesh stitched over the stump of a bone always made him look away. But this time, he stared at it. The distance between his fingers was wider on his right hand.

Wide enough to stop the bleeding?

It hurt like a fresh assault, but Barton stretched his hand over Jaycee's neck. The rounded amputation site applied pressure to the sputtering gash. He held it firmly. He told her she was going to be okay. He forced the image of the ponytailed little girl from his mind. This was not her. This was Jaycee.

The blood slowed. The EMTs signaled a victory. They instructed him to hold the pressure until they could bring her through the window. His hand began to quake, yet he held it still, keeping the blood in. They prepared to receive her on the other side. They had already wheeled out the man found on the floor.

They told him to let her go. They had her. Barton released the pressure. He fell backwards onto the ground slippery with Jaycee's blood.

He stared at his deformed hand, covered in red and shaky from strain.

And he grinned.

Chapter Thirty-Eight

Dr. Melinda Adler awaited the first ambulance carrying a trauma patient to Cedars-Sinai. The call described a male with severe head lacerations, a potential pelvic fracture, deep wrist gash, and spotty consciousness. Her team was assembled and ready to assist in saving his life.

The roar of the siren triggered a swarm of action around her. She ordered the presence of a neurologist to determine the extent of the injury and brain damage in case the head wound was the death trigger. Loss of blood was her second concern. The EMTs had already loaded this man up with four units, but his blood pressure was collapsing. She'd also been warned the patient was restless and fighting mechanical ventilation.

Finally, the back doors of the ambulance swooped open, and the gurney rolled out. Dr. Adler led the way, engaging in a rapid-fire verbal exchange with the EMTs.

"Pelvic binder in place, we have taken spinal precautions, and transfusions are not type-specific."

"Sinus rhythm," she asked, visually scanning the blood-drenched upper torso writhing on the thin mattress. "Electrolyte levels?"

"104 and just below normal, but falling," the EMT responded.

"Airway maintained?"

"Yes, but blunt trauma to head makes me question whether it's been compromised. Sedation recommended if he needs intubation. He's fighting oxygen."

Dr. Adler's team ascended on the patient. The wheels of the gurney spun rapidly toward the OR. The man's face was distorted by swelling and coagulated blood. Strips of flesh ripped outward where something made contact with his wrist.

"I'm going to take good care of you. Please, don't fight the oxygen mask, it's helping you breathe." She reached for his hand. This man, with bulging biceps and ropey muscles on his forearm, pushed her away to pull at the plastic cup over his mouth and nose.

"Sir, please don't…"

He uttered a deep, raspy, prolonged sound of anguish. Trying like hell, he wanted to speak.

They turned the corner into the OR, preparing to further stabilize to identify and treat wounds.

In 60 seconds, this man would be quiet and still, but he wouldn't go easily.

He grabbed Dr. Adler's sleeve, tugging so hard she pulled up short.

"Sir, it's okay, you're at the hospital…"

"Listen!" he blurted, lucidity fighting to break through the shock.

Dr. Adler had seen this before. Spasms of panic that struck when a life was sputtering. Many times, she was the sole witness to a barrage of secrets and confessions poured out as a person sought to clear a pathway to the heavens. As if coming clean to a last minute conduit here on Earth would grant resolution and safe passage.

She gripped his hand tightly, lacing her fingers between his. If this man wanted to be absolved in what could be his final moments, she would hear his confession. His eyelids fluttered over warm, blue eyes with naturally curled lashes. His nose, covered in blood, was straight and nicely shaped. His lips were cracked, but beneath them was a wide, generous mouth full of Crest White Strip-colored teeth. He was quite handsome. What a shame.

"Sir, I'm listening. Slow down."

God, it pained her to see him struggle like this. She contemplated bypassing his request and loading him up with narcotics to take the pain away. The hand embraced inside her own began to quake. He was fighting with everything he had left to speak.

"Bbbbb…" he tried.

"Okay, I hear you. B."

"eeeee…" the vowel shuddered on his lips.

"E." Got it, she told him. E.

"nnn…"

Dr. Adler quickly put the letters together. He was trying to tell her who he was.

"Okay, I hear you, your name is Ben."

"No!!" he exploded with rage, startling her as yet again his fingers found inhuman strength and squeezed.

"Sir, calm down, please. We are running out of time, I need to get you into surgery, you have very grave injuries." She tried to release her hand. The patient refused to let her go.

"Rod..."

"Rod?" Dr. Adler squinted.

"rrrrickkkk...rod...ricckkk." It was a jumble of hard consonants. His eyes went wide, the pupils revealed faint traces of red. Jesus Christ! Dr. Adler feared a brain bleed.

"I hear you. I will figure it out, I promise."

She handed him off to the radiologist for an emergency round of head scans but remained troubled. This patient clearly meant for her to know something important. She paused, quieted her head until all she saw were the letters. Ben. Ricky. Rod."

"Dr. Adler, stat!" someone screamed from inside the OR.

"Coming!" she scrubbed in, fast and efficient, and nearly tripped a trauma nurse walking behind her. "Corey!" she yelled. The young nurse snapped to attention.

"Yes, Dr. Adler," she said, hoping to get a spot in the OR with this exceptional trauma surgeon. She'd been waiting for the opportunity.

"Work this out for me," Dr. Adler stated. "Call the police and let them know we have someone here named Ben Rodricky, or he knows a Ben Rodricky, or something like that. Tell them he's been in an accident but very much needed me to hear that name. Go, Corey, get it done."

Oh, shit. Corey sauntered away toward the nurses' station to play secretary. She watched as a few officers lingered near the door. Another ambulance from the same scene was about a mile out. She motioned to one of them.

Barton walked to her.

"Something you guys might want to know," she told him. "The male is heading into surgery. He may be named Ben. Or wants to report someone named Ben. Weird last name, though…"

Barton almost came out of his shoes. "Roderick," he said expectantly.

"Sure," Corey told him. It was close enough.

Chapter Thirty-Nine

"Jaycee," the young nurse touched her hunched back gently. "Let me take you to your room. You need to rest."

"No," she snapped. "Today's the day."

"Okay, honey," she sighed, reluctant but empathetic. "But just a little while longer. I'm going to get a talking to from your doctor if I don't get you back."

Jaycee nodded but otherwise ignored the well-intentioned woman. It was her third day there, and while she was fast-tracking her recovery, Van's was unbearably stuck in place. His family was en route to Los Angeles, and she desperately wanted to give them positive news. They were just regular people, a teacher, and a dentist. They didn't understand all this Hollywood actor, serial killer, TV personality bullshit. All they knew was someone hurt their boy badly.

Barely conscious, Jaycee had asked to make the phone call, to explain to Van's family how he had fought so fiercely to protect her. How selfless and brave he was to get Ben's name out just before he was put under for surgery. It had been a critical key for police. Jaycee wanted them to know how deeply good he was.

She cried through her own pain and promised to love and care for their son for the rest of her life. She owed him everything.

Fresh tears flowed again. Come on, Van! Wake up!

She took his palm and laced her fingers between his. His skin was slack, colorless. She kissed his knuckles softly before placing his hand back next to his hip. She laid her head on the stiff sheet and talked to him. Her heart told her he was listening.

"I've been thinking," she began, her finger tracing a journey from his elbow to his thumb. "That maybe we take some time off. Just you and me. Maybe head up the coast." She saw it in her mind. She shared it with him. Their new life.

"Or, we could go east? Maybe see some snow in New Hampshire, or hit the dunes on the Cape? You'd love it, Van, it's so chill. Not uptight like out here, everyone watching everyone else, comparing peck muscles and hair color. It's just…cool…happy. I'd like to show you my happy place." She turned her cheek upward to search his eyelashes for movement. Just a flutter. That was all she needed. Just a sign that he was still in there.

Nothing.

Jaycee pressed her cheek on his chest, her chin tucked near his armpit. Everything she had never told him pushed on her like an avalanche. Now or never, she thought.

Tell him how you feel, Jaycee! Open up and tell him what's in your heart.

"I'm so proud of you, Van, and I'm sorry I never told you before now. You're a really good actor, and I doubted you. I'm sorry for that, too. I think it's amazing how you can memorize a script full of technical crime scene crap and make it sound natural and real. You are so much more to me, Van, than I ever told you. Without you being so

333

strong, I would've died! He would have won…" she broke down in sobs.

When Jaycee could speak again, she was empty inside. There was only one more thing she could say before the nurse swooped back in and returned her to the solitude of her own hospital room. Rising gently on still-wobbly legs, Jaycee leaned her upper body over the cumbrous metal bars and delicately laid her lips on Van's forehead. Squeezing her eyes shut, trying to tunnel all her strength into him, she took an airy breath and spoke through his ear, directly into his heart.

"I love you," she said, entirely at peace with this first declaration. She did love Van. She always had. In the end, when she was facing unimaginable odds, he was the only thing she wanted to save. She didn't do it to punish Ben, or skyrocket to fame with her story of survival and betrayal, or even to feel the thrill of coming out the other end alive.

It was all about love.

She turned to leave; her IV pole shuffled along beside her as she navigated over the large square tiles in her hospital-issued slippers. She had planned to go sit with Fiona again, the other bedside she kept vigil next to. Fiona had started holding her hand. Her frights were going away. Jaycee made sure her restless brain knew it was now safe, and the bad man who had hurt her was gone.

Something made her turn back. The invisible string that kept her by Van's side in the disgusting apartment pulled her back again. It forced her to retrace her steps to

Van's bed. She squinted. She almost missed an imperceptible wiggle of Van's finger. No, she must have imagined it. She leaned closer, seeking confirmation. The finger flicked again!

"Van?"

It moved. Another one joined it. Van's hand slid toward her. Jaycee's heart soared. She screamed for a doctor.

Van's wrist moved. Then his entire arm! By the time the doctor flew around the door, Van's eyes were twitching as he attempted to focus. It was often agonizing for head trauma patients to wake for the first time. Jaycee automatically stepped back.

Please, help him, she muttered on a loop. *Please, help him. Please, help him.* Her entire body was suspended between fear and limitless joy. What if he didn't remember anything? What if she was a stranger to him? What if their entire life together had been erased by the venomous actions of a maniac?

In the end, it stood as the most powerful antidote of all. A lone ember that burned long after the fire was extinguished, and the only emotion that could bring light to dark, hope to despair, and life to certain demise.

His eyes strained, trying to lock onto an object. The doctor was telling him where he was, who he was, all the cold hard particulars of what happened to him, but Van was restless. Finally, the doctor stepped back and pulled Jaycee in.

"Let him see you," he told her. "Let him see you first."

She watched his eyes make a trajectory from the windows, to the back wall of his room, and then, he found her. She smiled in between tears and said it again, the only thing she wanted to say, the only thing that mattered.

"I love you."

His parched lips quaked. He was struggling. Jaycee tried to tell him he was okay, and to relax; he didn't have to speak yet. His right hand was surprisingly steady as it reached for her. The words were right there; she could see him trying so hard.

"He may not remember you right away," the doctor warned. "Give him time."

She nodded. That was fine. She had all the time in the world.

"Season…" Van uttered just one breathy word to start. The doctor stared at him.

"What does that mean?" he asked. Jaycee shook her head.

"Six…" he continued. Jaycee gasped as a laugh bubbled up. Confused faces peered at them both. No one understood but her. He wanted it that way.

"*CSI*…New York…" he was weak but insistent. Jaycee waited. All the time in the world.

"…Boyfriend makes…it…out…alive."

She dissolved in tearful relief. Careful not to disrupt the tubes that pumped liquid into his veins, Jaycee embraced him as entirely as the space allowed her to. Van was fading back to slumber, exhausted by the strain of coming back to life. Before he slipped back under, he gripped her so tightly she could feel his energy and spirit rejuvenating.

"Jay Jay…" he said, as soft as a summer breeze. "I…love…you…too." And then he was gone again.

The doctor was smiling. The nurses were all crying around her. They had just witnessed a miracle.

"It will, uh, be a while before he's back to full strength," the doctor told her, somewhat reluctant to break the quiet of such a magnificent moment.

"That's okay," she told him, as she felt the broken pieces of herself working to fit back together. They would get through this. With tender patience, she would wait for him forever.

"I have all the time in the world."

Chapter Forty

"She'll need to stay in the hospital, at least, a couple more days," Clare told Barton over the phone. "Doctors won't clear her until she can hold her body temperature on her own. But the really amazing news is that Van woke up!" She wouldn't admit it, but Clare rather enjoyed their regular conversations. Barton was fast becoming her new favorite cop on the L.A.P.D.

Barton already had the update, but he humored Clare. He knew she was working through the guilt of having employed a killer. The media tempest had been brutal, even on one of its own. Clare was fierce; she would get through this.

"It's wonderful news." He paused. He knew Clare needed more. "We'll find him, Clare. I promise. He can't hide forever."

"And when you do, I expect first crack at his skinny ass, Barton."

He smiled into his phone. "Let me know if anything changes. Talk to you tomorrow." He and this smart-mouthed woman with a heart of gold would be lifelong friends.

Barton watched as morning hues of red and orange streaked across his living room and threw gentle highlights onto the quiet form curled into the corner of his couch. Debra had ridden out the incident right by his side, holding his hand as he sat up late with worry over Jaycee and Van, and helped nurse the frustration of knowing Ben, or Samuel Greene, had slipped away.

As her chest rose and then fell, Barton thought back to the early days when love was simple and pure. Could you ever get back what you willingly let go?

He shifted in his chair. Forever a cop's wife, Debra was instantaneously awake and alert. Too many late night phone calls prevented her from ever sleeping soundly.

"I'm up. What's going on?" She was already prepared to help him absorb another enormous loss. But James' face was peaceful. She felt hope rising.

"Van woke up," he told her.

A former wife smiled at the man she still loved. He was sipping coffee rather than vodka. He was motivated to find the elusive bad guy but had matured enough to appreciate the victories he had helped achieve.

Finally, Barton forgave himself for the ponytailed little girl and embraced the good man he'd always been.

She went to him. Their bodies threw off shadows that linked together in the warm glow of a fresh start.

Epilogue

Samuel Greene was well-practiced at many things, but most especially patience. He knew if something didn't come that day, it may arrive by the next. Patience allowed a person to live on a higher plane of understanding. He simply waited everyone out.

The southern road was windy and dark; he'd been alone on the highway for a while.

Time.

It was a gift when a man could be patient enough to appreciate it. Time allowed him to heal. To plan. Samuel knew that time was as precious as water.

As precious as she was. The only girl he'd ever cared for. The opposite of a Throw Away Girl, she was instead a mighty warrior. A survivor. His equal. Despite his best efforts, his *chica bonita* was rescued. In the end, she had won.

He felt that warm flood of anticipation trickle through him, an intimate and suggestive sensation he had begun to associate with her.

Their time would come. He would see Jaycee again.

Someday.

He had all the time in the world.

The End

Acknowledgments

Throw Away Girls is the product of me being a pest. To the recipients of my endless questions, texts, emails, and phone calls, I thank you for your expertise, your patience, and your willingness to share. To Detective Sergeant John Sonia with the NH State Police Major Crime Unit, you are the backbone of this book. From the minutia of crime scene analysis, to the dark thoughts hatched inside criminal minds, your input was indispensable. I look forward to crafting future sinister characters together.

Huge thanks to L.A.P.D. Detective II Kristin Merrill, who walked me through the particulars of her city, and her job, making sure the story I wrote on the East Coast fit into her West Coast reality.

My "great idea guy," Sergeant Greg Ferry, NH State Police, who often lead me down even more twisted paths than I started on. You gave solid ground to my imagination, and I so deeply appreciate all the times you allowed me to bounce my scenarios around your head.

WMUR-TV Chief Videographer, Jim Breen. Thank you for correcting me until I had all my buttons, bars, and signals straight.

Finally, Barbara Terry. Without you, *Throw Away Girls* would still be living a lonely life inside my computer. You have released it, and I am eternally grateful for your trust and support.

Author Bio

Jennifer Vaughn is a longtime member of the award-winning news team at WMUR-TV, in Manchester, New Hampshire. As the evening anchor, Jennifer has lead coverage that has earned Edward R. Murrow, Associated Press, and New Hampshire Association of Broadcasters Awards.

She is also the recipient of multiple Emmy nominations, the Red Cross Sword of Hope Award, and had her debut novel, *Last Flight Out*, featured in the Swag Bag at the Daytime Emmy Awards in Beverly Hills, CA, in 2013. Jennifer has had prominent roles in internationally-televised presidential debates alongside CNN, ABC News, and FOX News, has anchored election night coverage for both national and state contests and provided political analysis for national radio and television news outlets.

She's interviewed every sitting president and presidential candidate since 1999, supporting WMUR's extensive first-in-the-nation presidential primary coverage. Jennifer has covered everything from Super Bowls, world championship parades, ABC's *Extreme Home Makeover*, deadly natural disasters, and medical breakthroughs, though her favorite stories are the personal ones that showcase triumph over tragedy, and give hope to the human spirit.

Blessed with two great kids, Brody and Darby, and their cocker spaniel, Fletcher, Jennifer and her husband, Brad Dupuis, have embraced all that is unique about life in New Hampshire. When they're not on a baseball or soccer field, you can catch them playing tennis, ice skating, snowmobiling, skiing, hiking, or hitting the lake for a boat ride.

Giving back is an integral part of Jennifer's life. An avid contributor to charities that direct funds and support to cancer patients, Jennifer donated all proceeds from the sale of *Last Flight Out* to local organizations. Her family lends support and time to several important causes that better our communities, and country. Learn more at www.jvwrites.com.